Get Christie

Private Eye

Yvonne Snyder

PublishAmerica
Baltimore

First printing

ISBN: 978-1-60749-275-7
PUBLISHED BY PUBLISHAMERICA, LLLP
www.publishamerica.com
Baltimore

Printed in the United States of America

This book is dedicated to my son, daughter and grandchildren who have inspired me to pursue my love of writing and my dream of writing a book.

Also, I want to dedicate this book to my siblings, for their inspiration.

I say to all first time writers, never let go of your dream.

Acknowledgements

I want to thank my children for their love and encouragement that had given me the drive to pursue my lifelong dream of becoming an Author.

I want to thank my siblings, family, friends, and well wishers for their encouragement and strength during our time of grief at the loss of our mother last year. Through all my struggles they stood by me and I was able to continue on striving to reach that goal.

I want to thank my sister, Debra for her help with my editing to make sure that it was readable. She made sure that it was sent to the right people so I could meet my deadline.

I want to thank my church family for their spiritual uplifts and guiding me in the right way so that I would not stumble or fall while trying to make this dream become a reality.

And finally, I want to thank Book Publisher America who has paved the way to make my dream a reality. I am grateful to you, for allowing me to be apart of your family of writers. May you and your staff be eternally, Blessed.

In Memory of My Parents
Herman and Mary Snyder

Introduction

This is the story of Christie Higgins, a Black single woman in her early 30's who dreams of one day becoming a private investigator. After obtaining a degree in Communication, and landing an unfulfilling job as a journalist, Christie is determined to find her dream job as a private investigator. The problem is that Christie has no real experience in law enforcement and is uncertain on how to gain experience. All her past jobs include journalism and administrative work. Christie knows that the odds of landing a job as a private investigator, even an entry level job is slim to none for young women, let alone a young woman without investigating experience, yet she feels that all she needs is a lucky break. One lucky break to prove to the naysayers that she has what it takes to be a private investigator (P.I.).

Christie she will be telling her own story. She will come in contact with many people, and do adventurous things. Some of the characters they will have a tale of their own which will peak your interests in wanting to hear more about their lives. She will take you to two continents in which she will have traveled. There will be a period of sadness as well as happiness as she opens up a door that is full of secrets, mystery, and deceptions in her life and in the lives of the two men who care about her well-being. This story will keep the readers wondering what she will do next. Christie will tell you the readers about the things which will go on in her life throughout the story.

Chapter 1

After Christie had been sitting at home doing nothing for three months. She decided she needed to find work in her chosen field of study. She had graduated from a Community College and had received her A.S. degree in Communication and Journalism. Christie was ready to find her a job. She had spoken to some people at the College job bank and they said, "You should send out some resumes to places so they would be aware of your experience." This information was not a good suggestion for Christie at that time. She was not ready to find work. Now she was getting bored and each day she had wasted her time doing nothing in particular.

She had looked at her clock on the wall in her kitchen, when she had awaken. It was just 7:30 a.m. She had turned on her television earlier this morning to watch the early morning news. And she heard the weatherman say that the temperature was in its early teens this morning. The sun had risen, but it was still freezing cold. The weatherman said, "The temperature will have changed by the mid-afternoon." She turns up her thermostat because it was cool inside her suite. And she likes it warm before she takes her bath or shower. She had made her a fresh brewed coffee using her coffeemaker. She left her mug sitting on the counter, so that when she comes back inside she could get her a cup of this delicious gourmet coffee. She still had on her pajamas and her fluffy soft slippers. She had slipped on a soft pair of ankle socks. She went to grab her sweater coat from her hall closet. She had put it on quickly. She picks up her key and her small change purse from off the kitchen counter. She left her apartment suite, and had taken the stairs so she could get downstairs to the lobby faster than waiting on an elevator. She left her apartment to go outdoors to the Newspaper stand, which was right in front of her apartment building in the Bronx suburban area of NYC. She held her change purse and her keys to her suite in her hand. She steps outside in the brisk air to go to the newspaper stand. She quickly purchased the paper and go back inside to the lobby. She stood there for a few moments to glance through the newspaper. There was nobody in the lobby right now. The security guard had not arrived there yet.

As she was looking through the want-ad section, she saw there was an opening at this same Newspaper Company. She rushed back upstairs to her apartment suite to go to her computer that was in sitting over in a corner of her living room. She sat down after removing her sweater and draping it over her lounging chair in her living room. She begins to type out her resume and a cover letter. She had printed it and reaches to take out an envelope from her desk drawer so she could send it to them soon as possible.

As Christie put the resume and cover letter into a large envelope, she went back outside to the mailbox to drop it off. She knew that she was not really desperate for money. She had a trust fund that was set up from her parents estate before they had died. Also, she had sold her grandparents house and she had that money to do as she pleased. She just wanted to work to stay busy and to make some money.

It had been two weeks and the Newspaper Company, finally called Christie to come in for an interview. The human resource department receptionist said,

"She was to report to a Mr. Walter White, who ran the company. " They told her to come in on Monday morning at 8:00 a.m." Their location was right downtown in New York City. She wanted to wear something new for the interview. It had been a while since she had gone to a mall.

Christie decided to go to the mall. She saw on the front section of the newspaper that Macy's Department Store had a 20% sale on their suits and dresses in the women's department. She needed to bring in their coupon in order to get their discount. She gets her pair of scissors from off the kitchen counter. She started cutting the coupon from out of the newspaper.

Earlier, that day she saw that JC Penney had an advertisement of a new hair care product that she wanted to try on her hair, so she had cut out their advertisement too. They said, "To show this ad to the clerk upon your arrival and you will get a discount on this hair care product." Christie put both clippings in her purse. She was going to get her hair and nails done too.

Christie listened to the weather again before leaving her suite. The temperature was going to reach the high 30's today and drop down to a low 12 degrees by nightfall. This meant that she had to dress warm. Even, though this was at the end of March.

She was not in a hurry to get to the mall, but she wanted to get there before it gets dark so she kept on the same clothes that she had worn all afternoon. It was a cute outfit and it was casual.

She was wearing a gray sequin sweater dress that came with a pair of knit leggings that had laces at the bottom. And she looks in her dresser drawer for her pretty gray knee high socks they had laces on the top. She put them on and walks to the hall closet to grab her jacket and boots. She had slipped on her black "wet look" boots and put on her black "down" quilted jacket. She made sure she had her scarf and gloves too. She looked at her watch; it was 2:00 p.m. and it was about half past the hour. She knew that a bus would be coming in 15 more minutes. Christie picked up her purse, and grabbed her keys. First she made sure that everything was turn off in her apartment. She had made some coffee and ate a bowl of cereal. The coffeemaker was turned off. Christie doubled check to make sure that the windows and glass sliding door were shut securely. She had to be outside at the bus stop in five minutes if she wanted to catch the Suburban bus. She knew if she missed it then she would have to walk across the street to catch the train at the subway station. Christie took the stairs and she made it to the bus stop on time and she saw the bus coming down the street.

She had purchased a bus pass in advance so that she would not have to spend any money for her fare.

As she was walking through the mall she heard this beautiful song playing over the loud speaker. She wanted to go inquire of the name of the song. She went to the record shop. A handsome man was standing in the store in a beige suit; he had a badge on his suit jacket. He was tall and he was White.

He smiles at Christie, and said "Hello may I help you with something"? Christie asked him," What is the name of that song that was just playing inside the mall"? He smiled and teasing, he said, "I will tell you if you are going to buy it today." Christie nodded and said," that is why I am in here". He mentions to her the name of the song it is called, "I'll be Over You" He slowly walks away smiling and said, "Then I will go get the CD". He smiled. He was whistling another tune. Christie was not trying to be flirty. She followed him around as he went to the aisle where they had the artist song sitting on a shelf. Christie asked him coyly, "What is the name of that tune that you are whistling?" He smiled and said, "It is a favorite of mines". They both looked at each other, but he did not say the name of the song that he was whistling. They both stood for a minute looking at each other in the aisle where the song Christie was looking for was sitting on the shelf. Suddenly, Christie remembered why she had come into the mall. She had the newspaper clipping of the coupon at Macy's Department store still in her hand.

Christie thought to herself, *I must not get distracted; I have to get the whole works. First, I must find me a suit and a pair of high heels shoes.* Christie noticed that the salesman was holding two CDs in his hand. He was working alone. She thought to herself that business must have been very slow. His badge says that he was the owner. She asked him, "How much will these two CDs cost me"?

He said, "It is $38.00 plus tax, and I will throw in a third CD for free if you will buy one of our headsets". He had taken one of the most expensive headsets off the shelf behind the cash register. He said, "This one is the most effective one on the market". He told Christie, "I will wait while you go find another CD".

He stated, "You know you can get a DVD or Audio if you like instead".

She went back to the section that had DVD's. She saw the, "Theme song" to an old flick. It came with a set. She took it back over to his register. He smiled. He looks at the price. It cost more than the others.

He did not say anything.

She let him ring up her order.

He rings up the items on his cash register. He took off the price of the 3rd item from the total price. He put these items in a bag. He stated to her," You are all set now". She thought he was angry. But he smiled.

Christie said, "You must be trying to sell me all these products because I am the only one who is in here".

He stares at me with this little smirk on his face, he said," You are quite pretty and smart." He stated, "I think this is a crazy mixed up world that we live in and I can't figure out anything anymore". He continued, "I do not know you from Adam and you have no clue as to what I am talking about, so let me just quit stalling and spit this out".

Christie had to laugh at his remarks.

He stated to me, "I would like to take you out to lunch." "I do not blame you for not trusting a total stranger", he said. He was smiling. Christie saw that he was sincere and trying to be spiritual. He said, "I am a nice guy, and I will take you to some place to dine in the area". Christie did not see a wedding band on his finger. She was not trying to meet anyone right now. She told him, "I am in a hurry". She was not giving him the brush off. She had an itinerary she made during her visit to the mall.

He said, "It will be just lunch, dear. " He handed Christie her credit card back. But he had not given her the bag. Christie said, "I think you are handsome and very sincere. He said, "My name is Quinton Allen. " He handed her back her credit card. Then he asked her if she was married or seeing anyone. Christie stated to him, "I think that is personal". He smiles. He said again in a teasing voice to Christie, "How else will a man find out if a woman is available? "

He was looking at Christie in a serious way.

She was not trying to hurt his feeling. "Alright", Christie told him, "I was going to grab me a bite to eat at the food court when I am through with my shopping".

He said, "You have forgotten to tell me your name."

Christie had to laugh at herself, "My name is Christie Higgins", she tells him.

He held out his hand to shake her hand. "It is a pleasure to meet you, Christie". He was listening and rocking to the music that was being played inside the mall.

"Now about that lunch you agreed to have with me, "I will have to decline", he stated. Christie looked at him strange. She was getting ready to get angry. She took her bag from out of his hand and was about to leave out of his shop in a hurry.

He held her arm gently, "I wanted to eat somewhere else besides here, he stated." I did not mean today". He handed her his business card, "I have to work somewhere else tonight. I want to take you someplace beautiful, where they have live music playing and we can dine", he stated.

Christie was shocked.

He said, "I will need your address and phone number".

Christie retorted quickly, "Oh sure I give you my information and you never call or show up for that date".

He said, "You are making this difficult for me." He continued, "This is what I am going to do here just to prove to you that I am serious about that date. I will meet you for that lunch in the food Court". He asked, "What time will you be over there"?

Christie said, "In a few hours. I have an Itinerary and I am trying to finish my shopping within a certain time frame, if it is possible". She tells Quinton.

He said, "I can understand that myself. Give me a holler when you are ready to eat, I will take an hour break".

She shook her head in unbelief. Christie was thinking he was going to take 1 hour just for her.

He was smiling. He laughs and said," Alright make it 25 minutes". You are quite a little fashionable dresser, dear." He had stated. He was admiring her outfit.

Christie was smiling, too. She thanks him for the compliment.

He held out his hand to hers. He wanted me to shake his hand for some type of agreement.

She shook it. She said to him, "I have to go, Quinton."

He winks. Then he said "I think you are beautiful".

She thanks him. She walks away.

He was whistling another song while walking away. He was happy that she had accepted his offer.

Christie was thinking about all the things she needed to get done at the mall. She had wasted 20 minutes of her time on chatting with that sales man. She took a look at his card. He had the "Jacquar" car symbol on his business card. She knew that some men put their car title on their business card. It was rare that he was the owner and working by himself in a mall. Well, Christie thought aloud, "I finished part of my itinerary; now, I had to go find that suit. Then, I have to get my hair and nails done. I had promised that salesman, Quinton that I would have something to eat with him at the food court".

It was just 3:30 p.m. in the afternoon. She had made it to the mall in 40 minutes. She figured that she could be through in a couple of hours and have time to make that 6:00 p.m. bus that would be arriving for departure. It would have gotten dark about that time. She was thinking she could make it back to her apartment before 8:00 p.m. She did not have much time if she wanted to carry out this plan of hers. She hated to come home late in the evening by herself.

Christie walked over to Macy Department Store to the Misses and Women dress section. She found a pretty black pin stripe suit with a wide belt that was in her size. She especially liked it because there was a split in the back. She had to find a shell to wear underneath the suit jacket. She walked around looking at the blouse racks until she found a pretty pink camisole with laces.

Christie quickly walked over to the women shoe department. She found a pair of black patent leather high heels that was in her size. She had to take the items to the check out counter. She paid for the items using her credit card. She looked at her watch to see what time it was now. She realized that she did not have any earrings. So, she walked over to the jewelry counter. She saw a pair of gold loop earrings set. It came with a gold necklace, and one bracelet.

She asked the sales consultant, "How much will this earring set cost me?" The saleswoman said that it would cost $110 including taxes. Christie took out her credit card, and charged it. She put it in her shopping bag with her other items.

Christie thought she was through shopping until she saw a woman who was standing at a booth in the hallway trying to get her attention.

The lady beckoned and said, "Come over here for a minute." Christie was trying to make her way to where she could go to J.C. Penney Department store if she still wanted to get her hair and nails done today. She sighed.

The saleswoman introduced herself, "I would like for you to try out just a sample of this cosmetic product", handing the products to Christie.

"I will just put a little bit on your hand I think this will be just perfect for you", she said.

Christie said, "I am in a bit of a hurry." It was getting late in the afternoon. Christie's watch showed that it was 4:30 p.m. She had two and a half hours to go, if she intended on catching the Suburban bus back to her apartment. It would be arriving at the mall at 6:00 p.m. Christie said to her, "I will have to come back at another time. "

The saleswoman said, "This should only take a few minutes". She put a product on Christie's hand. The saleswoman said to Christie," You have such a beautiful face." Christie sighed. Christie knew that this was her sales pitch. Christie thanked her for the compliment. Then asked her, "How much will this product cost me"?

The saleswoman looks at her Item Sheet for a price and explained that it came with the lip liner and eye liner as an extra, for just only $165.

Christie knew she was ready to go. She said, "That is way too much money."

The saleswoman tells her trying to be persuasive," I will throw in a tube of this fine hand lotion." Christie sighed.

The saleswoman said, "For all these items here they are a $250 value at Macy's." Christie said," Yes you are right." She took out her credit card and purchased the cosmetic products. Christie raced by the woman who was selling perfume.

Now, Christie rush by the sale Associates who were standing around or at a counter, to get to the beauty salon. There was nobody waiting to be served. She walked over to the front desk. She said, "I would like to have my hair and nails done, right now if it is possible. I am press for time". "I must be finish here before 6:00 p.m.", Christie stressed to the clerk.

The clerk asked a hairstylist if she could wait on Christie now. The hairstylist told Christie to sit at her booth. Christie told her what she saw in the newspaper about a new hair care product. She almost forgot to show the ad to the clerk to get a discount. She reaches in her purse to give it to the clerk.

The clerk smiled and put it on the counter. She had to ring it up now.

Christie paid for the service using her credit card.

The hair stylist went to get the product. "This is a Permanent/ and Color Kit, they are combined", she said to Christie when she returned.

Christie asked how long it would take before she could finish.

The hair stylist said, "I am pretty fast, you will be out of here in two hours".

The hair stylist had finally finished putting the finishing touch on Christie's hair in an hour and a half.

Christie gave her a tip and went to the record shop to tell Quinton that she was ready to get something to eat.

Quinton had a customer who he was waiting on so Christie decided to walk over to the food court. Quinton was very busy.

Christie walked to the Food court to eat something by herself. She saw a man walking over towards her. It was Quinton.

He said to Christie, "Have you forgotten about me that soon"?

Christie said, "I had come into the shop to tell you that you I was ready to go eat but you were busy".

"I am sorry all of a sudden it got busy", Quinton replies, "This has been a very unusual day". He said, "I will get me a hot dog and a soda". He walks away to go get his sandwich. He came back over to the table. He sat down. "I never eat their food here. He stated, "I might be sick by the end of the day".

"You could have just gotten a salad or something that is light", Christie told him.

"I have not eaten anything today", he said as he shrugged his shoulder. I will do what I have to do, darling. I am more interested in how I can take you out on a date. "I have just been talked into purchasing two tickets to see a concert from some guy who is a ticket scalper while I was walking over here to find you" he stated. I have a feeling that it is going to cost me a small fortune, he stated. He shakes his head. Anyway, l will go pick it up from the ticket scalper after I get off work. I was wondering if you would like to go out with me to this concert on this Friday night."

Christie looking at Quinton before she answer, "I had to think about this for a minute".

He continues, "I am not asking for anything in return. "

Christie said, "Give me a call on Thursday night and I will give you my answer."

Quinton asked, "You are going to make me wait until almost the end of the week." I will have found me somebody else by that time. Or have sold it to someone else, he added.

Christie responds, "You are absolutely right, it is not fair for me to make you wait until the last minute. She stated, "I will go out with you on Friday".

Quinton was ready to go back to work. Christie said to him, "You said that you were giving me 20 minutes." She was teasing with him.

He had these beautiful green eyes. He said, "Do not push your luck, dear". He winks at her.

She was not trying to meet anybody, but it had been a while since she had gone out with a man.

Quinton said, "I will give you a call on Thursday night to tell you what time I will pick you up. "Oh, and wear something dressy", he stated to Christie.

"Do you have a looking glass?" Christie asked him.

Quinton thought Christie was so funny. He started laughing. He stated, "I am afraid you have lost me, Christie, Quinton replies.

"Do you know where I live?" She asked Quinton.

He said, "I have your address on my data base and I am familiar with the area. I had all your information when you purchase the items", he stated.

Christie had forgotten that she given him that information earlier.

Christie still did not have her nails done yet. She walked over to the Nail salon. The technician asked her to sit over at the nail booth. "I will polish your nails", Miss", she said. She gets out her supplies. She asked Christie to pick out a color. Pink was Christie's favorite color. It had taken 20 minutes. Christie looked at the clock on the wall. It had already passed 6:00 p.m. It was already dark outside. The temperature had dropped down to 25 degrees and she did not like coming home late if it was not her own neighborhood. She walked over to where the cabs were parked to get inside.

Chapter 2

It was Monday morning. Christie had gotten up early, she had taken a hot shower and she put on her makeup before she put on her new outfit. She was wearing her new earrings. She had to fix her hair back in place. After that she went to her kitchen to make a pot of fresh brewed gourmet coffee. She did not want any breakfast, but had heard that if she ate something it might help her make a good impression with the interviewer, and she will not have hunger pains. So, she fixed some bacon with two slices of bread. She sat down to eat and drank her coffee.

Christie looked at the early morning news on television to hear what the temperature was this morning. The weather man said, "It is supposed to reach a high of 35 degrees". This was the month of March, and that was still cold. Christie had to pull out her black wool hooded coat. She had bought it from Burlington's coat factory. She had a matching scarf and glove set that she wore with it. She was getting ready to head out in a few minutes.

A Suburban bus would be coming down the street in 15 minutes. So, Christie had to be at the bus stop in 5 minutes. She made sure that she had all her material with her for her interview. She had bought a briefcase that came with a long strap. She grabbed her purse, and her keys. She made sure everything was cut off in her kitchen.

Christie had turned off all the lights, except the hall light. She walked out of her suite. She locked the door, and took the stairs down to the main lobby.

She walked to the bus stop. She had the address to where the Newspaper Company was located. She had made it there on time. She had the interview with Mr. Walter White. He was impressed with Christie's educational back-ground. He said, "You will not be able to work by yourself for a while." "Most people they have a problem with that, and it will cause a problem down the line". Christie told him, "This will not bother me. I find it easy to work with other people. I have a good disposition, and I am quite friendly". He smiles. He said, "I will get back to you in two weeks to give you my decision." He shook Christie's hand. He walks her to the door. She thanks him. And she walks out of the office.

"I will place you on our Intern, program that will be for 3 months. I like to use the word, "rookie". That is my term, for not knowing anything". He had told Christie that before the interview. This is the probation period, before you are actually considered a permanent employee.

Christie Lands Her First Job

Christie landed her first job working as an Intern as a Weather and Journalist-Reporter. The company was called, "TODAY'S NEWSPAPER COMPANY" She was assigned to work with a male reporter. They both had to cover the stories on the treacherous weather condition. He was her supervisor. His name is John Atkins. He was always making the comment that this job is too tough for a woman. He would say, "Christie, I think it would be best if you just type this report, today." Christie would say, "John, I do not want to just be a journalist." She felt the tension in her neck. Her voice was about to crack. She knew this would only come when she was deeply stressed. She had to clear her throat. She felt that she should tell him about her educational background. He was not paying her any attention. He was reaching for their equipments, and he checks out the weather condition on the scanner.

They could detect where the storm was heading with their monitor. It alerts them with a flashing "red light". Their boss had said all of the equipment was his most prized possessions. He had spent thousands of dollars on his business equipment. Christie had to think of how to get him to see things her way. She said to him," John you know that I had gone to a New York Community College and have received my 2 year Associate degree in Communication and Journalism, so, I am qualified to do this job". She continued, "I do not think this is fair the way you are treating me. This is not what Mr. White has hired me to do". She tried to control her anger as she said to him, "You have no right to make me stand on the side line".

"How am I to learn anything, if I am to sit back and watch you do all the reporting", Christie asked him. He said nothing back to her. He gets out of the van. He had done all the work. He came back into the van after the storm had ceased. He still did not speak to her. He handed her the equipment to put away in the storage area. Christie was crying. She had spoken out of term. He was her supervisor. Christie knew she was being insubordinate. He did not scold her this time. He just drove them back to the Newspaper Company. They had to type out their report, and rush it to the press to be printed. They had never missed a story.

It was a gloomy day. The sky had turned dark. The wind was so strong that it shook their van. All types of news reporters were standing outside with their equipments. They used a tape recorder as well as jotted down notes. The company gave them a camera that sat on a stand. They could take some photos, if they wanted to use them as illustrations. The storm lasted all afternoon. Christie was inside the van, while John worked outside. He came back in the van. He said nothing to Christie, he just handed her the equipment to put away. He gets in the driver seat. Christie could not concentrate on anything else right this minute accept how hurt she was this time.

Christie's head was beginning to hurt. Her face had turned red. She had started cracking her knuckles. This was a habit of hers. She especially did this when she was tensed. John just let Christie rant and rave until she had calmed down. They had to do a report on the weather, everyday. Christie had gone head to head with this man. They constantly would express differences of opinions.

Christie knew that she was hanging on by a mere thread and it would be just a matter of time that she would push the wrong button. She could not have a decent conversation with this man. They never could look each other in the eye. He would just say to her, "I do not want to hear this sulking right now. You are giving me a headache". She did not want to look him in the face. However, he was very handsome. He was tall, and had his hair cut short. He had finger waves in his hair. He wore a mustache, with a goatee.

Christie knew this was an act of discrimination towards her. She felt like she was not treated as an equal pertaining to their job. She could have filed a complaint with a law firm. But, she did not want to hurt their boss who was very nice to her. So, she kept quiet.

Christie goes on a date with Quinton

This was Friday night. Christie was supposed to get home so she could go out on her date with Quinton. He had called her every night because he said that he was bored at work. She asked Quinton. "Where is your staff"? He gets quiet. He said, "I work better when I am alone." Christie felt like she was listening to herself talk. He said, "I have hired so many people and they were not willing to learn anything from me. They all felt like they knew better than him". He said, "I told them that they could find somewhere else to work and good luck". He then stated to her, "I am in the process of hiring some more people. I hope they are mature workers". Christie told him that she understood what he was saying.

Christie took a cab home to get ready for her date. She had laid out a brown formal gown, it was long and sleeveless. She had bought the designer gown and it came with a coat that matched the gown. The coat had fur around the collar and on the cuffs of the sleeves. Christie put on her make-up and earrings. She had a pair of brown high heels with tiny sequins.

Quinton came to the apartment to pick her up for their date. He gets out of his car, and he rings the buzzer to the suite. Christie watched him walk on the porch. He was dressed sharp. He was wearing a silver gray pinstripe walking suit that had a long tail. Christie especially liked his shoes. Quinton's shoes were silver gray alligator shoes. Christie used her intercom system to tell him she would be right down. He waited in the lobby for her. She picked up her clutch bag and her keys off the hall table. She walked outside to go to the elevator. She rode it down to the main lobby. He was standing there smiling at her. He said to her, "Hey, you are beautiful, Christie". She thanked him. "You are dashing, too", she said to him. He held the door open for her. They walked over to his car. He opens the door on her side. He drives her to the theater where they were seeing a concert.

The storm

On another day, the sky had blackened, and it was dark outside. The wind was hissing, like a whistle sound. Christie thought to herself we must be having a tornado storm. Her coffee cup and saucer on her counter started to shake. The wind had blown hard against her apartment windows. She could feel the draft seeping through the cracks of her glass sliding glass door. Then the air was coming through the vent. She turned on the television. The early morning news had come over the air. It was 6:00 a.m. The news anchor man announced, "There is a torrential rain storm approaching in the NYC area. There has been sighted a few hails, and thundering with lightning. Visibility is very poor, and driving condition is not safe. This is a news cast bulletin report, as well as a warning", he cautioned. "Please prepare to take cover at once." The sirens had not sounded off in the city, yet. But, the warning signals on the television were sounding off. They had announced a weather alert warning on all the stations.

The news reports were saying," A Severe Rain Storm Has Approach the City of New York." This meant that they would have a flood. Christie's phone began to ring. She answered it quickly. A man speaks. "This is John," he said to her. "Christie, I am coming to pick you up, right now." "Please be ready, and I want you to be down in the lobby in 20 minutes, if you still want to have your job tomorrow", he added. This sounded like a command to Christie.

They were in competition with other newspaper companies. So they had to be on top of things. And to make sure their information got to the press on time. Christie's duties were to write out what they saw in the weather. These were the things that she had described in her report: knocked down wires and light poles, trees leaves blowing strongly, debris falling, lightning and thundering, window and glass being blown out of buildings, flooding.

Christie had to get dressed in a hurry. She had already taken her shower. She still had on her pajamas set and wearing her hush puppy house shoes. She had rushed to her bedroom, and grabbed the first pair of black pants she saw hanging on a rack, she put them on quickly, and takes out a silver-gray designer turtleneck sweater from her dresser. She had gone to her hall closet to pulls out her tall, "wet look boots." She would wear them whenever she had to go out in the rain. Christie slipped them on after she put on her knee high socks. She had grabbed her black "wet look" coat with the hood. She had to wear it with a thin sweater coat. She had bought three of them. She pulled out the gray one. It came with a hood. She put it on quickly. She made sure that she had her scarf and gloves.

Christie walked to her kitchen to turn off her coffee maker. She was just about to make a cup of coffee. She had to make sure that all the windows were closed tight. She had to turn off all the lights. She had forgotten to put on her make-up. She had five minutes to do her face. She walked to the bathroom to put it on quickly. She grabbed her make-up bag. It was sitting on her bathroom counter. She had no time to style her hair. She just put a clamp on it, and twisted it into a ball. She always wore her expensive gold loop earrings. She grabbed them from off her dresser, and put them on her ears.

It had started to rain heavily, and was thundering. Christie heard a loud boom sound. A lightning bolt cracks across her window. She raced to put on her outerwear. She grabbed her umbrella. She put her purse strap across her shoulder. She was holding her keys, in her right hand. As well, she had her brief case; it came with a shoulder strap. She immediately put it over her shoulder. She always took it with her on her assignments. She locked her door. She raced for the stairs. She was downstairs in five minutes. She said aloud to herself, “Thank God.”

There were only three units in Christie’s building. She always liked being up high so that she could see the view of the river. She had told the manager of the apartment that she wanted an apartment on the 3rd floor. She made it to the lobby in time. John was in front of the building. She had rushed outside. She had to make sure she had locked the outer door. The other door was automatic. It locked itself. He had slid the door open for her in the van. “Get in quickly, Christie,” he demanded. He took off in a hurry. Christie said, “Good Morning.” He normally said, “Morning sweet thing”. He did not greet her back, this way.

He just uttered, “Morning” He could not speak to her, pleasant. He said to her, “Make sure we have everything together.” “This storm is a Category 1.” Christie had learned that these torrential storms came from the Caribbean Island. He started speeding down the street in the company van. It had two red flashing lights sitting on top. The company name was written was on the outside of the van.

It read, “TODAY’S NEWSPAPER COMPANY” He drives to the site.

John pulls up at the curb. Christie was monitoring the weather on the scanner. They had a tracking device that was sitting above the dashboard. She had to tell John the location of where the storm was approaching. There would be a flashing red sign, whenever it was heading in a direction. She had told him, "It is heading in the downtown, Eastside area of NYC." She quickly took out the tape recorder that was the property of the Newspaper Company. It came with a long stand. They sat it in an upright position. They also had flash lights in case the visibility was poor and they brought their microphone and recorder in case they needed to speak to a particular person and they needed to record the information. It came with a long extension cord.

Christie was ready to report on the condition of the storm. The employee training session had taught her in three days how to do an effective report. Our boss called it an in-service. All employees had to attend. An instructor had come out to their facility. They sat in the conference room. So, she knew what to do. She was about to get out of the van. John said to Christie, "You are to stay in the van." She was in a state of shock. Christie asked, "What do you mean, John?" She was so pissed at John. This was constantly happening. She had to stay in the van, and watch him do the report if he thought that the weather condition was too treacherous.

Christie said to him with tears in her eyes, "I want to cover this story with you, too." John gets out of the van. He takes Christie equipment from out of her hand. Christie did not understand why he was so mean to her. He said, "It is way too, dangerous." He stated to her, "I am just protecting you". He said to her in a soft tone. "Christie, will you please take a look around you. I can barely stand still with this wind blowing against me. If you think I am wrong, take it up with the boss," he exclaims. "I am going to do just that, John. This is so unfair," I exclaimed. He said, "I do not have time to argue with you, Christie. I am your boss." He had shut the door. I am thinking how I can pay him back for what he has done for me. He had said in a stern voice to not use the phone to call the Newspaper Company.

Christie was thinking that there probably is a power outage in some location. Even if she did get through to him, she was not going to be complaining to him at this very moment. She just ignored his remark. That made no sense to her. The storm had ceased after 30 minutes. He had made the report. He came back inside the van. He hand her the equipment to put away. She had to choose the right words to say to him, at that instance, she said to him, "John, I think that you are prejudice, and a female hater." "You think that we women are too helpless, and can not do anything. I do not even wear an apron to do the cooking, and cleaning at my place. I think you have a misconception of what we can or can not do".

"I will not bow down to you, Mr. Atkins. Let me take that back", Christie exclaimed. I will bow down to you, "Your Majesty." She made the gesture to him in the van. Christie had put a little smirk on her face. "Did I forget to kiss your hand and wash your feet", she uttered, "I seem to have forgotten to bring my sanitizer lotion". His face turned purple. Christie could not shut her mouth, "I will give you this one thing; I am not good with twisting the top off of the jars. I am grateful to have a man around to do these manly things. And, let me tell you one more thing", she had started to cry. She wiped her eyes on the back of her hand. "I think you are so afraid that I might do a better job than you". Christie was reaching for a box of Kleenex that they kept in the back seat. She held the box in her lap. She said to him, "You do not have to worry about me. I am not the type to run to the boss to tattle tail on you. I will still let you take all the credit for these assignments. You know that this is “dead wrong”. “Like my grandfather would say to me, “I do not have to say one word; your conscience will whip you.” I said nothing else to him. He gets quiet. Then, he lowers the boom. I felt like an earth quake had hit the State of New York.

John had taken off his trench coat. He drapes it across the seat. He looks at me with glossy red eyes, and said, “I have heard your rattling for 20 minutes. Now, you will listen to me!” He exclaimed, “You are an overbearing smart mouth, and a beautiful woman. You do not know the first thing about being a reporter. I care less about your education. I have not gone to a college. I work my way up by being on the job. I have worked at this Newspaper Company for 12 years to your one year. I think you are wet behind the ear, and this will affect your work performance”. Christie was crying. She wiped her eyes with the back of her hand. He said with empathy, “You ought to thank your lucky stars that some men think highly of you to want you to be away from danger”.

“Nobody has ever talked to me that way”, he exclaimed. “I have given you the utmost respect. I have even open up the door for you. You call me, prejudice. You are right, in that regard I do not think that a woman’s place is for weather reporting. If I was against females, I would act like you did not exist. I would not say these sweet little sentiments, to you. I would not speak to you at all.

I would ignore everything you said to me”. He was crying. “I have loved women my whole life”. He was wiping his eyes. “I love everything about women”. “Your eyes, the feminine things you do, how you dress, the style of your hair, the way you walk, and even talk”. He was crying so hard. “I am a husband, a father of twin girls. They love me with all their heart”. “You are not a professional.” “You are not ready to work in a workplace. I will never recommend that you work by yourself".

He had ended this storm that we were having of our own. "To set the record straight, I do not go tattle tailing to the boss every time I have a problem", he continued. "I am trying to save your beautiful self, from the embarrassment, and hurt that will no doubt come when you call to bad mouth me", he stated. "Mr. White is a nice guy and he is like a father to me". "I have seen some sides of him that will make your head spin. I have worked for him for 12 years. I have seen people running out of his office in tears, who had came in to do a grievance report. I feel sorry for you, Christie. You are a nice person and I really thought I could be your friend". As Christie listened to him, she swallowed a lump in her throat.

Christie was too hurt, and angry to apologize to him for her outburst. John said nothing to her when they were on their way back to the Newspaper Company. He did not apologize or say anything to her. Christie went straight to her cubicle. She still had to type out the report on the storm. She had a cardboard box she kept underneath her desk. She was sure that she was fired. John went to take out the form from his desk. He had to type in the information on the form. Then, he gets up to walk to his office. He had removed his trench coat. He was wearing a black pin striped suit. He had straightened his tie. Christie watched him knocking on the door, to Mr. White office. He was holding the form in his hand. Christie thinks this took a few seconds. Then she heard her name being called.

"Ms. Higgins, come in here right now!" Mr. White shouted. It sounded like the roof was about to blow off the building. Christie left her cubicle rushing to his office.

Christie knocked softly on his door. Mr. White opens up the door for her. He was holding a form with his other hand. John was standing there with one hand in his pocket. Christie stood there literally shaking in her boots. “Ms. Higgins, I am quite surprised in receiving this blasted Grievance form”, Mr. White shouted. He was shaking it in Christie’s face. His face had turned red. He had gotten angry. He held the form in his hand, tightly. As if it was going to fly out of the window. Christie felt a breeze. He says to her, “I get so sick and tired of receiving complaints every, blasted time,” he shouted. “I am appalled at the way you two are acting. You cannot get along with each other. I will not have this kind of behavior in my company!” he exclaims. “I am finish with you, John. Do not slam my door on your way out.” John left out of the office in a hurry. Mr. White cut off his television, and closed the blinds. Christie knew she was about to be chewed out. Mr. White pulls a chair out for Christie to sit down. Christie sits down.

“Before, I start on this thing, I want to say to you, ma’am, I do not appreciate people coming into my office, complaining how I run my business. I have hired,

as well as fired people over the years,” Mr. White stated to Christie. “I am constantly on the phone talking to lawyers that want to take me to court. He had calmed down, or so Christie had thought.

Mr. White takes out the company’s Office Manual Book. “I think you should have one of these at home. These books are not cheap”, he exclaimed. “I had to purchase them at a Printing company. I have 49 employees”, he had added. Christie could not say one word. He goes on, “I am going to go through every by law with you page by page”. Christie looks at him, hard. This was not a small book. Christie knew she could be there for several hours. Mr. White put on his glasses.

Mr. White begins to read the first page. His biography, about how he formed the Company. He even read the table of contents. He was reading page by page! Christie shook her head, in disgust. She knew that she would not get home until it was late. He made emphasis at each rule. He read, "Number 1, you will not speak to anyone that is in authority over you in a disrespectful manner." "You will get yourself terminated instantly if you do". There were at least 50 numbers. He had comprised it with questions and facts. He stated the Constitution and Amendment t He closed the book at the last number. " You know I had written out a check for your last two weeks pay. John had begged me not to fire you, now". Christie looked at the clock. It was 6:00 p.m. He still was not finish with her. He continued, "In spite of the way you have been talking to him, he felt you should have another chance. John is one amazing man. "

"I want you to know that I had chewed John out, too. I had told him in no uncertain terms, do not come into my office with this kind of mess," Mr. White stated to Christie. Mr. White continued with his ran ting, "I am running a business, not a circus. I do not want to ever see you in this office with this kind of problem again." He looks at her, pleadingly. "Do you understand me, Ms. Higgins"?

Christie said, "Yes this will never happen again Mr. White". Mr. White said, "You may leave my office now". Christie went back to her cubicle to put on her coat. She picked up her purse and briefcase. She was ready to go home. The others had left already at the end of the day.

Christie felt like jumping over the Hudson River Bridge. She had heard some words directed at her that she thought would never come out of his mouth. He was such a nice man. Christie thought nervously "I must have pushed the wrong button".

Christie could remember those stinging words, Mr. White spoke to her. By the man she thought could be like a father to her. She recalled with clarity the words Mr. White had admonished her with, stating furiously. "You were insubordinate". "He is your supervisor". "He can tell you what to do". Then, telling her about his life. "Before I had gotten my job, a woman was my boss". Mr. White continued telling her about his past employer concluding with his feelings for his former employer. "I never disrespect her, even if I thought she was wrong. Then one day she told me she was resigning and she said to me, I want you to have my job, Mr. White".

Christie was told to go back to work. She could not look at John. He had left the office to go smoke a thin cigar. He came back over to Christie's desk. He was still angry with her. He frowns over at her as she sits at her desk. He walks over to her and said, "I will take you home. Before, we go to the van. I want to say this to you. I had warned you what might happen if I went into his office with this grievance report. You had better take heed to my words. I may not have the education you have, but I am not stupid in any way", he stated vehemently.

John wipes his eyes with a Kleenex and said warmly, "I think I might have been too harsh with my words, I will admit to you that my temper will get the best of me, especially, when I said to you, I will never forgive you." That part is not true, John stated while shaking his head. Christie thought to herself, "I have been taught to forgive and to turn the other cheek"—this is the words of my Pastor, Dr. Horace Washington. He had quoted a partial passage that was from the book of Ecclesiastes. "Be ye angry and sin not; Let not the sun go down upon your wrath." Christie had read that passage, often. John interrupted her thoughts, "I will forgive you in time", Christie. Christie was crying all over again. John continued, "I just want you to know, that I will be going with you on all your assignments. I will monitor your work performance like I had before in the past".

John said to me. "I had never raised my hand to hit a woman. I promise that to myself and to my parents. But I think you should have had a spanking once in your life". "Or you would not have spoken to me this way." He had stated. "How dare you insult, me in this manner!" he exclaims. "What got to me the worse is when you uttered to me, "Your Majesty did I forget to kiss your hand and wash your feet?" Christie could not stop crying as John repeated the words that she had said to him in anger. John said, "I have to go home to my wife, and tell her that I had a brawl with a woman today. John said, I think I must have deceived my wife in a way. I had once said to her, that I would never say one unkind word to a woman." "You have made me into something that I did not want to become, today". John puts out his cigar. He said, "I am going home and take me a good cold shower". Listening to him, Christie felt like she had been set on fire, and she needed to cool down. John held the door open for Christie in the van. She got inside. But, she wanted to walk home. John dropped Christie back off at her apartment. Christie thought to herself that she had to make it her number one priority to find herself another job. She was desperate to find other work.

It had been two weeks since Christie had a date with Quinton. Quinton called Christie up on Sunday. He says to her, "I am bored and thought you might come over here to the Record Shop to keep me company. Quinton was the owner of three Record shops. Christie asked him which one of his locations was he was working at today. He said to her, “I am in China town district in downtown NYC.” She had gone over to that area before and it was very nice. There were many Asians in this area. I like the food and their shops. Quinton was waiting on Christie to arrive. He stood outside on the corner.

Quinton had on a black leather jacket and he was tossing some gummy candy into his mouth. He would sometimes give some candy to the children who were walking down the street. He kept a drawer full of candy for whoever came into his shop. He was very friendly. He stood there waiting until he saw Christie get off the subway. She had to go upstairs to walk across the street to his shop. He waves to her and smiled when he saw her in the outfit.

She had on a beige color leather pants set it had fur around the collar, and she wore a thin pull over sweater underneath the jacket. And her gray color high heel shoes. She looks casual but also she was making a fashionable statement with this outfit.

Christie smiles at him and asked, “What are you doing standing outside in the cold”? Quinton answered, “It is not that bad out here I was waiting around on you, dear” “Thank you, “I am hungry, Quinton”, Christie replied. “Come on into the shop. I will let you see one of my menus from the Chinese Restaurants”, Quinton said. There were three of their restaurants down the street from each other. One was the Golden Nuggets, the other one was called China Town Café, and then there was, The China Buffet. Sometimes they had someone outside who would give samples of their food. Christie went inside to take a look at his menu. Quinton takes out some money. “Since you are hungry you may as well get me something to eat, too”. “I want some egg fu young, rice with gravy, and an egg roll”, he said.

Quinton gave Christie a kiss as she was about to walk to the door. He knew that she had standards and he was not trying to start a relationship with her in that way. Christie went across the street to the Golden Nuggets restaurant. She went to the carry out booth. She was greeted by the cashier who spoke English. The cashier asks Christie what she wanted to order. Christie told her what she wanted. She gave the cashier $20.00. Meanwhile, Quinton was approached by a young man who wanted to get a job at the record shop. Quinton went in his office to get an application. Christie heard Quinton say to the young man, "I am looking for someone to work the afternoon shift. I have a guy who is coming in at 3:00 p.m. He will train you in what needs to be done. Can you come back this afternoon"? The young man said, "Yes, I can come back at that time". Quinton said, "Good". "I will need all your information for tax purposes". Quinton went to the office to get out the forms.

It took Christie 20 minutes to get her food. She walked back over to the shop. The young man who applied for the job was happy. He walked past Christie smiling. Christie had been angry about her job. She was ready to find another job. Quinton had told Christie that she could work for him at one of his shops. She told Quinton that working in a record shop was not what she wanted to do with her life. She wanted to be a Private Investigator. Quinton was surprised. He told her that he did know any women who were in that kind of career. Not to mention that she was Black. He was not prejudice. He sympathized with her, and said to keep the faith. He said to her, "I will keep my eyes and ears open for you". He asked Christie, "What kind of soda do you want to drink"? Christie said, "I will have a Sprite". John went to the back to the vending machine. He brings out two sodas. They sat out front in two folding chairs he brought from the back. She had stayed over to the shop all day. When Christie got home she was tired. She had gotten her mind off of her problems for the moment. Things were going pretty good with Quinton and her.

Until one day Quinton calls her up from home. He sounded terrible. He said, "I really like you a lot Christie". "I have to be honest with you. I do not just want to be your friend. I am use to becoming more affectionate to women". Christie knew what that meant. They both were not in agreement with each other on this thing. She was not surprised. She said to Quinton, "I understood. I appreciate your being honest with me. I will see you around". He asked her, "No hard feeling Christie? " Christie said, "None whatsoever, Quinton you will meet that ideal woman." He corrected her, "You were the ideal woman, but I am not willing to cooperate on your terms". So that was the end of Christie's dates with Quinton.

Christie had to keep her standards, especially if she wanted to meet the right man.

Christie looks for another job

Christie was thinking that this was the straw that broke the camel's back. This was her last straw. She had to get away from the Newspaper Company, expeditiously. She started leaving resumes in all the law offices around town. She even put in a resume with the News Media at Channel 7 News Station. Still no one would call her for an interview. Christie was sitting at her cubicle when her phone rings. She picks up the phone, and answers saying the company's name. " Yes, this is Christie, how may I help you?" It was a call from the News Station. A secretary from the Human Resource office, said," We have received your resume." Christie said to herself, "Thank you, Lord". The

Secretary of the Human Resource was screening all their calls, she said to Christie.

"We are currently looking for News reporters. We are conducting interviews for all our applicants. You are qualified for this interview", she tells Christie. "This will be an open interview." That means names will be called in random. You will have to listen for your name to be announced. "We will be having our interviews between the hours of 8:00 a.m. to 3:00 p.m. We will hire the right reporters immediately on the spot. Christie looked at her watch. She thanks her for giving her this information. Christie had her lunch break in twenty minutes. She had an hour for lunch.

The News Station was right downtown from where Christie worked. She could get there in ten minutes. She continued to finish her work. She stopped when it was time for her lunch break. She grabbed her coat and put it on. She rushed out of the building after punching out at the time clock. Christie began to walk in a hurry.

When Christie got to the News Station, she could not believe her eyes. There must have been hundreds of people. They were waiting in a long line. It had extended all the way around the block. There were men and women of all races standing outside. Christie asked a lady, "Is this where we line up for the Interviews? The lady answered to Christie, "Yes, but you are in the wrong place." Christie asked her again, "Where do I stand?" The lady had an Afghanistan drape around her shoulder. She points, and said" It is way around the corner". It was 18 degrees outside. But it felt like 4 below zero. Christie asked herself," is this worth my time"? Christie thanks her and walks away.

Christie tried to keep her scarf tied around her mouth. There was a wind chill factor warning the public to make sure that they had on warm clothes to block off the wind, too. Christie walked around the corner. A man was standing ahead of a line. He was shivering. She asked him, "Is this where the line begins?" He nods his head. He then speaks to Christie.

"You have to go stand across the street." He turns around to show her. They had formed another new line. Christie was becoming agitated every minute, now. She cracked her knuckles. She had this habit since she was a child. She went across the street. She asked a woman who was ahead of her in line, "Where does this line end?" She said to Christie in a flippant remark. "It had better end here. I have been here since 8:00 a.m., and I have not eaten anything today".

Christie shook her head in disgust and rushed to stand in the line. She had skipped her lunch. A man was standing outside, who worked as a Security officer. He shouts to the applicants, "Please move along in the line". He did not need a "bull horn" he had an audible voice. Christie asked another man in the line how long had he been waiting. He exclaims, "It took me like 20 minutes to move from this spot".

Christie thought, she had to get back to work. She was going to get in some trouble. She stopped the Security Officer who was walking up and down the line. He says to her, "Yes ma'am?" It was freezing. Christie asked him, "Is there anyway I can phone back here, to see if my name has already been called?" He answers, "You are not planning on staying?" "I have never heard of anybody doing that, here", he said. You had better let them know, inside that you can not stay". "I have a job, and I am on my lunch hour", I explained. He said, "That is too bad. Some people had called off work when they received their call." Christie was steamed. She tells him, "They called me from work".

"Is this my fault", he asked. Christie felt bad about lashing out at him. She was under a lot of pressure, and deeply stressed out. She said to him," I am truly sorry, sir." He walks away. Christie had stayed for 25 more minutes. She told a representative who was walking up and down each line. She had a clipboard that she was using to sign people names off of the list. When she had gotten to where Christie had been standing. She asked her, "What is your name?" Christie answered," My name is Christie Higgins. Christie adds, "I will not be staying here any longer." The representative checks Christie's name off the list. "Have a nice day", she tells Christie. Christie walks back to her office.

Christie was still working at the Newspaper Company in spite of how sad and pathetic she felt being there after the incident had gone down with her supervisor and the way that her boss had treated her in his office. He was not the same man that called her, his baby girl. Christie still greeted him every morning. She had stopped buying pastries for a while. She made sure that she picked up a copy of the newspaper every day so that she could check out the Help Wanted section.

Christie's newspaper ran ads of various kinds every day. She bought herself a copy of the newspaper. Inside was an ad that read, *"How would you like to become a PI?" "You will not be discriminated, because of your race gender, or height." If you have what it takes, you ought to contact us, right now."* They had a 24-hour hot line. An operator was screening the calls.

Chapter 3

Christie had to take the subway back to her apartment. " She reached in her purse to take out her keys. There were two doors she had to unlock before she could get inside her building.

Christie rode the elevator up to her suite. She had taken off her outer wear. She hung them up in the hall closet. She was starving. All she had eaten was a bag of potato chips, and she had a soda. She had skipped her lunch to go to stand in a line for 45 minutes for an interview. Which, she had not taken because it was too long of a wait. She arrived home about 5:30 p.m. She went straight to her phone in the kitchen. She had been residing in this area since she was 27 years old. This was a suburban area of New York City. It was urban renewal. She had a terrace balcony. She was facing the Hudson River side.

This was where all the wind was coming from off the river. It was cold in her apartment. She went to turn up the heat. She had to open her drapes that had been closed all day. Although, it was chilly outside the sun was shining. She was about to go make the phone call to see what the advertisement entailed. She had her newspaper out. She had put a circle around the area in red ink. She had put this section in the front so she could get to it when she got home.

Christie picked up her cordless phone from it holding stand. It was sitting in an upright position on her kitchen counter. She could have it mounted, if she so desired. She held the receiver in her other hand, getting ready to make the call. She walked over to look in her refrigerator to see what she could find to eat. She decided to fix herself an egg and bacon sandwich. She was waiting on someone to answer their phone. She had no ideal what kind of place that she had called, now. She wanted to check her messages.

Christie's light was flashing on her answering machine. It sat next to her "Princess" telephone that was sitting on a brown round table. It was in her living room. She was starving. She held her stomach. She dials the number and she utters to herself, "You all had better hurry up". She was thinking aloud to herself. Then, a female operator clicks in on the line.

She had spoken pleasant. She said, "Is this call in reference to our advertisement that we placed in the" Today Newspaper, Want Ad section?" Christie replies, "Yes, that is correct." She said to Christie, "Are you aware that you have contact a college?" Christie was about to hang up. She had no plans of going back to a school, she thought to herself. She answers the operator's question, "I had no ideal what this call, entailed." Christie wanted to hang up. The operator said to Christie, "Wait a minute, honey. Please, hold on for a minute".

Christie heard another click. Another person said, "MACKINSON & HILLARD COLLEGE." Christie asked her, "What kind of school, is this a college?"

The operator explained that this school was designed for people who desired to become Private Investigators, as well as a Detective. She asked Christie, "What course will you be taking?" Christie stated," I want to become a Private Eye." The operator told her, "Let me put you through to the right department. Please hold on a moment". Christie was getting agitated from all the delays.

Christie cracked her knuckles again. Her knuckles were sore from this dreadful habit. "Listen here, Miss", Christie started. The operator had clicked off the line and put her on hold. Before Christie had a chance to protest for these long delays, another female voice said, "Can you hold for another minute?"

Christie was being sarcastic. She told the operator, "Your job must be very exciting." The operator was silent. The operator then responded, "I know you are trying to become offensive, ma'am. I will let that remark slide". Christie apologized for her remark saying, "I am sorry for my snide remarks. I am frustrated right now, and in a bad mood." The operator accepted Christie's apology explaining, "I am still trying to get the man who is the head of our Criminology & Investigation Department to pick up". Christie said, "Take your time." Although Christie was getting impatient and tensed, she tried acting much nicer. They were just doing their jobs.

The operator came back on the line. She asked Christie, "Do you mind if I could try to reach someone else's office. Christie said "Sure." Christie starting thinking, "Everything else in my life is going haywire". Christie started mumbling to herself. Christie and said again, "This must be a fun job you have, dear". Christie grins to herself. "I actually like my job, the operator stated.

Christie's sandwich was sitting on her saucer. It had gotten cold. So, she put it in her microwave oven. She had nothing cold to drink, so she was going to make herself some hot tea. She was thinking she had made a mistake in calling this number. She should be putting in more resumes at the Law offices. She thought that they might be hiring at this one other law firm. The other law firm was not in the Bronx area. She would have to take a subway. She had put a circle around their advertisement in the Want Ad Section of the newspaper so she could find their number on Monday.

Christie was thinking to herself while she continued to wait, that she was not into," doing this school thing, again." This was farthest from her mind. The operator put her on hold, for the final time. She was about to say," Please give my name, also my number to whoever that person is that you are trying to reach. I will be here all day". Until, a woman came on the line.

The woman said to Christie, "Hello, we do apologize, for all these delays. The man who is the head of our Investigation and Law Enforcement department had a family crisis. He had to leave the college. I will be screening all his phone calls. I am trying to reboot my computer. I have to take down your data', she continues, "My name is Tracey. I will be asking you a series of question. I will need to get a profile, on you. After I am finish we will go straight to the process of registering you". Then she said, "Please do not hang up, dear. I can feel your frustration". Christie guessed that the other operator had told Tracey what she had said.

"I know where you are going, I have been there myself, Tracy said, "I thought that going back to school, was my worse nightmare." Christie had nodded her head and was listening, now.

"After I graduated it changed the way I felt. I had gotten my degree" said the female spokes person. Tracey continued, "Let me tell you, honey. It was worth every dime I had to spend on this school. I had to go out in all kinds of bad weather. I had worn out shoes, and coats that could not be repaired anymore. I stayed in while everyone else was out having fun. My husband would encourage me, “Keep going Tracey, you are almost there.” He was my Pastor, at that particular time.

Christie had wiped her eyes. She reached for a box of Kleenex that sat on her counter. It was down to the bottom of the box. Christie is thinking, “I like this woman”. Christie listens as Tracey explains, “I had fallen in love with this man, and we got married.” He is a wonderful man.

“Who did you say you were? “ Christie asked the woman.

“I do apologize. Sometimes I get hyped up when I am excited” Tracey elaborated and stated, “My name is Dr. Tracey Washington. I am the Administrator”. Christie had begun to smile. “You have a doctorate degree in Administration?” Christie asked her.

Tracey laughs. “Yes but not in Administration, I have a degree in Psychology. I am also qualified to teach Psychology”. Christie was so impressed with Tracey’s education and running the College.

“I was expecting a man to be the Administrator.” Christie said, still thinking that this was a College. Christie’s tone had changed, considerably. Tracey spoke nice. “I know you thought a man should be in charge.”

“Well, it has crossed my mind.” Christie stated. “Actually, I believe that all women should be treated as equal.” We should not be made to feel inferior to a man, Christie continued, “Moreover, I admire your determination”.

” Wow, you have said a mouthful” Tracey exclaimed. She was very appreciative of what Christie said to her. Tracey laughs.

“Thank you. I think I needed to hear that, today” Tracey stated. Tracey goes on to explain to Christie, “Today we are quite stressed out. I have received a lot of call offs from the staff. I am running in every direction trying to help someone else who had to suddenly leave, she explains. Tracey said with a bit of tension in her voice "I am so glad you did not hang up, Christie." Tracey was trying to get familiar with Christie. "Can I ask you what is it you are trying to become?"

Now Christie had become comfortable.

Christie and Tracey were communicating well with each other. Christie felt like they were good friends. Christie said in a proud voice. "I want to be a Private Investigator. This has been my life long dream" Christie expressed in joy. "I believe I can do a good job." Christie was smiling and continues, "I love to work on my own."

"I think I understand that now." Tracey said to Christie, "You can call me, Tracey". Tracey then asked Christie another series of questions.

Tracey asked, "What are you doing now?" Christie sighed.

Tracey asked, "Are you still on the line?"

"Yes, I am still here" Christie replied. "I just had a flashback of my horrid life". Christie tells her," You must have heard my annoyance."

Tracey said, "Yes dear."

Christie explains, "I am working for a Newspaper company as a Reporter and Journalist. Christy was getting thirsty. She liked talking to this woman.

Tracey asked Christie, "Have you been working there, long?" Christie answered, " I have worked there for 1 year. The pay is good, and the job is interesting". Tracey asked Christie, "What is it that you do not like about this job?" Christie was trying not to show her emotions over the phone. She asked Tracey, "Do you have time to hear a story?" Tracey said, "I am free until 11:00 a.m. this afternoon. I have another caller to speak to at that time". Christie knew that she was going to be talking to Tracey for 3 hours.

Christie's heartbreaking story

Christie paused to think about what she was going to say to Tracey for this length of time. She began to tell Tracey about her heartbreaking story. She made sure that she chose her words carefully. She was only telling the parts that got to her the most and made her go on this rampage.

"Well, I am very observant, I love exploring things; I have been ranked the highest in my class at the college where I had attended for doing the best research on a project. I love taking pictures to captivate my reader".

"I specialize in doing things in a secretive way", Christie added.

Tracey said, "That is interesting, but not entirely unusual. "

Christie continued, "I have these ideas and suggestions that I think, will help my assignments at work. I try to tell my supervisor. He would dismiss the idea. I would ask him if I could go by myself on an assignment. He'd say, "No, that is not even an option". He would sigh and tell me, "I still do not understand why they even hired a woman to do this job. He would say," You should be in the office typing out the reports I give you." Christie told Tracey that this remark had burned her up. She would get so angry that smoke could have come out of her nose.

Christie told Tracey that she was so angry with her supervisor. Christie admitted that she not very good with her temper. "Tracey, I do not normally lash out at anyone. I was just getting fed up with his treatment towards me". Christie continued explaining her point of view regarding her supervisor to Tracey. Christie acknowledged that she had told him, "You must be prejudice, and a female hater."

Christie told Tracey that she could not even remember if she had stopped to get some air when she argued with her supervisor. She told Tracey that she continued to rant and rave at her supervisor. She wiped her eyes. She knew that she had said, "Some cruel words to him." Tears were coming down her cheek heavy. She reached for another tissue, as she recalled her words to her supervisor telling him, "You are so afraid I might do a better job than you." You do not have to worry about nothing; I will let you get all the credit for this assignment".

"Then, she had called him "Your Majesty." She told him in an evil way," I will not bow down to you, John". She had to rephrase it cuttingly by saying, "Let me correct that statement. I will bow down to you, John." Christie recalled that she made the gesture. Christie remembers something and smiles. Christie had forgotten something important that she said to him. Christie tells Tracey that she uttered something else terrible to her supervisor when she asked him, "Did I forget to kiss your hand or wash your feet, adding, I seem to have forgotten my sanitizer lotion. I must bring it every time, we are together".

Christie said to Tracey, "I had become someone, who I know does not exist in my world." I am a loving person, and I never say anything mean or terrible to anyone. However on this day, I was evil. I had become the cruelest person in the world, I felt like "Satan's daughter." I did not care how much this hurt him. The way I was carrying on with my steaming words. Christie had stated these words to Tracey. And she added. "He had gotten vehement," too.

Christie continues, he could not say anything back to me for a few minutes. He had cut off the engine. He removes his trench coat. It was a freezing temperature outside. Christie guessed that he had gotten hot.

We were both on fire, though. He turns to face her. His eyes were turning blood shot red. He gave her this look that made her think that she was getting ready to be slapped across her face. She did a duck to dodge the blow. He did not hit her. They had set that van on fire with their words. If someone had heard them, they should have called the police or fire department. He was not the type to be vulgar. He has this sweet disposition about himself. The way he carried himself when he was in the office was always professional. But, he said these stinging words to me too. They had hurt me as well as his treating me like I was helpless. She had stated.

Then, he stated to me, “On the other hand, I pity you.” He had said, “You are a beautiful black woman”. He sniffs. He pinched his nose. I will never forgive you, Christie”. She said, “I have never heard anybody say these things to me before.” Christie was crying again, now.

“You are lucky, that I do not have you fired.” He said to me, “You are being insubordinate. Nobody has ever talked to me this way, he stated. He said, “I will be writing you up.” He said, “You can start boxing up your things, immediately.” I will have this on Mr. White desk. ”

Christie tells Tracey that she had never seen a man cried so hard, except at a funeral. He was holding his face in his hands. He had never written me up before. He then said, “I had promise myself, and my parents not to never hit a woman. I know you thought I was getting ready to slap you. He wiped his eyes with a handkerchief. He said to me, “You know I must have deceived my wife in a way.

I promise her that I would never get into a fight or brawl with a woman. “I have to go home to tell her that I got into it with you, today,” he stated. He quotes a passage from the book of Ecclesiastes. "." He said that his Pastor often quotes this passage when delivering his sermon." He said that his Pastor name is Dr. Horace Washington.

Oh my stars! That is my husband who is his pastor. What did you say his name is, again? Tracey had stated.

Christie hesitated to tell her his name. She said to her, "His name is John Atkins."

"He is a member of our church. Oh, yes. I know him, and his wife, Tracey stated. I heard her sniffing. Christie continued telling her story.

"I had hurt this man terribly, by that remark". He says to me, "I have always loved you females, and have cherished the ground women walk on." Christie was trying to keep from crying again. John told her," I cannot imagine what it will be like without a female on the earth. "I love everything, about a woman. John was giving me all the characteristic of a female. John said, "Her eyes, little feminine ways, the way she walks, talk, especially the clothes she wear. He looked at me with the saddest face. He was so handsome to me. He was tall, slender built. He wore his hair cut short with fine wave. He was sporting a mustache with a goatee. Christie said, "I always love to see him walk in the office. I never in my wildest dream thought we would not become friends". Christie was wiping her eyes again. He said to her, "I do not know if I had ever shown you these pictures of my girls." He takes out his family picture. He had handed it to Christie. Christie had taken one look and frowned.

John said, "I am a Christian, a loving husband, and a father of twin girls. How in the world could you utter, such a thing to me"? He had shown her a picture of him holding one of his daughters on his back, and the other held onto his leg. Christie's eyes were turning red. She went to wet a face cloth from the bathroom. She was holding a cordless phone.

He said to me, "I have always given you the utmost respect."

Christie ran cold water in her sink to wet her face cloth. She put the wash cloth over her eyes. They were burning, now. She continued to tell her the story.

She said, "He lit a thin cigar and smoked it in the van." She stated, "He was so quiet. " She said, "I just knew he was going to hit or shake her something awful she told Tracey." However, he started the engine, she stated. He drove so fast that they had spun around the corner and left a streak mark, she stated.

Christie recalled that she held onto the door handle. She had never seen him react this way. She told him, "You are going to get us killed". He still did not say anything else to her. They got back to the Newspaper Company. He normally opens the door for her. He left her to go inside. She followed behind him. She went inside to go to her cubicle. He had removed his trench coat, she stated. He was sitting down at his desk taking out a form to type it out, she stated. He did not even look over at me, she stated. She had a flashback of his last words sitting in that van.

He said, "I was wet behind the ears. I do not know anything, although I may have an education, he stated. My whole sordid life had gone down the drain", she stated.

Christie had stated to Tracey, "That she never knew that words could hurt this bad."

Tracey responded, "Honey, my husband would tell me all the time that he would rather get cut with a knife than to have someone say an unkind word to him."

That is true, Christie replies. Christie acknowledged that her supervisor had treated her as if she was not even there. Christie blew her nose. He could not stop talking to her though, she stated. He did say that he had lost his temper, she stated.

It was like Christie was listening to a tape recorder that would not turn off. She was crying so hard. She wished she could take back her words. She was very sorry and remorseful.

She stated, "Her supervisor had said, "I even hold the door open for you every time I see you." His last words were like a torch that had been lit from a kindling stove. He frowned up. "As long as I live I will never forgive you, Christie." He had stated. He could not look me in the eyes, she stated. Christie eyes were turning red. They had started to burn. Christie could hear sniffing coming from Tracey. Christie had walked to the sink to put some cold water on her eyes. She knew Tracey was crying, too. She could hear Tracey sobbing. She knew that she had said something horrible things. She should not have said these words to her supervisor, or to any man. Christie loved everything about a man. Christie was not a weak person, she considered herself to be a strong woman. Yet, she still loved doing feminine things. She could be pretty, even beautiful. Sometimes she felt ugly.

Tracey said, "I can relate to what you are saying right now."

Christie was crying out loud. She had taken a roll off the toilet paper holder. Her supervisor was going to tell their boss. This time he meant it. In the past he would just let it bounce off his shoulder by saying to her, "I am not having this discussion, today." He would ignore everything she said to him. This time, he had taken out a long form to write her up.

Christie could see him wiping his eyes with a Kleenex that was sitting on his desk. He went to the office with the form. He had on a black pinstripe suit. He got a lot of attention from the females in our office. He just smiled at them. Or, he would say," Hey how is it going"? Christie really liked him. Christie was told to report to the office, immediately. She just knew she had been fired. She had taken out a box to put her things inside.

He was standing there with one hand, in his pocket. Mr. Walter White was our boss of the Newspaper Company. He says nothing to John. He was reading the grievance form. He shook his head in anger at me. My supervisor knew I was going to get it, now. I look over at our boss. His words were coming out like the thunder. He had looked over at me, and shook his head. He yells at me. He said, "Woman how dare you come into my office with a bunch of junk like this." He said some things to me that Christie would never forget. This was not the same boss she knew that was so sweet and kind.

He uses to call me, "Baby Girl". But, not this time. He said, "Ms. Higgins, "I had written out a check for your last two weeks pay, and was terminating you this very minute, he exclaimed. she had stated. But, John was begging me not to fired you", he said. Christie was crying out loud.

John had asked our boss to give me one more chance, she stated.

Christie knew that she had said some terrible things to this man. Yet, he begs their boss to reconsider firing her. In addition, she had to take home an Office Manual Book that was thicker than a dictionary to read it over again. Not to mention she had to come to his office everyday for a week. She had to attend an in-service meeting entitled, "Professional Conduct". This was mandatory.

To my surprise there were 48 employees attending this in-service meeting, Christie stated. Including, John. She added. He was ordered to attend, too, she stated. He was so angry with me, she stated. I had put my head down on the table to cry, she stated. I could not fight back my tears, now. I could not say anything to him for a long time, she stated. "I will make this point by saying that I had learned a lot at that in-service meeting," she stated. Christie stated to Tracey, "I may still have a temper, but I am striving to work on it so that I can be a better person."

"You know in spite of the fact that I do have a college degree in Journalist-reporting," she stated. I still do not know everything there is about reporting in a Public place", Christie had stated. "What I mean is I have been taught one way, but when it comes to being out in a public place it is totally different". This is what John had told me in his anger, she stated. "Having an education meant nothing to him; it is the work performance she had stated to Tracey." Tracey agreed with John. "He was telling you the truth, Christie", Tracey said.

Christie tells Tracey that from that day forward she had made it a point to look for another job. She could not stand to hear the truth. She had to prove to herself that she could do something better on her own. She did not need someone to dictate to her what she could or could not do. She had doors slammed shut in her face. Nobody wanted to hire a black female Private Investigator. Some men would laugh in her face. They said," You are living in a dream world, darling." Then they would say something hurtful like, "There are a lot of female jobs and companies that will hire you instantly". Christie kept having flashbacks of John words.

Christie Getting Her First Lessons in Life

Christie recalls, "I may have an education but when it comes to working on the job. I do not know anything". He said this to me everyday, she stated. He had been working there for 12 years. He said to me, "You can forget about going anywhere alone. He said, "As long as I still have a job working here, I will be monitoring your work performance more than I ever had in the past". Then, he pinches his nose and his eyes had turned glossy. He said to me, "I do not care if you like me or not." He frowns. He said, "If I hear anything out of your pretty mouth except, "What should I do first?" Or, "I have a question"? "I will write you up without any hesitation". "I will see you, downstairs in the van".

He put on his Trench coat. He walks down the stairs out of the building. He was smoking a thin cigar. Every time we go out on a site, he would greet me, "Morning, Christie. Before, you say one word. I am in charge" he had stated to me. Then, he points to his badge.

By now, Christie was getting thirsty, and her mouth was getting dried. She went to get some water from my out of her refrigerator. Tracey said to her, "This is the saddest story I have ever heard in my life. I cannot stand to listen to anymore sad stories", she stated. "I hope that there is a happy ending". Christie told her that it will be, eventually. Christie continued to talk to Tracey. She ran the water in her sink to rinse out her glass she had taken from her dishwasher. Christie had not taken out the dishes that had been in there since yesterday.

Christie still had her sandwich in the microwave oven. Christie said to Tracey, "I am not a bad person, Tracey." The tears were falling from her eyes. Her pulse had risen, and she was steamed. Christie said, "He made me feel so terrible. This is what makes me so upset". When he said, "I will forgive you in time." He said, "I am not perfect by any means. I still have some miles to go, and a few hills to climb. I am struggling to reach that goal". Christie said that she was thinking to herself that this man is very smart. Why hadn't he gone back to school? She could not look him in the eye anymore. She wiped her eyes on a napkin. She needed to go to the grocery store to buy more Kleenex tissue, and other items. She was so fed up with this job.

"I know I do not have any work experience" Tracey, Christie stated.

Tracey sniffs. She said to Christie, "I have to get me a box of Kleenex from my closet. Christie had to wait a few seconds". Tracey came back to the phone. "Please finish telling me your story", Christie. I could hear some gospel music in the background. It was turned down low.

"All I want is a chance", Tracey. Christie felt like crying all over again.

Christie finds a church

Christie had to find a church that was open late in her neighborhood. It was a Word of Faith Center. They had welcomed her inside. She had gone to sit in the back row. She sat there and listened to the Minister deliver his sermon. She felt like he was talking about her life. She was so overcome with emotion she had cried through the whole service.

Christie felt someone put their arms around her shoulder. It was a Nurse. She had taken Christie back to the Nurses Room. She gave Christie some water, and she begins to minister to her. Christie was crying very loud. Christie said, "I do not know what to do. I am not a bad person. I cannot stand myself these days". Christie had to stay in the Nurses Room until she felt better. The nurse told Christie to not stop being kind to her boss. Christie told her, "I still could not say I was sorry to my supervisor. " The nurse said, "One day it will happen.

The Minister looks at Christie with a smile. He said, "I knew you would come in here one day. Please come back for our Sunday morning service". Christie said, "I will try to come back. " Christie wanted to start going to church. Christie shook the Minister's hand on her way out the door. She walked to her apartment.

Christie has a change of heart

One morning Christie asked her boss if she could come into the office to talk to him. She had stopped at Dunkin donuts to buy some pastries. It was for anybody in the office who wanted some. She took it to his office. She had bought two large Dunkin coffees, too. She sat the box of donuts and coffee on his desk. She really liked her boss. He was about 62 years old. He reminded her of her grandfather. He had this," pot belly." He had told her that he loves to eat and drink out of jugs. He loves to tell her old stories about his childhood experience. Christie often would think about her grandfather when she saw her boss.

"You know I was raised by my grandparents. My parents had died when I was young". I am sorry, Christie, Tracy said. Thank you. Christie stated. Christie said, "My boss is so funny, too. He would crack me up", she added. He would come out of his office, after eating a hearty lunch, snacking on the pastries she had brought him from the Bakery Shop. He would hold his stomach. Then he said, "You are trying to make me so fat. I already cannot fasten my pants." Christie told Tracey that she would always stop on her way to work at a Bakery shop to buy him donuts, he was like a father figure to her.

Tracey sounded chipper and pleasant. "I wish you could come out to the college soon so I can meet you in person. I have really enjoyed talking to you and listening to your story". Christie had to laugh in spite of being frustrated. Communicating with others was the least of her traits.

Christie had a college degree in Communication and Journalism. Christie did love to talk. "I hate to keep interrupting you" said Tracey. "That is alright", Christie said to Tracey. In spite of knowing that how much she was talking, Christie continued to go on with her story. "My boss loved calling me," Baby girl". He is also black. I think he is from the "old school". He is very professional, too. He has three degrees on his wall. Christie said that she thinks that he has been working in the business for 30 years. He does not look his age. He has gray hair, with a gray mustache. He is above average height. He had told her. "I am 6 feet tall and I was weighing 180 pounds a few months ago". Christie had to laugh. She could hear Tracey laughing, too. He said, "Yesterday before I began to eat like a horse." He pulled out a chair to sit next to me at my desk. I told him about my concerns. He said to me." "What is on your pretty little mind, Baby girl?" I had to smile. I had chosen my words carefully.

"This is not what I want to do with my life. I had told him. I want to be a Private Investigator". He sympathizes with me. I told him that I like working by myself. "I understand just how you feel." he said to me. "I will look into this matter and come up with a solution". I hugged him. He left to go back to his office. I could hear some blues music being played. He had a different type of mood each day. So, today was his "Blue Mood "day.

"I know how this must sound to you, I uttered to Tracey. "As you can see, I am terribly, frustrated. Deep, down in my heart, I do know that something better is coming. I pray and read my bible often. I do not get a chance to go to my church, that often. I had become a member of this church. I could not make it to the week-days service. I had gone on Sundays". I am getting off the subject again.

"I am glad you said that", Christie. "This is important, too. I do need to know. What is your faith or religion?" Christie said that she was Baptist, but now she was with the Word of Faith.

"That is good. I have attended their denomination, too, Tracey stated. She was a "Church of God In Christ," denomination. Then, Tracey made a comment. "You must be real pretty".

"I do not think I am beautiful. Other people do, though", Christie replied. Christie had to ask her, "Why did you say that?

"The supervisor had called you beautiful, Tracey stated.

Christie shrugged her shoulder.

"Most men will not say that, if they did not really think that we are beautiful," Tracey stated. "Based on the information you have told me, they seem to be very protective of you". They probably think you should be doing feminine type, work. Tracey explained to Christie the different classifications.

"You forgot to mention being a Secretary or Administrative job" Christie stated to Tracey in a nice tone. Tracey said, "Yes you are right. There are some women, like me; that love working in an office or firm."

It must be your "looks," that plays a big factor in why you are treated this way.

Tracey stated. "I am sorry for keep interrupting you. I am carrying on like a Psychologist. Incidentally, I do have a degree in Psychology".

Christie said, "I could tell by the way you keep analyzing certain points in my story. Tracey agreed. "Yes, you are right. We have 15 minutes left. So, try to speed this story up".

Christie continues, "However hard I tried, I had not seen any drastic changes being made for me." Not in the way I had hope. She added. "I still had to work with my Supervisor". John had said, "I was still in the Intern program." He said, "You may be doing a swell job but it is the complaint that has put a halt in moving you up the ladder." "Actually, this is my first year, she stated.

Mr. White had told me, "During my interview that sometimes it takes 6 months to a year before you are considered a permanent worker." He said, "If there is a grievance report in my file when he does his evaluation—he will put me on a trial basis after the 3 months Intern program is over. I was on trial for 3 more months. Finally, I was released from this trial basis period in 6 months. John, he had recommended that I be offered for a promotion because of my work performance. "He was still angry with me about that incident." I was promoted to become Junior Journalist-Reporter. I was still not able to work alone".

"That is wonderful", Tracey said to me. Mr. White had made John the head supervisor over the Newspaper Company. He told John, "When I retire I had planned on making you the owner. If you are interested in that position and is still with us at the Newspaper Company. John had smiled. "That will be considered an honor. I will think about it" he had stated.

Christie tells about her exciting moments

One morning I got a call. It was Mr. White. He said," I have an assignment for you, Christie". This will be your first job working alone.

"What, about John?" I had asked Mr. White.

"He will be doing another assignment". He had stated.

She stated, "I had gotten so excited." I was hurrying to get dress and to get downtown to work, she stated to Tracey. Christie said, "I walked into his office with a big smile on my face." I gave him a big hug, she stated. He was not smiling this time, she stated. He pulls the chair out for me to sit down, she stated. I was too excited to sit down at that time, Christie stated. He said to me, "I think you had better sit down Christie."

He hands me an assignment, she stated. "I look down at the sheet", Christie said. "There must be some kind of typo here," Christie stated. This is not my assignment, she stated. I am a Weather-Journalist/ Reporter". Christie stated.

Mr. White looked so sad. He felt like this news might hurt and humiliate her.

I could tell by his expression on his face, she stated.

He stated to me, "After much thought, I decided to let you go on this particular assignment by yourself." Christie read the sheet. "I am to do a report on a Mother Orangutan giving birth," she stated to Tracey" "I was in a total shock," Christie stated. "This is not surprising to me one bit I had said to Mr. White. " Christie had frowned up as she continues to tell her story. She felt a tear fall from her eye.

He said to me, "I want you to go to this location, right now." It was to the NYC Zoo. "They are expecting your arrival".

I smiles at Mr. White. Then, I said. "Thank you, Mr. White I will go right away." I had rushed out of his office, crying, she stated." "I did not look back until I got to the restroom door," she stated I had myself one good cry, she stated. "A van was waiting for me outside," she stated. "I hurried to get my things from out of my desk, she stated.

"I started to laugh out loud, she stated. If anybody had been in there, they would have said that I had flipped, she stated. Tears were falling from her eyes, again. It was actually funny, she stated.

"I was ordered to do a photo shoot and cover the story," This was actually a big story in the NYC area," she stated. Christie knew that all kind of News Media and Newspapers in the country wanted to cover the event at the Zoo. It was being televised, too. Christie was the only black female there to do the report. Christie had set up her equipment. They had shield off the area. The Zookeeper had on a heavy guarded uniform and gloves, and he held a stun gun in his hand. They announce she was about to give birth! They had put a big plastic blue sheet over the female, orangutan. The area was blocked off from the public. A truck was waiting outside in the parking lot. They were ready to transport them to the Veterinarian hospital. They had armed policemen standing around.

The orangutan was still a dangerous, wild beast".

Tracey was not crying anymore or laughing. She was amazed by this story. She asked me. "Are you okay"? "Yes, I am alright", Christie replied.

Even though Christie was hurt as well as humiliated she felt like he had done her a tremendous favor. She was smiling. She was in the Newspaper. She had some photos of the mother orangutan and the baby. They allowed her to hold the baby orangutan. She had covered a full two page article about where they originated from, in the Southeast Asia rainforests and there are two species.

They set the Zoo up just for the highly endangered ape so that she could feel at home. This was a big project for the NYC Zoo. Christie had done her research on the female ape and went to writing out her story. They had her s on the 7:00 p.m. news. They did a special news report. Christie had got so much recognition for this job. Christie dabbed at her eyes. Christie said to herself, “I am tired of crying”.

Christie wanted to crack her knuckles so bad. She reached for a pen; it was sitting on her counter. She had gripped it tightly. This is what she used when she could not crack her knuckles at work. Mr. White said that she had a terrible habit. He told her, “I will give you more assignments alone, because you have done such a good job.” Christie wiped her eyes. “Everyone was smiling at me,” she stated. John had a bouquet of roses for me, she stated. He put a note on my desk, she stated.

He said, “I am so proud of you”, Christie.” Christie was so happy. She felt so sorry for what she had said to him in the van.

I had taken out a piece of typing paper and began to write John a letter of apology, she stated. “I had puts it in an envelope,” she stated. “I signed my name on it, and put it on my desk,” she stated. He had gone on other assignments.

“When John got back, he read my letter,” she stated. Christie could not stop crying.

He rushes over to hug me, and we were both crying hard,” she stated.

I think Mr. White was in his office crying too, she stated. He had closed the blinds. Tracey was crying so hard. Christie could hear her sniffing. She told Christie to hold on a minute. Christie thought Tracey was going to be sick.

“I cannot stop crying. I wonder what is wrong with me, today” Christie was thinking. Tracey came back to the phone. “That is wonderful”, Christie.

“Yes, he and I acted much better towards each other”, Christie said to Tracey. “I had learned that he was just trying to protect me. But I was too stubborn to realize it", Christie told Tracey.

The Baby Elephant was Magnificent

My boss thought that I was so good with telling stories about these mammals. He got a call from the Zoo saying that another mother was about to give birth. It was an Elephant. He asked me if I would mind covering the story again. I told him, "I had enjoyed it the last time. I will go there to do a full report". They had all types of reporters from every news station. Also, various Newspaper Companies.

They allowed us to be in the area where they were holding the mother elephant.

The only thing I could not stand was the screaming. The two Veterinarians watched the baby come out naturally. I had more photos and I did a two page article on this Mammal. I got a special plaque. I was rated as Number 1 employee of the month. "That is wonderful, Christie. Tracey said.

To conclude her little story, Christie continues, "I had never had any children of my own. I felt like I was having this baby. This mother, Elephant" she was moaning and groaning. She was in labor. She was screaming so loud. They had her in a holding area surrounded by a cage. Her mate was in another cage. There were two Veterinarians, as well as two nurses from the Animal Hospital who had came there to help with the delivery, inside the cage. They were not afraid to be inside this cage. The Elephant delivered a female baby elephant. I was smiling, now. I asked them if I could take a picture with the animal. They said, "Yes". It was so amazing to me. I wiped my eyes again.

Christie's Conclusion of her little tale

I was so thrilled and filled with joy. I even got a raise. "I was happy then, Tracey. Now, I am not happy working on this job", I said sadly.

I had received a promotion, with a salary. I am now a Supervisor. This has made Tracey cry again. "That is wonderful", Christie.

I said, sadly, "This is not what I want to do. I only took the position because they said it was open". I was shocked. John was leaving in two weeks. Tracey took out a Kleenex. She asked me to hold on a second. My boss, he still sends me on non threatening assignments.

My friend, John was hired by a News Station in Boston, Maryland. He became a News Anchorman. Everyone was sad to see him go. We gave him a small party after work. We had met at a hall that Mr. White rented for the occasion. I met his wife, and saw his girls. I see him on television often. He calls, and sends me an e-mail.

"What is it you really want to do", Christie? Tracey asked.

"Well, it is my heart desire to become a Private Eye, Christie stated.

"You are qualified to enroll in this school. You will receive a two years, A.S. Degree in Criminal Investigation. Also, you get your license to practice as a PI. [Private Eye]

"In addition, with this degree you can become a Detective and can work at any law office, and the FBI may give you a chance to get your foot in the door as a Detective, too, provided you stay in school for two more years".

Christie said, okay. She thought about what she had just heard from this woman. "Did you say I have to stay in school for four years"?

"Yes, that is correct". Tracey said.

Christie thought she was going to pass out.

"This will take me too long to reach my goal." Tracey, I am 33 years old. By the time I get out of school I will be 37 years old in four more years". Christie stated.

Tracey, responded to my remark, “You will still be young enough to start a new career”.

“I am just 40 years old, myself”, Tracey responded as though she was reading Christie mind. She said, “Go with the gusto, dear.” “I know you can do it, Christie.

Christie found herself, laughing. “How do I sign up?”

“When we have end this conversation a woman by the name of Carolyn, will be contacting you. She is the head of our Financial Aid department”.

“I will not need any Financial Aid. I will be paying for my course using my own money”.

“Christie, it will cost nearly $100,000 just to stay in school for that length of time”.

“I will be paying you in monthly installment. Christie stated. I do not want to take out any loans”.

“I do understand.” Tracey said, “Do you know that we are paid by our students quarterly.”

Christie replied, “Yes, I am aware of how you all handle your tuition”.

“If this is what you desire, we will accept that kind of payment plan.”

“Yes, that is what I will be doing”, Christie said.

“In addition, you will have to come down to the school to register for the course”.

“Christie could not believe she had let someone talk her into going back to school. This will cause her to have to wait even longer to fulfill her dream of becoming a PI. She was not concerned about the cost. She had to go to the bank to get a statement of her transactions. She still had her own savings account and the trust fund from her mom and dad. In addition, from what she had received from her grandparents old house. Christie could use this whenever she wanted money. She did not really need a paycheck to survive.

Christie was thinking about how hard it is for other people to believe that she could do this job. "In addition, the numerous times she had tried to get in the door." She kept hitting her head up against a brick wall. It was due to her determination and drives to succeed in becoming a Private Investigator. She had cried for her last time. She had thrown the last of her roll of toilet paper in the waste paper basket.

She really did not want to go back to another College. However, this was her only chance to be a Private Investigator and her life long dream.

This was the only reason why she was going back to College. She had to go to school to become a Journalist, Reporter. She had to take a course at a Community College. Her Counselor at the College where she attended would say to her," One more training will not hurt you."

Christie told Tracey that she had an Associate degree in Communicating and Journalist.

"Oh, that is wonderful. I will put down that you have prior schooling, too", Tracey stated. "The more schooling, the better it will be for you when you submit your resume for an interview", she explained.

Chapter 4

Christie goes back to School to become a Private Eye

They had Christie to sign up for a school that took 40 months. She was asked to report to the school at 5:00 a.m. every morning. She had an Army Sergeant, Instructor that taught her basic training. She had to do this gruesome drills and training. As soon as she arrived at the school they had her go out in the field. She was allowed to wear a sweat suit with a hood on cold days and shorts with a tee shirt on hot days.

Her Sergeant had a whistle and a stop watch. He would tell the recruits to do a series of push-ups, sit-ups, jumping jacks. They were timed. Then, they were allowed to get a drink of water. Afterward, they had to run around the field. Christie did everything she asked to do. When it came time for the recruits to climb up and jump over the wall, the women were allowed to get help from the men. Christie had her mouth got her into more trouble. She said, “This is not fair.” to her Sergeant. He was her Superior Officer.

She had said something to him that she knew was against the rules. She said, “I think I am able to do anything here that these men can do.”

My being reprimanded by a Sergeant in the Army

She had forgotten the in-service she had at work, "Rule number 1.— Do not undermine anyone's authority.

Christie had covered her mouth. She had lost her temper.

He blows his whistle at me. He said," I want to see you in my office, right now! I thought I was about to get thrown out of the course. I had to sign a Grievance Form. "It had stipulated, "Do Not" try to change or undermine anyone who is in authority while given an exercise, unless I write out a letter stating that I wanted to be allowed to change an order. I could go to the Administrator with this letter, and there would be a hearing process. Then she could change the order as she desired or saw fit. He had made me feel inferior. He said, "We are no different from these soldiers, police, and other law officers. Everyone has to do the same thing". I would ask him, "Why are you treating the women different from the men? He would get so mad at me. Everyone had left to get cleaned up. I had to go to his office.

He said to me. "You are such a smart mouth, but beautiful." He pulls a chair out for me to sit down. He said to me. "I am going to tell you something, and you are going to listen. "

I knew that I was about to get a lecture of my life.

He started off telling me, "You profess to know a whole lot when it comes to reading books. To me this is all well and good. But, when you are dealing with the real world you do not know "Jack". "When you are on an assignment you will be given strict orders in what to do. If you do not carry out the assignment like the commander said, you will get fired without any hesitation. I am your commander, and I tell you what to do".

I thought he was finish giving me a lecture. I stood up.

He said," I am not finished with you."

I had another class in 30 minutes. I had to bite my tongue from saying this to him. I knew I was going to be late. We were only allowed three tardy excuses before we were dropped from the class. I was frowning. He said to me, I am in charge here. I am a Superior Officer of the United States Army of Division 101. He cited me his rank number. I just listened to him.

"You will not override my decision. Do you understand me"? He tilts my chin upward with the palm of his hand. I said, "Yes sir".

As soon as I got home I called Tracey. I had to ask her why on earth did she hire a Sergeant who had been in the army to teach us this type of training to be a Private Investigator and Detective. I had heard these words before.

I was thinking he is going to lower the boom on me. He looks at the clock.

"Tomorrow before you come to my classroom you will do three laps around the field".

His class started at 5:30 a.m. in the morning! I would have to leave my apartment at 3:30 a.m. in the morning, I was thinking, if I did not take the subway or get the bus. To take a cab to the Campus would cost me $30 because it was in another suburban township. The campus was in the wooded area. It took me 1 to 2 hours to get out there. He was still talking to me. I was in a daze and worrying about my next class. I could not go there with this kind of odor on me. I would have to get a towel to wash up quickly. He said to me, "I will be out on the field watching you, Missy".

I had bit my tongue to keep from correcting him. It had started to bleed. I bit my tongue hard to keep me from telling him, “That is not my name”. I picked up my book bag and left his office in a hurry. I had 10 minutes to go to the shower room and get dressed for my next class in 3 minutes.

I had to run to the building where my classroom was. I knew I was going to be late. I just said a prayer. I thought he was so mean.

He was tough on everyone, except the women. He would give us something that was not so rough. I still had to work on controlling my temper. I had tried to tell him that I was sorry for what I had asked him on that day. I was the only Black female in my class. There was a White female, and an Asian girl. She was the youngest in our classroom. I had asked her, “How old are you?” She spoke some English. She said that she was 19 years old.

It was during the last stage of my training. I was taught how to shoot a gun.

In addition, I had to learn how to do Kung Fu, and Karate. We had a Chinese Teacher. He did not care if I was a woman. He would still toss us hard on the mat.

He had told us that if he treats us any different, we would be killed by our assailant. I could not wait to get home to take me a hot bath, and rub myself down with some of my favorite liniment, Witch Hazel.

It had been two years since I had a date with a man. I was feeling sad because I wanted to work in my career as a Private Eye. I decided to dress up for my second hour of class. I put a dress in a garment bag with a pair of high heels. I brought along my make-up bag. I was not paying attention to the way the Sergeant was looking at me. He still acted tough during the exercise. Afterwards, I went to take my shower and change into my clothes for my next class. I put my other clothes in my locker. I had a school bag that had wheels at the bottom so I could pull it to wherever I wanted to go instead of lugging it on my back. The Sergeant was standing by the door of his classroom. He said to me, “You look very nice Christie”. I thanked him. I went to my classroom. It was at the end of the day when I was on my way to catch the Subway to go to work at the Newspaper Company. I was so dog-on tired, and sore too. I was walking towards the Subway station. I saw a sharp red Corvette with a black convertible top driving slow as I was walking.

Then a window let down automatically. A man spoke to me.

“Ms. Christie, may I give you a lift”?

I stopped to take a look inside the car to see who this was that knew my name. The voice sounded familiar. I asked him, “Is this Sergeant Ronald Ackroyd?”

“Yes, dear it is me”, he replied. “I was wondering if I can give you a lift some where”.

He was not in his uniform. He had on a brown dress pair of pants with a knit sweater and a leather jacket. He had on a pair of leather shoes. He looked different in civilian clothes.

“How far are you going”, he asked me. I said, “I have to go downtown to the Newspaper Company”. He said, “I will give you a lift”.

I was thinking that maybe he was just trying to make up for being so mean. He said to me, “I would like to tell you something that I could not say at the school.”

He had stopped driving.

“I promise to take you straight to your job. This will not affect our relationship in class. You will still get the same grade for your work performance”.

It was cold outside and I did not really want to take a train.

I could have caught a cab. I walked to his car, and he opens the door from the inside. I put my bag on my lap after I had put the handle down in its folding position. I sat down in his leather cushion seat. I fastened my seat belt and he starts driving. He said to me, "I know you are probably wondering about why I am being so nice to you all of a sudden". I said, "Yes sir it has crossed my mind.

"I really like you Christie and my treating you stern is to help save your life. I have been in the Service for many years. I am not married or seeing anybody. I am in my early 40's. I am not a lonesome man, but I would like to date women from time to time. Since you are about to graduate I thought it would be nice if I could take you out on a date. There are no strings attach to this offer".

"And this will be strictly our business". He added, "If you decide to accept this offer to go out with me one night."

She was graduating in a few weeks.

"If you do not find me to be suitable company I will not get angry at you, Christie".

"We do not have to wait until I graduate, Ron".

I had called him by his first name. I covered my mouth. I said, "Excuse me Sgt. Ackroyd".

He laughed. "You may call me Ron if we will be going out on a date". I said, "Yes it sounds like fun". He asked me what I liked to do for fun.

I had to think about it, I had not done anything for fun in a while.

"What would you like to do if someone taught you"?

I said to him, "I always wanted to shoot some pool". He laughed. "I know a nice pool hall that has a Pub Restaurant inside and we can get a bite to eat or drink a brew. I said, "I do not drink beer. He said, "then you can have a Root Beer. " I had to smile. He was happy. He asked, "What are you doing this Saturday night"?

"I do not have anything planned", I answered.

I was going to church on Sunday with Tracey. He was good friends with her husband Horace. I had found that out that they were neighbors, too. I asked her, "Why did you hire him to be an instructor?"

"Horace said that he was really a nice guy".

He had a beautiful house by the Hudson River in a secluded area. Tracey had shown me his house when we were out riding one day. I was still not impressed because he gave me such a hard time. He made me work harder because I had made a comment to a classmate about him, and he overheard me.

I was very sorry and I tried to apologize to him. He just dismissed it.

"Do not let that happen again", he said in his deep voice. I was shocked that he wanted to take me out on a date. He pulled up at the Newspaper Company. He got out and opened up the door on my side. He opened it, and held out his hand to help me out of his sports car.

I took his hand. And I stepped out of his car.

"Thank you for the lift", I told him.

He smiled. "I will pick you up on Saturday at 7:00 p.m."

He had my address and phone number in his computer system.

"Unless you prefer I call before I come".

"No, I will be ready at that time".

"Okay, he said to me. "I will see you in class on Wednesday. You can sleep in a little bit longer and come to the field as soon as you arrive."

We were getting ready for our rehearsal where we were going to be dressed in the uniforms the school provided for us on graduation day. The uniform was just a nice jogging suit. They were navy blue in color. They came with a hood. We had to buy our own gym shoes. We had our names pinned on the uniform. We had to buy the pin, too. I was going to be a Detective, too. I had my suit in my garment bag. I was taking it with me to class.

Sgt. Ackroyd was to be dressed in his Army uniform. He was presenting to us a certificate of completion at a private ceremony outside on the field. He had a large box in the classroom that he had to take outside to the field. Some other officials were going to be there when he presented the plaque and certificate.

The plaque had our title engraved in gold. He showed us what it would look like if we graduated. This was to give us an extra boost to work harder. He was also a Professor. He taught us Criminology 1, 2, 3, and 4. I had his class for 4 years.

He waved at me as I went inside the Newspaper Company. Then he drove off.

"This was going to be interesting", I thought to myself.

I think this was my first time in four years I had dressed up coming to work at the Newspaper Company. I was extremely exhausted. I walked inside and everyone greeted me. I spoke to everyone. I walked to my cubicle. I was now the Supervisor. I had taken John's position. I knew exactly what to do. I went out to some sites to watch the new journalist reporters do their job. I had my assignment on my desk. I was now covering stories about other topics of interests. Some were at a hospital delivery room. I was fascinated with seeing new born babies. I went inside his office to speak to Mr. White. He said to me, "You look very nice tonight." "Thank you", I replied.

"I had been meaning to speak to you about this resignation you gave me that was in my mailbox", he said to me. "You should continue working with this newspaper company. I think you have a great career ahead of you if you stay here with us. I sure hate to lose you."

I gave him a hug. I said, "You know I love you and that this is best for me. I appreciate everything you have done for me". He looked sad. "I understand, dear", he replied. "If you need me for a reference you can give me a call".

I smiled. "I may just do that, Mr. White". I had to go out with a new Reporter. "I will talk to you later".

Christie resigns and get ready for her graduation

He smiles. He said to me. "You have come a long way, dear."

I was walking towards the door of his office.

"I really appreciate hearing that, Mr. White". I held the door knob with one hand.

"I am going to miss you", I stated. He sniffs.

I went over to give him another hug. I left his office in tears.

I had a date with Ron tonight at 7:00 p.m. I was dressing up. I had bought a fitted satin skirt with a wide belt. I already had a silk white ruffle blouse. The weather had turned warmer. It was almost 70 degrees. It was the first week of May. I was graduating in two more weeks. I had already taken my shower and I was putting on my make-up. I had on my earrings, necklace, and bracelet set. I had put my hair in a ball. It was 6:45 p.m. I dressed quickly. I was ready to go out on this date. It had been a while.

Ron was very punctual. He rings my buzzer. I told him, "I will be right downstairs in a few minutes".

He said to me, “No you will not come down to the lobby”.

I said,” that is absolutely right.”

“A gentleman always comes up to greet his date at her front door. I am not a cab driver”.

I had to laugh. I buzzed him inside of my building. He walks to the elevator. He rode it up to my floor and walked to my suite. I had the door open for him. I was standing there waiting.

He smiles. “You look beautiful and I hope I did not offend you”.

I thank him. I said, “No you were absolutely right that was the way I was taught by my parents.” He smiles. “I am from the old school, dear”.

I had put on my cute sweater. I picked up my purse and my keys off of the table. I was walking out to lock my door. He double checks it to make sure it was locked. He had twisted the knob with his hand. We walk to the elevator. He said to me, “We do not have to go the pool hall tonight. I have a friend who is a Jazz Pianist who is playing at a hotel Night Club. She asked me to come see her performed if you do not mind going with me”. I said, “Sure tonight I am at your disposal.” He smiles.

He was not driving his Corvette sports car tonight.

A limousine was out front. A chauffeur held the door open for him.

“Is that your ride”? I asked him. He smiles. “Yes, I sometimes have a problem driving. I called for my driver to take me around”. He said it as a matter of fact. I looked at him hard.

He was wealthy. I was helped inside the limousine. He sat across from me. The chauffeur shut the door. He told the driver where to take us. He had on a sharp

White pin striped suit with white leather shoes. He was not the same man that made me do laps and push ups for speaking out of term. He still had his hair in the same hairstyle.

He gave me this warm look as he was talking to me. There are some things I have never shared with too many people", he stated to me.

"I am afraid I am confused", I answered.

"Well, I lived a different lifestyle that is different from where I worked at the College. I have acquired a variation of interest that fulfilled my daily life".

I was still confused.

He said, "You will see what I am talking about the more you go out with me." I had to smile.

We arrived at the destination. The chauffeur gets out and opens the door for us.

There was a crowd coming inside the hotel. He supports my back and we walk inside the hotel lobby. There was a large posture with the artist picture on it. It said she was featured with a special guest. He led me to the elevator to go up to the floor where she was performing. We went to the entrance door. A doorman let us inside.

A hostess greeted us, and shows us to a table. Ron thanks the woman. He pulls a chair out for me to sit down. He scooted my chair underneath the table.

The Master of Ceremony (MC) was coming out on stage. The lights were dimmed. "You can have whatever you want to drink and they have food here too", he said to me. A server came to our table. The MC was standing in front of a microphone.

"Good evening ladies and gentleman. I want to welcome you to the beautiful Twilight Room. Tonight we are very excited about having this dynamic Jazz Performer with us so without further ado will you please help me to welcome the Beautiful Natalie Ewalds".

We clapped for her and she came out on stage. She had on a white flowing gown. She came with her own band and back-up singers. She was part Asian.

She smiled. She said to us, "I am very happy to be here tonight. " I am going to sing a few selections of Jazzy tunes". She was looking up at Ron face. She smiles.

"Now, I can go on with my show. I am going to ask a very good friend of mines to come up and help me out with this selection and maybe one more selection a little later".

Ron shook his head and smiles.

"I would like to ask if Ron Ackroyd will please come up on this stage".

He was laughing. I was looking at him in a strange way. He walked down to the front of the stage. He walked up the stairs. He gave her a hug and they were talking to each other in a low voice so we could not hear their conversation.

"You told me that you would not ask me to sing tonight", he stated to her. She laughed.

"I was not completely honest with you, Ron", she told him. The musicians and back-up singers were smiling. One of the musicians made a gesture with his hand to his neck. He said, "To cut it out." They both smiled.

"I am sorry about that, you' all. We had a little misunderstanding", she stated to us. She gives to the audience a little background about Ron. She said, "We have known each other for years. I met him while he was in the service. He used to put on a show for the Servicemen until he completed his duty. Then he took his singing business on the road".

She continued telling us about Ron.

"Ladies and Gentleman I have standing beside me a dynamic, Jazz Recording Artists who has appeared all over the world performing. He is a former Sergeant of the army, now he is a Professor who teaches at a College here in NYC. Will you help me to welcome this sensational performer?" She was clapping too. I was clapping and smiling as I watched the show from our table. He did a bow. The musicians and back-up singers knew him too. They were clapping too. He points at them. He said, "I have been caught off guard." It has been an unexpected surprised. He stated to us, "I will get her later, y'all". He was smiling. The musician began to play one of his favorite tunes. He rocks and pats his chest.

He looks over at Natalie who was crying. He asked her, "Will you help me sing this song, darling"? She goes over to the microphone and begins to do a dance to the music that was being played. He sings a familiar jazzy song. He was singing his part first. She was still doing her little dance. The crowd was getting up to dance. I was rocking in my chair. He steps aside as she begins to sing her part. He was dancing too. He was so professional and reserved at the school. He was not the same man I saw every week in school. He was so full of life.

He was smiling and dancing on the stage. He was pointing at the back-up singers who were on jam. They were two men and one woman. Everybody was clapping and the men were whistling. He does a bow after the song had ended. He held up her hand so she could take a curtsy. He gave her a hug. Then he left the stage to go back to our table. I stood up to give him a hug. I was so excited to be dining with a performer. He said to me, "You must never tell a soul."

I said, "I am telling everybody". He laughs.

He replies, "You would do that to me"?"

"Yes I will do that to you", I replies. Then I smile.

He smiles. "I guess it is payback time", he stated to me.

I had stated, "Yes you had better believe it". I laughed.

He laughs. And he shook his head at me.

A server asked us what kind of drink we desired to have either a cocktail, or a beverage.

"I am not much of a drinker", Christie stated to Ron. He orders a bottle of Chardonnay wine. "Do you mind if we drink some wine"? Christie said," No this is your party". He smiles.

"Are you hungry we can order something from the food menu"? He had asked me.

"I may get something later", Christie replied. He nods his head.

Natalie was on jam. She was singing the hit song, "A Love of your own". She was rocking to the music. I liked this particular song. I was singing with her to myself.

"She is terrific huh"? Ron stated.

"Yes, she knows what to do up on stage". Christie stated.

"Also you are quite good too", she had told him.

He smiles. "Thank you, dear." He stated.

"I cannot believe that you use to do this sort of thing", she said to him.

Ron he tells her a little bit about his background. He said, "I was quite young and had not one clue as to what direction I wanted to take in life," he explained.

I had joined the service and they would ask me to do something to cheer up the service men and women. I had contacted this organization to ask them for help in putting on a show. They said, "That they were going to send some people who would help me." Natalie and her group were some of the performers who came out to help me. That is how we met".

The server brought over the Bottle of Wine with two wine glasses. The server poured us both a glass of wine. "Can I bring you a menu from the kitchen", she asked him. He said, "Sure we want to see what you have on the menu". She walked away.

"I think I should make a toast to your finally completing the course", Ron stated to me. I had to smile. He held up his glass and I held up mines. I clicked his glass. He said to me, "Best wishes on your new career"

"Thank you", I said.

Natalie told us that she would take a five minute break and she would be right back so we could hear another selection from Ron Ackroyd. She looks over at him. She said, "He think he is finish with this show. He said, "I will get you darling." We both laughed. Everybody clapped for her and she went back stage. They had taken a 15 minute break so that they can change their clothes. She came back on stage wearing a silver sequin gown that was flowing and hanging down to the floor. The MC had came back on stage. He was smiling. He said, "I know you all are enjoying this as much as I am and without further ado, will you help me to welcome back, the Beautiful Natalie Ewalds and her back-up singers. We stood up to claps. She smiled. She thanks us for the warm reception. She walked to the microphone. "I want to ask the performer to come back up to sing this particular song. Before I tell you the name of it, I must say that he had written the lyrics. And we had it recorded back then. She was wiping her eyes with her finger. I believe it is one of the prettiest songs I have ever heard in my time. And the only one I know who can sing it this way. She said it is called, "I want you so Bad". We had worked on this project for about a year and finally we were able to see it on the shelves at the record shops. She smiles. She said, "Come on up to this stage, man." Ron laughs. He went to the microphone the musicians were excited. They were waiting on him before they plays the music. He smiles at the back-up singers who were clapping too. He said," I have to find a way to pay you back for this humiliation, dear." She just laughed. She had already stood in position with the other back-up singers. He does a dance to the music that was bad. She was dancing with the other back-up singers. It was a beautiful ballad.

Christie thought to herself; I believe that he is one of the best male vocalists of all time.

Ron sings the song. Natalie was singing her part and hitting a high note. She continues to do the dance routine. She was smiling. Ron held up his arm and he was ending the song. The back-up singers ended it beautiful. He turns around to face them and the musicians. He put his hand on his chest and gave a bow to them. He face the audience again and gave a bow to us. We had given him a standing ovation.

I shook my head in disbelief at how beautiful he could sing. I had wiped my eyes with my finger. He goes back down to our table. He looks at me and say, "Do not start any stuff lady." The crowd was screaming and whistling. Natalie wanted him to do another song, but he shook his head. She went on with her show. He put his hand to his mouth to blow a kiss at her. She smiled.

Natalie asked another male vocalist from the back-up singer to do a selection. He goes to the microphone. He was handsome, too. She had introduces him as Mr. Stanley Cravit. He said, "We all are so happy to see Ron again and it has been years since we have done a show together. I was on my way to the airport to go on a much needed vacation, and Natalie had called me to ask me to come to her house in Connecticut. "I asked her what was this all about?"

She said, "Just get here man. She was laughing.

I change my airline ticket and flew to Connecticut. She came up with this idea and asks me to go along with it. I said, "If you pull this one off—you are a good one dear." She smiles. We had to get Ron to come to the show. Once we got him here—the rest was in our favor. Ron was laughing hard. They were laughing too. He said, "I know where to find y'all." We were laughing too. He asked him to come back up on stage again. Ron goes to stand in position with the back-up singers. He joins them as they were rocking. The vocalist had a nice style to his singing. He danced while he was singing. Ron kept up with their moves. The show was fantastic. They had a photographer that the owner of the establishment had called to announce about this performer arrival. I was having so much fun with my Instructor.

We stay until the club was ready to close. The Chauffeur was outside waiting on Ron to come to the Limousine. Ron had to go backstage to give Natalie a hug and a scolding. "I want to say that it was fun just like old times", he stated to Natalie.

"How long will you be in town", he asked her.

She said, "I am leaving tomorrow morning. I will be on tour for 9 months.

"What about you, Stanley?" Ron asked his friend.

He said, "Once again I have been asked to join Natalie on this tour." He gives him a hug and a hand slap. He stated to Ron, "You were dynamic boy."

Ron smiled. He replies, "So were you, man."

Natalie said, "If you want to catch my show again you have to go to Las Vegas".

He laughs. "No, way darling", he replied. "I do not want this to happen again, your embarrassing me". She said, "Aw you have to come we will sing your song. "

He smiles. You know I have retired and now I am a Professor. He gave her a gentle hug. Stanley he could sing in my place.

Stanley said, "Not like you man." He had a deep voice.

Ron said, "You all have a safe trip". He looks over at Natalie. "You have not changed one bit". He said to her, "Whatever you are doing—keep on doing it." He hugs her for one last time. They got inside a White Limousine. He bid them goodbye. He takes his hand and supports my back. He walks me to his Limousine. The limousine drives me back to my apartment building. He walks me to the front door.

"I hope you will forgive me for not seeing you to your suite", he stated.

"I know you are tired from all that singing and dancing". She stated.

He laughs and say, "You are going to rub this in my face every chance you get Christie"?

I said," I may cut you some slack." He gave me a hug. "Have a good night, dear". He watched me get inside the elevator before he left to get back in the Limousine.

The Graduation

I was about to graduate. I had passed my classes with good grades. In addition, they gave me a Bachelor of Art degree as a Private Investigator. Now, I was qualified to be a Detective. I had a degree and a license from the school for both professions. Tracey had become one of my dearest friends. I could not wait to send Dr. Horace and Tracey Washington, an invitation to my Graduation Ceremony. She and I had cried all day. I could hear her blowing her nose. I had known her for four years. I had gone out to buy me an outfit to wear to the Ceremony. Mr. Walter and Judy White were invited too. They were there to congratulate me. He was riding in a White Baby Limousine. He said that God had smiled on him over the years. He would anxiously wait for his retirement in a few more years. He was almost 65. He still looked good for his age.

I was surprise to see John, too. He was sitting up in the front row next to Mr. White. He had told him to save a seat for him. I had cried so hard. They were smiling. He had a camcorder taking a video of me. What had got me—everybody was standing up to cheer me, my entire class mates. They asked me to be the Valedictorian and spokesman for the class in the Criminology Department. I was quite emotional. I had bought me a beautiful dress. It was pink with tiny sequins. I had on pink high heels that were the same color with tiny sequins. I had my hair in curls. I waited until they all sat down from clapping. I had written out a speech. I dabbed at my nose as I read it. *As I remember my first day starting at the school. I am thinking this is not where I am supposed to be. I had stated this to the audience. How long will it take me to fulfill my dream? I have all the education I need in this world and in another life. They were all laughing at me. I have temper tantrums. I smiled.*

I received an award. It was an honor of Recognition of my accomplishment. I really was not expecting John to be there at my graduation.

John told me in his letter that he works long hours 6 days a week. His wife had just had another baby. She had a girl that was 6 pounds and 7 ounces. He sent me a picture. She was beautiful. He asked me to be his children's Godmother. I happily said, "Yes, it will be an honor. You are like a brother to me, John". He hugged me when he saw me. I had asked him to help me move out of my apartment in two weeks. He said, yes.

John now lived in Boston, Maryland, in the suburban area. He had bought a new house. He said to me, "I want to come to see you walk across that stage." If I can get away for a day, I will be there on Thursday afternoon". That was the day I was graduating. John said that he will drive up to the Auditorium. I had sent John and his wife an invitation. We had made up, and talked to each other daily about our jobs.

When I heard my name being called over the speaker, I was practically running up on that stage. My classmates were cheering me on, too. I smiled at them. I hugged all of my Instructors. I even hugged my Sergeant. He was smiling at me, with tears in his eyes. I always thought he was handsome, too. He had his hair cut in a crew cut. He was tall, and had a muscular built. He congratulated me, too. I went down to my seat. I had to cheer for my classmates. I had screamed myself hoarse.

We all went out to dinner to a Four-star Restaurant.

I was riding in Johns car. He had a brand new Mercedes Benz. It was sharp. He had a convertible top. It was June now. The temperature had gotten warm. I still had to cover the weather. He had become one of my dearest friends. He told me I could come for a visit anytime. I bid him goodbye when he dropped me back off. He said something crazy. "I will come back to teach you how to drive". I was laughing so hard. He kept his word. He was at my apartment door. He said to me." Are you ready to go? I asked him if he was feeling, sick?" He said, "No". He had an old raggedy of a car. I said to him, "This is not your car". He fell out laughing.

He took me out for lessons. I passed my driving test. He was going to help me find a car. I said, "Nope. I am not driving, right now". I was happy taking busses, cabs, even the subway.

Christie's Mentor

Maybe I will give Tracey a call, today. I would normally go over to their house on weekends. I did not want to go anywhere today. I felt like watching some videos, and the Travel Channel that was coming on tonight. I had put a circle around a date on my calendar on my bedroom wall. Tracey invited me to go to a concert at her church. It was on Wednesday night. This was supposed to be next month. I had gone to church with them often. He was my Mentor. He said to me, "Do not give up on your dream, dear." He talked to me over the phone at the church for almost an hour last week. He said, "This is not just a man's world." "Everything we have in this world belongs to all of God children." I had to get my thinking straight. He said to me, "There is no such a thing as a man's job, if I want to do this thing, to do the best I can." I started to cry again. I had used up all the roll of toilet paper. I had to go back to the kitchen to grab a napkin.

He told me, "Do not let the devil steal your joy." I was wiping my eyes, and blowing my nose. I still needed to go to the grocery store. He told me that my attitude with men had caused me to lose my self respect. I told him that I was hurt by their shunning me. I am strong, but I can still maintain my femininity.

I was being pathetic today. I had never been so emotional. Mr. White had sent me an e-mail from his home computer. He said to me. "Please do not quit us, Christie. There is so much you can learn from me". I had worked for him for four years.

Chapter 5

At the school were recruiters who gave each of the graduates' helpful suggestions on how to start a business. I made a few calls to local office supply companies, Office Max, Office Depot, and Staples. I had discovered that it would cost me $10,000 for all of the things I needed to get my own business started. I decided to shop at Office Depot to buy my furniture and supplies for my home office. They were one of the largest stores in the United States.

I decided to use the money from my trust fund to purchase the things I needed to set up my own office. In addition, I needed to find me a larger place. I told them to hold my things for a month. I began to search for another larger apartment that was still in the Bronx area. I needed to write out a list to take to the Office Depot Warehouse. I picked out a brown wooded desk, and a leather swivel chair, a home computer system, a file cabinet, and I ordered another private phone line, with another phone, some office supplies, a fax machine with a copier machine, In addition I ordered my own Website. I told them I had no place to keep these things. They told me that they will store the items for 30 days.

Christie moves to a new Loft

I saw that someone from the Newspaper Company had covered a story about "The New Condominiums and Lofts" that had been built in the Bronx area. I quickly went to make a call to a Real Estate agent. I told him I wanted to take a look at the New Lofts. He told me, "I can come pick you up, this evening.

I will send a limousine out to pick you up at your apartment". I had to hurry home to get cleaned up, and change my clothes. I had resigned.

The Loft was about 20 minutes from my apartment. These Lofts were beautiful. This was a new subdivision and a new development project which the City had approved. I wrote him a nice letter of resignation. I had put it in his mailbox at work. I had put all my things in a big box. I was crying.

I had a cab waiting for me downstairs. I had bid my co-workers goodbye. I said to him, "If I am ever going to find my dream in this world, I have to take that first step alone. I love you and I will still be in touch". He said to me, "You are like the daughter I never had, Christie". He caught up with me at the front entrance. He and I both cried for a few minutes. I was now about to go find some assignments of my own. Christie moves into a Luxurious Loft in a rural area

John and Mr. White helped me moved into my loft. I moved out of my apartment in two weeks. I had a mortgage for 30 years. My mortgage was $3,000 a month. That was $36,000 a year. My loft was large enough to accommodate my office. I had so much space that I could put some other things like a mini spa. It was

something that had not crossed my mind.

As I was checking my credit card statement I did not see where I had purchased a laptop.

My instructor said to me, "You sure do need to have your own personal laptop.

This is where you should keep your data for all your assignments".

I had forgotten to buy a personal laptop. I had to go back to Office Depot. I had become friendly with the sales Consultant. I said, "Hey Stanley".

He smiles. He said, "Now do not tell me you need something else?" I said, "Yes I do. As a matter, of fact I need a personal laptop. Should I purchase a camcorder, too"? He smiled. He said, "Come, let me show you what we have here." I was thinking. I have spent a grand total of nearly $15,000. It would have been more if he had not knocked off $3000.

I had to thank him again. "You have done so much for me these last two weeks.

I will be charging this to my credit card, too". He smiled.

I bought me a newspaper and saw an ad for a Private Investigator. They left a number where they could be contacted. It was a 1-800 number.

I almost hesitated calling the number. I remembered the last time I called an 800 number, and I was connected to a College. I said a prayer. I made the call to the person.

They answered, "Wade & Rudolph Law Firm. How may I help you"? A woman spoke to me. I stated to her, "My name is Christie Higgins. I had seen your Want Ad; I am inquiring about the ad that has been posted". The woman told me to hold. I was still praying. A man came to the phone.

"This is Mr. Timothy Wade How may I help you"?

"I am calling in regards to your Want Ad section. I am a Private Investigator, I stated.

I thought he was going to hang up. I said," May I come in to speak to you this afternoon? "He answered, "I have an hour before my client comes. " Can you get here right now"?

I said, "Yes I will leave my place right now". I asked him where was he was located. He told me right downtown in the Bronx. I said, "I will be there in 20 minutes". His office was in my neighborhood. I hung up. I rushed to my bedroom to find my black and white suit.

It was white on the collar and the cuffs. It was a skirt suit. I put on my pantyhose stockings. I had already taken my bath. I got dressed in a hurry.

I put on my black high heels; they had a white bow across the toe. It was summer time. I only wore a rain coat if was a rainy day. I put on my make-up, and earrings. I grabbed my purse and briefcase. I kept all my information on my laptop. I had a copy of my resume with a cover letter. I walked out of my loft.

I saw a cab coming down the street, slow. I waved my arm. The driver came to a halt. He pulled up at the curb. I got inside, and I asked him to take me to the address of WADE & RUDOLPH, Law Firm. It was in the Bronx area. I could have walked there.

He pulled up at the place. I paid him my fare. I got out, and walked inside. I stopped at the front desk. I asked for Mr. Timothy Wade. The reception said to me, "Is your name, Christie Higgins"?

"Yes, that is my name", I replied.

"He is expecting you".

She used her intercom to notify him that I had arrived. I was escorted to his office. She left to go back to her desk. He smiled and shook my hand. "So, you are interested in this position", he asked me. I said, "Very much". He pulls a chair out for me to sit down. I sat down. He offers me a cup of coffee. I said, "No thank you". He began to tell me what I had to do for him. He takes out a form. "I will need to see your license and other credentials", he said. I take the items out of my purse. I hand them to him.

He smiles and said, "I am impressed. I have never met a woman Private Investigator. Not to mention a black one". He was Black, too. I said, "I really am qualified to do this work". He said, "I can see that Ms. Higgins. I think I will give you a chance". I smiled.

"I will need you to fill out this form".

He went to his receptionist to ask her to make him a copy of my credentials. I took out my ball point pen. I had written out the information that was on the form.

He came back to his desk. He pulls out some other forms. I could not believe I was hired, instantly. He told me that I could start today. I thought he was joking. He told me that I needed to find this person. It was a, "You have been Served Notice"

"We have had a hard time tracking this person down", he said. I asked him, "What kind of Summon is this?"

My first assignment as a Private Investigator

This is a Divorce law firm. His wife has filed for a divorce. I sighed. This could

get pretty ugly, I was thinking.

"This is one of the most expensive cases I had ever handled.

" If you can find this man, I am prepared to give you $25, 000".

I took out my laptop to do a database search on the information that he had given me. He said, "You have 5 days to find him". He handed me an envelope.

"This contains the Summons. You must put it in his hand, and make sure he signs it. Then, bring it back to me right away. I have a mailbox that is on the outside of this building. Good luck, dear".

This was Friday afternoon.

"I will give you my cell phone and house number if you have a problem".

He handed me his business card. I typed into my data base to do a detective search.

It cost me $5000 for this program. I had to wait 2 weeks to have it delivered to my house. It came with a couple of discs, instructions, and I was taught how to install it into my computer. It was a Software Program. I had found my answer, immediately.

He had a common name, Brad Smith. The search had given me 10 names like his that lived in New York City. I would have had to check out every last one, if I had to use a white page directory. This program was very effective.

The Summon

I decided to contact this Brad Smith that was working at an Elementary School.

I hailed a cab, and went to the school. I went inside the school. I stopped into the office. I showed them my license.

I had not received my badge from the Federal Bureau of Investigation that issues badges to Law Officers. They told me it would take 90 days to receive mines. They had to send for it from the Headquarters in Washington, DC.

I told them I needed to see this man immediately. I asked the receptionist, "What does he teach? She said, "He is a Science Teacher". "That is nice", I replied.

I waited on him to come to the office.

I had all of his information. He did not have any children. I asked him if he was the one who lived on the street in my report. He said, "Yes, I live on that street". He asked me, "What is this all about?" I told him that he was receiving a Summon. He started to leave. I held his arm. I told him this was not easy for me, either. Then, I said to him, "I will keep coming back. You may as well get this over with now, sir."

He started crying. He takes the envelope. I had him sign the form.

"I am very sorry, Mr. Smith", I am just doing my job", I explained.

I take the form and I go back to the law firm. It was getting late in the day. I dropped it into the Attorney's mailbox.

I did not hear from him until Monday morning. He was so surprised. He was laughing.

"I will give you a check, today. Can you come to the office?" I said, "I could be there about 3:00 p.m."

This was an easy assignment. I thought that he had some more assignments for me. When I got there he shook my hand. "You did a magnificent job, dear", he stated to me.

"I will give you your check".

I sat down. He took out the envelope. He put it on the desk. I looked at it. I smiled. I

asked him, "What will you need me to do next"? He said, "That is it for now. I was just pressed for time to get this case to court. I have your number. I will contact you when I need someone for an investigation".

I was disappointed. This was not what I had expected from him. It was a one day job.

I had been let go, on my first assignment. I thanked him, and I walked out of his office. I took a bus home after depositing my check into my account.

I had to get another newspaper. I left my loft to go across the street to the Newspaper stand. I went back to my loft and began to look through the Want-Ad section. There was something there that looked interesting. I put a circle around it.

I was hungry and wanted something to eat. I had a taste for Chinese Food.

I asked them to deliver it to my place.

I called the next person. I asked them, "What kind of job is this"?

"We are a Collection Agency". I thanked her. I hung up.

I hated to deal with these types of people.

I was at home doing nothing in particular and it was a Friday morning. I had woken up early to make me a pot of coffee. I was going to look at a video of some places I wanted to visit one day. My phone rings. I looked at the clock on my wall. It was 7:00 a.m. I had not sent in anymore resumes. Tracey and Horace had gone away for a weekend. I had not spoken to John this week. I thought maybe that it was him. I answered the phone.

"Hey John, how is Maryland"?

Spending Time with Ron

"This is not John, darling".

"Oh, I am sorry", I stated.

"Is this Ron"? He answered, "Yes you are correct. I have been thinking about you since our last date and decided to see what you were doing for the Memorial Day weekend"?

"That is today, Ron. He laughs. Yes, I know. Well, do you have any special plans? No, I am sort of glum today".

" Aw, that is terrible. I have an idea that might cheer you up. Come spend the weekend with me and we will find something to exciting to do. I have a RV with all the necessary things I need while I am traveling to whatever destination I choose to be on the map. I can be at your place in an hour. I just need an answer so I can start making preparation. Did I startled you with that suggestion", he asked me.

I was too silent.

I said, "I am sorry Ron. I was lost in thought. Yes, it sounds like fun. What do I need to pack"?

He laughs.

"Well, it is supposed to be hot this weekend. You will need some cool clothing. I may stop at a restaurant that has a dress code, so I would bring a dress with me. Secondly, you can bring a swimsuit in case you want to go swimming if we stop at a National park. That ought to do it for the time being, the rest is using your discretion.

Now, I will throw something in a bag and asked On-star to draw me a map of someplace within 300 miles from here.

"I will give you a call when I am ready to come pick you up, he stated to me. I thanked him. He had hung up.

Ron Acquired another Side

I went to my bedroom and I walked to my closet to find a dress that I could bring with me. I had a green plain silk dress with a round collar and it had a belt that was silver. I had seen it at Macy's. It came with a white jacket that came to the waist. I like the way it looked on me, so I bought it.

I went to my dresser to pull out two pair of Capri's sets that were cute and casual. I was going to wear the red one today. It had big buttons on the top and had shingles at the bottom. They were different colors like the buttons. The pants were plain with a split at the bottom. I had a cute pair of sandals that were red.

I was bringing my green strapless pumps. I began to pack these into a bag. I went to grab my cosmetic bag to apply my make-up. I put on my outfit. I had not gone to get my hair done this week. So, I just put a clamp in the back and twisted it in a ball. I carried all my things to the front hall. I sat them on the floor. I was wearing a Denim jacket. I take it from the hall closet. I forgot about my swimsuit and a pair of gym shoes. So, I went back to the bedroom to grab these two things. I checked to see if I had my sun block lotion, and insect repellant spray. I threw these items into my bag, too. I went back to the kitchen to finish drinking my coffee. Meanwhile, Ron called On-star from his RV. He got a map of a 300 mile radius.

He drove to get some gas at the gas station. He picks up some food and snacks and also some beverages with a bag of ice. He had a freezer and a refrigerator in the RV. He already had his bag in the RV. He called me from the gas station.

"Alright, I am ready to head out to your way." "I am 10 minutes away," he stated.

"I am ready", I tell him.

"Good. I will be there in a jiffy", he added.

I thought maybe I should get my sun visor. I had bought it at the Dollar Store. It was red and matched my outfit. I put it on my head.

He had made it to my Loft in 7 minutes. He pulled into a parking space in the parking lot. He parks and get out. He had on a pair of Army pants with a green tee shirt and a cap that said, "Sgt. Ackroyd." I made the comment, "You are dressed for this weekend". "He smiled.

"Yes, this is Memorial Day weekend. Not to mention I am a Veteran", he stated to me. "How are you feeling", he asked me.

"I am feeling much better", I answered.

"Good", he said.

H gave me a little hug. Then, he picks up my bag. I locked my door after I pick up my keys and my purse. He always twists the door knob to make sure it was locked secured.

Sergeant Ackroyd and the little game he played

"Alright, we are going up North as far as it will take us that is within a 300 mile radius", he stated to me.

"I have On-star giving me direction. So, I may not be able to communicate with you too much while I am driving".

The Motor Home was beautiful. He carried my things inside. I sat up front in a leather cushion seat. I had an armrest and neck rest. I could lie back in a lying position. The couch let out into a daybed. There was a bedroom with a bathroom and a kitchenette. I have never ridden in one of these before I told him. He smiled.

"It is like being in a hotel on wheels." That was their logo they use for their Advertisement. He started the engine.

"You can move around and fill free to get whatever you want".

"Thank you, I replied to him. He was a perfect gentleman. He headed for the highway. He took out a DVD of a movie. He put it on so I could watch some movies. He could only get a glimpse of what was playing. He could hear what they were saying though. He stopped to pay the toll. We were on our way to our first destination. There was a National park within 30 miles.

He said, "We can check out the beach and grab a hot dog or some ribs. Are you gain"? I said, "You bet, I am hungry." He laughs.

He drove us to the National Park. I am not making this up. When we got there they had a Family Reunion. He asked me, "Do you want to have a new family?" I said, "Are you feeling alright Ron?" He smiled.

"I am fine. I have done this plenty of times". We got to eat free food and drinks. And hang out with strangers.

"Watch what I do or say, Ron stated to me.

"Never leave me alone".

I thought he had been drinking. "Ron, this is being dishonest". He said to me, "It is fun and harmless. Some of these folks cannot remember all their relatives and I could be a long lost nephew or cousin. Work with me. I will not do anything to harm or embarrassed you, Christie".

He drove to the site of a family. He got out and opened the door for me. This was not my idea of having fun. He takes my hand. You are my wife and we came from Alabama. Our last name will be Davis. Jordan and Davis were the names of the Family.

If this is what he was going to do for this trip I was ready to be dropped back off at home.

"Listen Christie, I know this sounds strange. I have no family and I am alone.

I would not do this if I thought it would hurt me. I am not an odd ball". He smiles.

Someone started walking towards us.

"We will stay for an hour", he said.

I went along with this fabricated tale.

"Hey, he said in a happy voice. I am Cousin Ron Davis and this is my wife Christie Davis". We just heard about the Family Reunion and decided to mosey our way out here to celebrate with our kin folks".

He was good at this too. The man gave him a hug.

"Come on out here to meet the rest of the family. You sort of look like Uncle Billy he has nephews we had not seen yet", the stranger said. He was smiling. He looks at me.

"Uncle Billy was not there today. He took sick", the cousin said to us.

"Oh, I am sorry about that, man. I do not believe I caught your name", Ron said. He smiles.

"Forgive me. I am Curtis Davis. Uncle Billy, other nephew". Curtis calls for his wife.

"Come over here and meet my cousin Ron. His wife came running over.

"Honey, this is your cousin Ron and his wife Christie. They are a Davis too".

"Hello, I am Jacqueline". She hugs us both.

"Come on we are about to bless the food. We have some sanitizing lotion where you can wash your hands". I looked at Ron's face. He was so handsome. He said to them, "We cannot stay too long we have to go visit my wife's relatives too".

"Well, we will fix you up a carry out plate. Come on and we will say grace".

We went to where the family was standing in a circle. Ron felt I was uneasy. They were very friendly. We hugged people and we were led to the food line. We got our food and we bid the family goodbye.

"If you are in the area of Tallahassee, we are listed in the phone book", Ron said to them.

Then we walked to his motor home. I could not wait to get in that motor home! I told him in no uncertain term, “Nobody will put me in an awkward position”. You can turn this vehicle back around to take me home, I exclaimed.

He got quiet.

“I am very sorry”, he said to me with tears in his eyes.

“I am so sorry, Christie. I meant no harm”. He put his arms around me.

“I do not want to lose your friendship over this thing. I will never do this again”.

I put my head down. “Alright, we can continue on this trip”, I stated to him.

He smiled. He drove off and we stopped to eat the food and use the restroom at another location. We went sightseeing at a small town where they had a Parade or some kind of activity. Then we were going to have some dinner at a restaurant later in the evening. There was not a dress code. We wore our same clothes. Someone had saluted him. He saluted them back. Another person made the peace sign. They were very courteous and respectable. It was getting late in the evening. He told me I could sleep in the bedroom. And he would sleep on the sofa day bed. He got out two sheets. I was actually having a good time with him. I had not brought up with he had done earlier. He said that he wanted to just tell me something about his past.

Ron's sad Tale

Ron said, “That he had never had much time growing up with his parents. His father was very poor and told him that he had to get a good job if he was to stay in their house. Ron said he cried. He had just turned

17 years old and he saw a sign on the billboard that said, "Uncle Sam Wants You" It was paying $1,400 a month. He was not old enough to get in on his own without his parents signature. He could hear his mother screaming all the way down the street when he told her that he was already signed up. He just needed his dad's signature in order to take the physical examination. He walked with his dad to the recruiting office.

Ron said, "That he had never seen his dad cry so hard when they told his dad that he could tell him goodbye right then." He said, "I was sworn in and was to get on the bus to go to the base in West Virginia." He said, "I was trained for 6 months then they shipped me to Korea." He had sent letters to his parents and then one day he told them that he was coming home. He became a Sergeant. They were so proud of him. He smiled. He sent them money every month. They both lived a long life and they died shortly after each other.

Ron said, "I mean before I could hang up my suit and tie, I was getting ready to go to another funeral. I have never heard anything like this before. All my relatives were dying right behind each other. This is why I pretended to be apart of someone else family. I had no right neither the permission to put you through this thing."

Christie understood now. She was crying. But she told him, "I still cannot deceive people in that way. I cherish families, and I was raised by my grandparents because mines had died when I was young". Ron, nodded, and said, "I had read your profile from the computer data base in the office".

I was crying so hard. I hugged him.

"I had no ideal that this was your reason for playing this game. It was not a game—to me", I told Ron.

"Anyway, I will not do this to you again. Tomorrow we will drive

100 more miles to wherever we can find some place that is happening around town", Ron said.

I thought I was becoming serious with Ron. I woke up early in the morning and I came out into the other room. He asked me what was wrong. He had turned me away. He said, "He was not the marriage type." He did not want to ever get married.

I asked him why?

He said, "It is too much agony and it is best that he keeps things the way they are."

I said, "I do want to get married and he is the wrong man for me." He cried. I had him to take me back home earlier on Sunday. I have not dated anybody else for a while.

I could not find anymore assignments that I was interested in doing. This had gone on for several weeks.

Tracey and I Go Out For an Evening Together

I had gotten tired from looking in the newspaper want ads and on my Website on the Jobs Webpage. I wanted to get out for a while and to do something fun. I was going to go to church on Sunday. But, today was Friday. I call Tracey. I asked her was there anything she would like to do, tonight? She said," There is a Play that is appearing downtown. It is a musical religious type of play." "What time will it start? I asked Tracey.

"She said, "It will start at 8:00 p.m. I have two tickets. I will come pick you up, dear", she replied.

"What about Horace", I had asked her.

"He does not want to go anywhere, tonight," she stated.

"I am glad you call me, I tell her. It was just 6:00 p.m. I had time to take an hour nap, before I got dressed. She was driving a SAAB it was a convertible. It was silver gray with a black top. I had slept for almost an hour. I set my alarm to wake me up. I went to my closet to pull out a black long sequin gown. It was sleeveless, and it came with a matching jacket. I went to freshen up. I was putting on my make-up when she called to tell me she was in front of my loft. I slipped on my high heel shoes. They had sequins on them, too. I had picked up my clutch bag. I walked out of my loft. I went to her car. I got inside, and we hugged each other. She drove downtown to the theater. We went inside. She had on a long black dress. It was an African gown. It was elegant. It was very pretty on her, too. She was tall, and had blonde hair. It was cut in a style. She was quite pretty, too.

Chapter 6

I had been up early in the morning. I never shut down my website. I did not want to miss any of my messages. There had appeared a "Pop-up Alert" on my monitor. It stated. "You have a Message." It said, "Please Reply." It is Urgent".

I accepted the message. A man speaks on his phone. It was attached to his computer. He said "Go to my website. So I could continue this message, I immediately went to his website. He explained how he would conduct this conversation.

He had a video camera on his screen so I could see him. He was getting ready to talk to me. I had named my company, GET CHRISTIE/ PI, INC. I had a phone attach to my computer. I had answers it, professionally, "Get Christie/PI, Inc. This is Christie", I said. "How may I help you?"

A man he answered. He had a device where I can see him as he talked.

"Hello, how are you today," he asked me. I said, "I am fine". He said, "That is, Good." He smiled. He had on his pajama set with a satin bathrobe. He had it tied around his waist.

"I hope you are able to listen to this entire message. It may take a little long, he said.

"Yes, I can talk to you as long as it takes." I said.

"Good, I will proceed", he said. "I am Mr. Mike McGuire. I want to hire you to do an Investigation on my daughter. I want you to find out about her boyfriend. I want to know with whom he is keeping company, and some of their activities. Things that is relevant to this investigation," he stated.

"You will need to gather as much information as you can on some of the things my daughter is doing, too. I have not seen her in a year. She has not spoken to me, either. I am worried about her well-being".

He was still talking to me about his daughter. I was typing this into my database as he was talking to me over the phone.

"I am here in NYC. In addition, I think you will be perfect for the job. As you can see, I have done some research on her too. She is residing in the Bahamas Island. I have found out that she lives in a village called, "The Atlantis Coral Beach Resort in the Bahamas." It is a luxurious resort and in a secluded area." That is quite expensive, too".

I typed this information into my database. I was listening to him talk.

"I wanted to know everything about this man and his company as you possibly can get for the length of time you will be there in the Bahamas Island", he said. I had gotten happy. I had to smile.

"My daughter's name is Stephanie McGuire. She is 31 years old. She is Black. She is 5 feet 7 inches tall. She has long brown hair. I want to show you a picture of her when we get through discussing this situation. You will have to be discreet. This might be dangerous, so I want to hire you a bodyguard", he stated.

I tried to protest. Christie's instructor at the college had told her to take deep breath, before she flies off the handle. She sighed. She wanted to do things on her own, not having someone looking over her shoulder.

"How can I be a PI to someone, and have a bodyguard walking along beside me. This makes no sense to me", I exclaimed.

"I understand how you feel, he stated.

"You are not experience enough, and do not know anything about the life that my daughter is living over there", he stated.

"That is true, Christie replies. She had calmed down.

"If I accept the assignment I do not want you calling me everyday". This was my rule. He said nothing. He had dismissed this rule. He continues telling me what he wanted me to do.

Then he said, "That is not my job, dear. I expect you to call or send me data on your report each day. This is how you will get paid, based on your information". He sighed.

"Are you interest in this job", he asked.

"Yes, I mean, yes, sir, I replied. He asks me. How much is your fee?

I want $50,000 I stated to him. He gets silent. He was surprised.

He knew this was not my first assignment. I had another assignment but was let go in one day. He asks me, "Is that all"?

"I was thinking more like, $75,000. I will pay you $30,000, now. And you get the remaining $45,000, when the job is finish", he stated. He smiles. And he mentions to me. You know I could not get anybody to do this kind of work for fifty grand. It would be like a circus to them.

"I would like to put this into your savings account. It will take me two days", he said to me. I wanted to do a dance. But, I kept my composure. "This is wonderful", I replied.

"I will need your account information", he said. "Then, I will transfer the funds into your account. Just as soon as I can get to my web page. How soon can you leave for the Bahamas Island", he asked me. I had a calendar on my wall. I looked at it. Then I said to him. "I can leave on Sunday afternoon, or in the evening." He said to me, "I am still getting that Bodyguard". He was letting me know that he was still in control of the situation.

I sighed again. "You know we are in a disagreement, Mr. McGuire", I said to him.

He replied, "Yes I know. I want very much for you to handle this assignment".

"Maybe I will find someone else. I do not have too much time", he said. I cried, to him, "I will co-operate with you, Mr. McGuire. You can get me a Bodyguard", I had stated to him with tears in my eyes.

"Good. That is all I wanted to hear. His job is to make sure that you are safe", he stated.

"Yes, I understand, I said to him. I am not feeling that well, these days".

He had said to me, "I will have to cut this conversation short. I have some errands to run. So, I have to call you back this afternoon to get your banking information".

"I want to thank you for giving me a chance", I told him.

"I hope everything works out for the both of us, he said to me. I replied. "So do I, Mr. McGuire". He told me to call him, Mike. I said, "Alright".

He said that he was getting off the Website. He wanted to show me some pictures of his daughter. He was still on the phone. You will need to take more pictures, too. I want them put in your data for me" he stated.

"Yes, sir, I replied.

I had seen that he was devastatingly handsome. He might have been in his late 40's or early 50's.

"I have to go, he said. I will call you back about 4:00 p.m. or 5:00 p.m." He ended his conversation with me.

Christie's dream had become a Reality

I have now become a Black female PI from New York City. I just turned 37 years old. I had grown my hair longer. It is now shoulder length. I just dyed my hair Auburn color, and it is relaxed. I put a hair clamp twisted up in a ball in the back.

I took out my pair of gold loop earrings that was in my jewelry case. It was 14 carat, and I had spent S100 on them. I was still in my pajamas set. I was just about to sit at my desk to type in some data for my new program. It was late in the evening. The temperature had dropped down to 12 degrees. I turned up the heat in my loft. And I sat down at my desk to have a sip of gourmet coffee that I had bought from Dunkin Donuts. I proceeded to put on a video of the places I wanted to visit one day.

I pulled out the video of the Bahamas Island. I also had a video of Africa. I had read in Ebony Magazine a feature article about Africa. This was one of my past time hobbies that I did in my spare time. I have not watched any television or movies in several days. I have a cable service. I have my television guide sitting on the coffee table. There was something I had planned to see tonight. It was on the "Travel Channel." This is what I was interested in watching on television tonight. I was thinking I should turn on my radio. I wanted to hear different culture's music. I am in a Caribbean Island mood. I have to look in my radio guide book to find a Caribbean station. I put on the station that said it plays music from other countries. And it has a mixture of Jazz, R&B, Contemporary, and Gospel. This was a new station. Some were beautiful songs, and others put me in a different mood. There was a DJ who was from the Bahamas Island. Christie loved to hear him speak in his native language. He had an accent.

He would captivate his audience by saying, "I hope you are in a good frame of mind" today, I am going to be playing a variety of music that will make you wish you were here.", he would tell his audience.

"Have you turned off that television, yet? "Alright, I want you to sit back and prop your feet up. Welcome to Paradise".

It was Sunday morning. I had to see what time it is, now. I looked at the clock and saw that it was 8:30 a.m. in the morning. I heard my neighbor's dog barking. The same cat was lying at my door. I had never wanted any pets of my own. However, I still loved them. So I thought that maybe he was hungry. I went to my kitchen to take out the milk. I took out a small dish and poured some into it for the cat. I sat it outside my door. I was thinking, "This might as well be my cat". I was still trying to decide what am I going to eat, today? I did not have anything I really wanted to eat that was in my refrigerator.

I had to find myself something to eat for dinner. There was a Mini Plaza that has all kind of fast food places right across the street from Christie's loft.

She was still downtown in the Bronx area of NYC. This was the suburbs and many Professional people lived in this area.

I was about to get up from my desk to get the flyer they send to me every week. There was a Pizza Hut right across the street. I was just about to order me a pizza. I put the DVD disc in my DVD. It was one of my discs of the Bahamas Island. I made me a library to put all my books, videos, discs and other things for my reference. Mike had told me that he would call back that afternoon. This is a big Island. There is so much to view and things to do. He was smiling. He must have felt better.

I want to arrange for you a vehicle. "Do you drive? Or have a license?

"Yes. But I take busses, subways, and cabs, I replied. He said, "I will find you a driver who will have his own car."

"This will not be necessary. I like to be private", I stated. "This is not, what I had in mind. He said, "Very, well." "You can do things, the way you normally do it in NYC. I have called to get your banking information, he stated.

I had my bank book out on my desk. I had given him my banking information.

He said, "It will be in your account on Monday or Tuesday. Have you made your reservation, yet"? I said, "Yes".

"Mike, I had a lawyer to draw me out a contract, stipulating what I want from my clients.

"Oh, I will mail you a contract of what I just mention to you", he responded to what I said, about a contract.

"I will accept the contract", he stated. "And you can mail it to me or send a copy to my e-file. You have my webpage, he stated. "I will have my lawyer to send you out an agreement contract. Or, we can do it electronically".

"I will do it by electronic, too. I said to him. They were in agreement, now.

"I just want to say something else to you, Christie. If you give me what I ask for, I will make sure that other doors are open for you. I know a lot of people who maybe can use you as a Private Investigator. I will start making recommendations once we have ended our business together", he stated.

"Keep your eyes open, and stay focus," he told her.

"That makes a lot of sense, Mike", I stated. He had gone to the doctor. They had given him more medicine. I had no idea he was very ill. He was in a lot of pain.

He did look tired, earlier. He said," I would like to put this sum of money into your savings account. It will take me five days".

I asked him, "Why will it take so long?" You told me that it will be Monday or Tuesday". He stated, "Any time you deal with large sum of money. You may have to wait five days for it to clear." This was not a NYC bank account.

Christie thought. I already knew this.

"Yes, I understand", I said to him.

"If you need some of it right now, I can write you out a smaller check for $3000. In addition, I will transfer the rest when it is clear", he said to me.

I said to him, "That will not be necessary. I have money. I will use my own money to take this trip".

"I like to hear that dear", he stated.

"I have been saving my money for a long time".

I would not tell him about how much I had in my bank account. I still had $300,000 left from my trust fund. I had to use some of it to go back to school.

He had taken one of his pills. He was not on his website. He just took down my information to put on a piece of paper. He asked me, "What time will you arrive in the Bahamas Island"?

"Oh, I am traveling with British Airways. I have booked a non stop flight for 10:00 p.m. I said, happily.

"That is, good," he replies.

"You know I have a temper. This is not one of my best qualities", I said to him. I was smiling. I am still working on it.

He said to me, "Everybody has something that they can improve".

"I was upset when you mention a Bodyguard".

"My job is to make sure you are safe."

I had to apologize to him.

"I am sorry for my outburst. I am accustomed to wanting things my way. I apologize". He smiled.

"This is a new learning experience for me, he stated. We will work on that as the days passes by. You will find me to be a good person to work with, Christie".

"I already see that, Mike," I said, sadly. "Nobody else wanted to give me a chance. I had gone to school for four years. Not to mention I went to school to become a Journalist/ Reporter". He said, "That is wonderful. You are very smart". I smiled. I said to him, "Thank you".

I was thinking he must be wealthy because of the large money he was paying me on my first assignment. He lives in a mansion. There was a huge gate around his estate. He had a surveillance camera and a Guardhouse. He was a wealthy Black businessperson, with his own Enterprise. He also had some properties, stocks, and bonds. He had other assets that he had invested in over the years.

I was listening to some gospel music, now. And I was sipping on a glass of wine.

I had gone to the grocery store. I was so emotional today. I felt that this would make me feel much better. And, it had given me a sense of peace. It had gotten dark outside. I had to pack my bags, too.

I was scrambling in my closet to get my four piece luggage set. It was a pretty color brown with designs. I could not pack my bags fast enough. I had to take out some of my clothes I had worn last summer. I would buy some new things when I got there.

Christie arrives at the Bahamas

I had arrived at Bahamas Island on a Monday morning. They said, "That it was 85 degrees, now." It would reach a high of 97 degrees by, midday. And their time was the same as hers in NY. It was 5:30 a.m. when I looked at my watch. The sunset was not out yet.

I had a cab to take me straight to "THE GRAND INTERNATIONAL HOTEL. It was a very elegant classic hotel. They had some Ancient sculpture's, inside. It had similarities of the White house with the white bricks exterior. It had big poles propped up on each side. The poles were on the outside. It was also white on the outside. The island had beautiful, "Mango" trees. The hotel had a huge lawn. There was a huge driveway for the cabs, limousines, vans, and cars to park.

I had made reservation for the 30 days. The weather was humid, but not scorching hot. I was sweating profusely. I needed some water. I had worn me a sleeveless dress with a spaghetti strap. It was made out of Nylon type of material, with a slip underneath that was sewn in with the dress. I had on my white pumps.

I bought me a bottle of cold water from the vending machine. They told me at the front desk, " We have beverages set up in all the suites. As complimentary service, for are patrons who are staying at our hotel".

They said all the suites had a small compact refrigerator, and a microwave oven. I just needed to go buy the ice from the Ice Compactor room. I thanked them. I was smiling with happiness.

I was anxious to take some pictures, and do some sightseeing. I had a bellman take my bags up to my suite. The hotel was beautiful. I wanted to do some browsing around before settling down in my suite.

It was my first day in the Bahamas. I saw a shop on the main floor that was open. Inside was a beautiful lounging set for me to wear. They had put it on display in the window. I had notice it from the front desk. I had to register and wait on a bellman to take my luggage up to my suite. The lounging set was made of nylon material. The color was a pale green with flowers. The lounging set consisted of a long gown that was sleeveless, it came with a matching silk robe, and there was a pair of shorts, with a shell top. I saw there was a pair of high heels slippers, too. They were the same color as the lounging set. I asked the sales consultant," How much does this lounging set, and matching high heel slippers cost me? The sales consultant said that this will cost $1700 plus tax.

"It will cost me how much for this apparel?" I repeated my question. "I will charge it to my credit card." Not touching any of the money, I was receiving from working my assignment.

I had seen many men who were walking around inside the hotel. I could not speak the native language of those who were from the Island.

I had hoped someone could speak English, too. I knew some spoke Creole, French, Spanish, and other languages because there were many different cultures on the Island. I had my language book that I kept with me, too, for a guide, in case I got into some trouble communicating with them. However, I was not looking for anyone right now.

I had gotten much attention as I walked around the hotel. Nobody had approach me yet. I just went to different types of restaurants and decided to walk alone the long boardwalk that sat over the water. They gave me a directory at the hotel. I carried a bottle of water in my back pack. I had put on a short set and a pair of sandals. I wrapped a scarf around my head. I wore my loop earrings. I had made sure that I put some sun block lotion on my arms and legs.

I saw some bike riders who were passing by as I was walking. Some were walking along, holding their binoculars in their hands. There were a series of birds that flocked around in front of their path. I took out my camera to take a picture.

I was getting tired from the nature walk. I put my binoculars back in a small case. Mines were like the ones they used at an Opera show. It flipped around. I went back to the hotel. I began to walk towards the elevator. A woman was standing at the elevator door. She was about my age, I thought. She was holding the door open for me. She props her arm, and feet against the door so it would not shut. She smiled. She was beautiful. She was 5 feet 6 inches in height. She had black hair. It was long and wavy. She started to strike up a conversation. She was friendly.

"Hello," she said in her accent.

Ann

"My name is Ann Francez. I am Puerto Rican", she mentions. She spoke English, well. Christie replied. "Hello. My name is Carmella Davis", she said to her.

I did not want anybody to know my real identity. However, she had to tell the hotel for security purpose. I shook her hand gently.

"It is a pleasure to meet you, dear," Ann replies.

"I am delighted to meet you, too," Christie replied.

We both were just standing there. Then, she asks me. "What floor are you going to, honey"?

I had to look at my key card. "I am staying on the 14th floor", she said to Ann.

I almost forgot where I was going. I said to Ann. "I am staying in Suite number 1425".

My mind is on this beautiful scenery, and the lovely music that the hotel is playing. I had stated to her, "Oh, yes indeed," Ann replied. I know what you mean".

We strike up a conversation.

"Do you like going to Clubs," she asks me.

"I like to hang out occasionally. I do not go out too often. I am mostly a homebody," Christie stated.

"Since, I am here in the Bahamas Island. I will visit the clubs. That is, some times. I may not be able to hang too out that much.

Carmella—[she is Christie]

Christie said to Ann, "There is much to see and do here."

I had been working on my laptop computer. I had not even looked out my window. The sun was going down. My suite phone rings. I answer the phone.

"Hello, this is Carmella," Christie said". She answers, "This is Ann." She said, "I want to go out tonight. I was wondering if you will come with me".

I stated to her "This is my first day here. I do not know, about tonight"?

I was trying to get my data base together for this assignment, I said to Ann.

I had told her a fabricated story. I have to get my book started because of my deadline.

"I do understand that, dear, she said to me. This is your first day here in Paradise, she stated. You are here to have some fun, girl." I intend on enjoying every minute of mines."

Ann stated to me. "I am only going to be here for one week." How long will you be staying here in the Bahamas Island? She asks me.

"I don't know how long I will be here." My journey here might be longer than I anticipated. It depends on my completion of a project," Christie stated.

"May I ask you a personal question? Ann had asked Christie.

"What kind of book that you are working on, Carmella"?

I had hesitated in telling her this fabricated tale. I had hated to do this to my new friend. "I am working on a Mystery-Romance Novel. I came here to think of a story idea".

I was so sorry for this deception. But, I had to do it in case she was tied to Stephanie's boyfriend, or his company. I did not want my cover to be blown.

Ann beamed. She said, "Girl, I sure do envy you."

Christie said to her, "If it was not for my parents, and grandparents that left me some money, I might be here for only a week." It cost a lot to travel here from the United States. This was the truth. My parents and grandparents did leave me a trust fund. I did sell their home to get some money, too.

"Where are you from,"? I asked her. She replied, "I am originally from Puerto Rico. But, I live in Malibu, California".

"That is nice, I stated to her.

I was using a different name. Ms. Carmella Davis. However, the hotel had my real name registered into their system. Christie Higgins.

McGuire had hired a Bodyguard to make sure I was safe while doing this job. He had heard that a young woman had been strangled here at the Bahamas Island, three years ago. This happened before his daughter had arrived here to work as a model. He was still worried about his daughter. In addition, he became afraid for this Private Investigator's life.

He would not give me any information on the bodyguard. Other than he lives in the Bahamas Island. I was still very upset because I did not like anybody looking over my shoulder. Watching me like a hawk. I was the only PI doing this job.

This was my second day here and I wanted to see the Island attractions.

I had a circle put around this destination. I saw some tourists wearing straw hats, and carrying straw purses. I asked a woman, "Where did you get that straw hat and purse you are carrying?" She replied, speaking to me in her own language.

I take out my language guide book.

"Oh, you do not speak Creole. She spoke, English.

Gerald—The Bodyguard

There is a place called, "The Straw Market. How do I get there?" Christie asked her.

The lady in the straw hat answered, "You will need to ask your hotel what time a bus departs to go to this place".

"Thank you," Christie said to her. She went back to her suite and was putting on a pair of Capri's pants set. It came with a pretty orange blouse that matched the pants and had designs that look like beads. The blouse dropped off one shoulder. She was wearing her low orange pumps. She called the front desk and asked what time a bus was departing to go to the "Straw Market". They told her to be downstairs in ten minutes. One was departing shortly. She rushed to the elevator. She almost bumped into Gerald. He had on his maintenance outfit. It was a blue pair of shorts and a white polo shirt. He came out of somebody's suite. He smiled. He looked down at my face. He was teasing me. He said, "I have caught you trying to get out of here." She smiled. "Yes, I am trying to catch a bus to go to "Straw Market".

"Oh, that is nice". He speaks with an accent. But his English was perfect. Gerald said, "I am going to the "Blue Lagoon Island," and "Lucayon's National Park. Just as soon, as I get to the Houseboat."

He seldom calls it his "Yacht", he told me. He said, "I must change my clothes, first." "No woman will want to be around me. My aroma is not too sweet," Gerald added.

She smiled.

Gerald said, "I was wondering, if you would like to join me? I can take you over to the "Straw Market" on the way back. I have rented a Jeep. If you have a swimming wear you can join me". I had bought me a swim suit, she had stated to him. She laughed when he said, "We can go snorkeling together." She had seen the video of this sport. She just wanted to hear him explain it to her. He was very knowledgeable about many things.

What is, 'Snorkeling? She had asked him". He smiled. He answered, "That is scuba diving".

She stated, "I do not think so, I can watch you on land". He laughs.

"You will have to go underwater to see me," he stated.

She was laughing hard she had to hold her side. She was being humorous. She stated, "I will have to hold my breath." Christie was laughing at her own humor. He laughs, too. He had explains, "No, they will give you a mask, Gerald said.

I shook my head. I was being humorous. I said to him, "I cannot drink up all that water." He laughs.

"Come with me, darling, he said in a serious manner. Go grab your swimsuit, beach towel, and sunscreen lotion. I will be driving to Harbor Island, too. We will have some fun. I have to go take this receipt to the front desk. I will wait on you".

My First Adventure Trip

Gerald had his hair braided. Twisted up, I thought his hair was beautiful. I went back to my suite, and grab my swimsuit, towel, and beach blanket. I put it in a big Duffle bag. I made sure that I had my sunscreen ointment that I carry with me whenever I go to the beach. I went downstairs to the lobby. I stopped at the Front Counter. A consultant said, "Hurry miss, your bus will be departing, now. I asked the driver to wait on you". The consultant was a native Bahamian. Gerald was the lobby waiting. Gerald speaks to the consultant in their native language.

"She is coming with me, Gretchen". He knew the lady.

"I had no idea, I understand," Gretchen replied.

Gerald lived in a beautiful area. It was called, "PORT LACAYA, Resort & Yacht Club." He has a gigantic yacht that he spent almost $400,000 on where he was living at on the Island. He kept it in the middle of the ocean on nice days.

His rental jeep was out front.

"Do you mind riding out to my place, first?" Gerald asked Christie.

"No, I am in your hands". He smiles. He held the door open for me, and I walked out. I still had no idea that he was my Bodyguard although I had run into him so many times on the island. This was my first trip going somewhere with him.

Christie has a Flashback

Christie recalls, she had already called on him on the first day of my arrival, when her shower knob was too tight. She could not twist the knobs to adjust the temperature setting. They were too tight. She could not take a shower, neither a bath. She calls the front desk. They called for Maintenance Service. They did not have their own Maintenance staff. They had to call a Vendor company to come out. Gerald worked with the Vendor Company. He had on light blue shorts with a white polo shirt. It had his company name inscribed on the shirt.

He was already at the hotel working in another area. He came over to adjust the knob that was in my bathroom. He is a tall man. He is 6'1 inches in height. He is slender and is muscular built. He had a lovely tan. He wore his hair in braids. He was really a license Maintenance man, too. He knocks on my door. I let him inside. I looked at his face. I did not realize how handsome he was at that moment. He smiled.

"Hello, ma'am," he said. He asks me," Did you call for a maintenance man?" I replied," Yes, I did." He flashes his badge. He had the order sheet from the front desk. He said, "You are having problem with your knobs in the bathroom? He smiles. He could not understand why I was not speaking back to him. He goes to my bathroom and I followed him.

He observed my bedroom. I had my new outfit lying on the bed. In

Addition, I had a small hand pistol in a brown leather case. I had my laptop on my bcd, too. I had to use this for my assignment to send my data information, to Mike. I kept a small notepad to take notes, too. I had not noticed that Gerald had been looking at me in a strange way.

Christie was Feeling Sick

Gerald gave me a pleasing look. I had been staring at him very hard. He smiled. He began to twist his hair. I asked him, "Why do you twist your hair?" He smiled.

"It is a nervous habit that I had as a child," he told me.

Christie recalls the first day she saw him in her suite. He had asked her, "Did I forget to say our friendly hospitality greeting, "Good Morning? Or say, Welcome, to the Bahamas Island?" He was still smiling. He said, "You are making me nervous". He spoke something in his language. I still was not saying anything. I just kept staring at him. I was in a daze or trance. I definitely was not where I should be at that moment. I was stunned by his striking features. I had lost all sense of perspective. He has a remarkable tan. He shook his head. And he had to ponder for a minute on what to do. He was trying to talk to me, but I was not listening to him. He snapped his finger. I came out of my daze.

"As I was saying it would be helpful for me, Gerald said." "Can you show me, what you were doing to the knobs?"

"I had tried to twist them, the way the directions said on the knobs, to turn right for hot, and left for cold." "I think they are stuck in position," Christie said.

"I cannot turn my knobs for the shower stall, and neither the tub".

"That is actually a Jacuzzi," he said. The hotel does not have a maintenance staff". He explained, "I was asked to report here by the agency where I am employed". He told me his real name.

He said, "I am Mr. Gerald Labrodoreax." You may call me, Gerald or "Island boy". He was a native Bahamian.

I did not think he was born here, though. He had a stunning color. I would have to ask him if he was born here, later. He spoke their native language of "Creole," or Spanish. However, he could speak English. He was finish with the maintenance work in ten minutes.

"You are all set, miss," he stated.

Christie just realized that her bedroom door was open, so she reached over to shut her bedroom door.

"Thank you," she said to Gerald.

She walked Gerald to the front door. We continued to talk. She thought it would be courteous to offer him a cold drink. She smiled at him.

She said, "I could offer you a bottle of water or perhaps a cold soda".

He smiled at me and he shook his head. "That is very nice of you to offer, but I must get back to work," he said to me.

"Come to think of it" I am quite thirsty, he stated. "I think that bottled water will work for me". She smiled at him. She turned around to get the bottle of water from out of the refrigerator. She walked back to the front door and she hand the bottle to him.

He said, "Thank you, dear." He added. "I really have to run." He wanted to get out of there, before his own cover was blown.

Now she could tell how nervous he became, plus, he sighed. She shut the door.

He wiped the sweat off his forehead. He hopes she did not find out, what his real reason for being around her all the time. He did not care if she knew about his other jobs. He had already told her about his other jobs but not that he was a Bodyguard. He worked for the Coast Guard and thc Police department whenever they needed him.

Christie has a high fever with Deliria Symptoms

On Christie fourth day, She had felt something strange was happening to her. It was like a "flashback" when she had been out in the sun too long. Her face was flushed. She seems to always be in a daze. He had to snap his finger to bring her back to wherever she was at that moment. "Are you feeling alright, my love." He asks me. He had not called her name, yet. She shook her head. She said to him, "I am feeling sort of strange, now. It is like I have already been here before, De'javu-. He shook his head. He said to me.

"I do not think that is it, darling." He knew some medical terminology, too. Do you feel like you are having a "Heat Stroke? Some people experience this, when they have been out in the sun for a long time, he had stated. To some people they may have, "a mirage." He gives me a description of the symptoms. "You think you see a fountain that is on dry land on a deserted Island. I ask him, "How did this happen to me, Gerald? He had replies, "I do not know, baby." I have read so many books, he stated.

Do you feel like you are in a "Delirious state of mind?" It is a light-head symptom. To some they are like in a daze or trance. "I do not know." She replied and it is weird."

I am no doctor, but I think you are suffering from "Heat Stroke", Gerald said.

"I have been doing a lot of walking in the sun," I stated. I asked him, "Have I lost my mind?" No, you will be fine, he tells me. "Soon as I get to my boat, I have something that I know will help you. I keep it for when I am in contact, with a person that might be experiencing this condition. I sometimes, have this problem myself," he stated. It is like a "Sea sickness pill. You probably can get it over the counter. It will help you to relax your mind". "Has this ever happen to you"?

I asked him. He replied. "Yes, it has. Especially, whenever I stay out in the sun too long". She said to him, "I keep thinking we have, just met on that first day." You had fixed my knobs.

"Oh, honey. I am sorry, he said. That had been over three days ago. I think I will summon the House doctor at your hotel, to see if he can come take a look at you as soon as we get back to your hotel".

We had gone to his Village. It was a beautiful scenic ride. It took about an hour. She took pictures along the way. He stayed at the Marina. This place was where boaters reside. There must have been hundreds of boats and yachts. They had a Yacht Clubhouse, too. It had all the amenities that his yacht did not have, and a spa with a huge ocean side pool. They had long pier to walk on to get to his boat. It was surrounded by hundreds of rocks stacked on top of each other. Some times the tourists would walk down to the bottom of the rocks. Some likes to sit on the rocks. Inside there was a restaurant inside, too. It had a spectacular view of the ocean. They were playing beautiful music.

She had never been inside a Yacht before.

It was huge, and beautiful. He had his name written on the outside. It reads:

"Gerald—Island Boy, Labrodereax". He held my hand to help me climb in the Yacht. He said, "Be careful, my love." There were steps you have to take to get to the lower level". It had resembles a mobile home. He told me to excuse the appearance. He had his clothes lying around the room. He was picking them up. I forgot to straighten up. He went to his medicine cabin. He takes out his pill box. He came back in the living room. He had a bar, television, stereo system. A built in leather couch that was round. It was white. The floor was marble. It looked like we were stepping on water. He had pictures on the walls. The yacht had a glass sliding door, to go out on the deck. Up on the second level, was for him to use for steering his boat. He had a black brass leather chair that he sat down on when he was moving his yacht. It resembled the inside of a car. He had all the things he needed to check on the weather condition. He had a dispatcher radio to notify the Coast Guard if he ran into trouble.

He brought me a bottle of water. He put two pills in my hand.

"This is harmless. You can go about your normal activity," Gerald said.

"Thank you," I said to him.

I took the pills. We left after he showered, and change his clothes. We went to the Blue Lagoon Island, first. He had a small duffle bag with his swim wear. He had a scuba diving outfit. He had convinced me to go underground. He had teased me. He said, "You are such a scary cat." He smiled at me. He stated, "I have seen some children doing this sport". I said to him, smiling; "You do not have to rub it in, Gerald. I cannot eat anything if am going to go swimming". He said to me, "With my good friend, Amos." He smiled.

Gerald goes swimming with the dolphins

"Who is Amos?" I asked him. "That is the dolphin name", he said.

It was so fascinating. There was a huge steel tank down below. It was installed, so that those of us who were not scuba diving could stand and watch them. They had a stairway and elevator in case, we got sick. It was the most fascinating place. It was inside a big building. It sat on an acre of land. There were millions of cars, cabs, tour busses. They were parked outside. We had to stand in a long line. He had to register his name at the desk. They directed him to another area to change his clothes. I said a prayer. I went scuba diving. I was actually underneath the bottom of the Ocean. I took pictures using my camcorder. I wanted to put all my pictures in a video library when I got back home.

Later he bought me an Island fruit drink called, "pina colada". We walked over to the" Poolside" bar outdoors. I had taken pictures everywhere we visited during my tour. We had done some sightseeing of this other Island in the Bahamas,"Harbour Island," too. Then he took me to "The Straw Market." I had a lot of fun with him. He finally took me back to the hotel.

"I am calling that doctor, now," he tells me.

"No, I am feeling much better." She said, "Let us wait to see how I feel later". He said, "Alright. I am worried about you, dear". I went back to my suite. Gerald had decided to call for me a doctor, anyway.

Gerald was waiting in the lobby for the doctor to return his phone call. The doctor was not in the hotel. He had gone fishing. They left him a message at the front desk to page, Officer Gerald Labrodereax. Gerald had left his business card.

I went back to my suite to take a shower, and take a nap.

Christie goes out with Ann

Her suite phone rings. She answers it. "Hello, this is Carmella." She was not using her real name.

"Hey, girl, this is Ann", the caller on the other end responds. "I was wondering if you wanted to go out with me tonight. It has been four days since

I have seen you," Ann stated.

"No, that is not right", Christie stated. "We were just together yesterday, walking downtown looking in the shops."

"Oh, that is not true, honey." Ann said. "I was not with you yesterday I had gone to a beautiful Resort with a tour group." Remember you said, "You had to work on your book," Ann reminds Christie.

She said, "I am sorry I really did have to do that yesterday, "I am not trying to ignore you, Ann," Christie said, "I have not been feeling all that well. "

That was her last conversation with the woman. She finally agrees to go out with her new friend, Ann.

"Do you want us to go out, tonight?" Christie asked her. Ann said, "Yes".

Christie said, "I have to go find me an outfit. I will see you tonight. Give me a call about 6:00 p.m."

Christie stopped in a nearby clothing shop to find an outfit to wear to the Salsa Club that she had finally agreed to go to with Ann.

Stephanie

While Christie was in the expensive shop, she saw the man's daughter, Stephanie.

Stephanie was there modeling an outfit.

This was Christie's first time seeing his daughter. She began to do her investigation work. She asks her, "How much is that gown you are wearing, miss?" Stephanie, smiles. She did not respond.

The sales consultant said, "That particular gown cost $5000, ma'am." Christie is

Stunned by how high the price of that gown was in this shop. Stephanie did not speak to respond to her question.

Christie thought to herself; did Mike forget to tell her that his daughter did not speak English? She was puzzled.

The sales consultant explained to Christie, "We have a Policy here, Ma'am." We are trying to keep things done here at the shop decent, and orderly. Moreover, making sure these girls are doing their job here at the shop. We prefer that our models not speak directly to the customers".

Christie said, "I am very sorry, miss". Christie understood, now. She remembered having this same conversation on the second day she arrived. This was not Stephanie. She was not speaking to the same sales consultant. Stephanie was doing a shoot at a site.

Christie gives her attention to the model, she apologized to the sales consultant.

"I am sorry, Christie replied.

"No harm is done, dear," the sales consultant replied.

"We had a sign up in our window, but the storms we have here knock them down," the sales consultant said. "Many of our customers make that same mistake, she states. Is there something I can get you?" she asks Christie. Christie shakes her head. "No, thank you". Christie walked towards the door.

She was trying to make her way out the front door. Christie saw Gerald was standing there in a Police uniform. The uniform was just a pair of shorts with a powder blue polo shirt. It said, "Police" on it. It was engraved in white. He said to me, "Hey, I was worry about you".

Christie felt worse

Christie was sweating profusely. And she felt like she was light-headed.

"Are you alright, darling?" Gerald asked her.

"She said, "I think I am still feeling sick and I am supposed to be going out, tonight." I was trying to find me a dress, she stated to him".

Gerald stated, "They have plenty of shops in your hotel." I think you should stick around the hotel," he stated to me.

She agreed with him. She said, "You are probably right".

It had gotten up to 95 degrees. They said, "The temperature would rise up to the high nineties by mid-afternoon." It was already getting scorching hot.

"Come on I will drop you back off at the hotel", Gerald said.

She said, "I had no idea you were a Police Officer". He said, "Yes". He was not smiling at me this time. She had forgotten that he had told her this yesterday when they were together.

"I like protecting people," Gerald explained. She still could not visualize that he was her bodyguard. Christie was thinking to herself; she still did not see or run into this Bodyguard that Mike supposedly arranged for her protection. "She had no idea that Gerald was her Bodyguard.

Gerald stated to her so not to make her alarmed. He said in a calm voice, "I told you yesterday about my two jobs" when we were on my Yacht. She could not remember any of this that happens yesterday. She was puzzled.

He had told her the truth about his two jobs except being a Bodyguard.

"Have you ever ridden on the back of a Police motorcycle,"? Gerald asks Christie.

She replied, "No". Gerald said, "It will be fun just hold onto my waist".

She had remembered a jeep. "Where is your jeep?" She asks him. He said, "That was not mines. I had rented it. "

"Then, where is your bike,"? She asked him. He said, "It is on my Yacht. He has said to her, "He had not broken down to buy a jeep of his own."

Why am I remembering things that has already happen? She had asked Gerald.

And not remembering what had just happen yesterday? He was trying to keep her from worrying. He said, "You are caught up in the ambience of being on this Island. He had stated this to change the subject while he thinks on how to handle the situation. He was being, evasive.

He stated, "You are mystified by your surrounding. As well as being in the presence of a true romance person", he stated. She smiled. As she listen to him talk to her while we were riding back to the hotel. He puts a listening device behind his ear. So, he did not have to use his hand. He had a receiver attached to his shirt. He asks to speak to the hotel operator. This is Officer Gerald Labrodereax.

He had stated, "I want you to notify the doctor there, and tell him I am bringing in a woman who is register at the hotel." He said, "I want him to come take a look at her in her suite." He said, "Tell the doctor that this is urgent too."

They had put Gerald on hold. Then a front desk clerk speaks to him. She said, "That the doctor was not in right now." He had gone fishing.

He asks the front desk clerk, "How long will he be gone? She told him, "I do not know Officer."

Gerald said, "I want you to keep paging him." "We will be arriving there very shortly" he tells the clerk. He had on a tam cap. He still looks good with a cap. I held his waist, as he was driving to the hotel. He drives in a regular speed. He speaks to Christie "The doctor is not in now."

I told him that I had heard his conversation; that I had to go out to buy me one of those devices he was using for my assignment. She had forgotten that she had not told him her real identity. She told him, "I will just go shopping in my hotel and I will wait on the doctor to arrive."

He tells me, "That is a good idea and that he has to get back to work, anyway." He had shaken his head.

Gerald said, "The doctor will give you a sedative that will help you." Then, you should feel normal again. "I am sorry this has happen to you, dear" he tells me.

He took me back to the hotel. The doctor came right away. He apologizes for not being there to receive his first message. "My name is Dr. Timothy Wilkes, he tells me. He was not a native of Bahamas Island. He was Black, too. He follows the both of us up to my suite, and he gives me a shot. I fell asleep instantly.

Dr. Wilkes asks Gerald to tell him what happen to her. Gerald closes the bedroom door so that I could not hear him talking. He tells the doctor how Christie has been acting. He had told Gerald that the shot should work drastically. He had given her a medicine that would make her rest. He uses this medicine for patients that have anxiety attacks. He put the vial of medicine back in his black bag, and dispose of the syringe needle he kept with him in a disposable box. He tells Gerald if she acts different or runs a high fever, "I want you to call me at once. " "If she continues to feel this way we will send an ambulance to take her to the hospital", he tells Gerald. Dr. Wilkes tells Gerald that the shot will relax her mind and she should rest for several hours. The doctor assures Gerald that when she awakens from her sleep, she will feel like her normal self. Dr Wilkes asks Gerald, "Can you stay and watch her for a couple of hours?

Gerald shakes his head. He said, "I am sorry I have another place to be".

"That is alright," said Dr. Wilkes. He had stated, "I will stay with her, then". I want to monitor her condition. I have the hospital on stand-by in case she feels the same way.

"Thank you, Gerald replies. Gerald bids the doctor goodbye.

Christie slept for several hours. When she awakened, she saw a strange man in her suite.

He greeted me. He was smiling. He said, "I am the Hotel doctor." He did not speak in an accent. He identified himself. He shows me his badge.

He said, "My dear you are suffering from "Heat Stroke or the medical term "Deliria." He said, "I have given you a mild sedative by way of an injection in your arm pit. He stated, "It might be a little tender in that area." But you should be fine, now." He had told me that I had some messages on my phone. He said, "I took the liberty of ordering you some food." He stated, "I must go home, now." My wife is waiting on me".

She said, "Thank you, doctor." She held out her hand to shake his hand.

He held my hand gently. He replies, "You are quite welcome dear." He said, "I am on call everyday if you need me." If an emergency should arise, have the front desk calls the ambulance. They will take you over to the hospital. I am on staff there, too. Have a nice day". He smiled.

Christie was thinking to herself. First, I had to check my messages. Tracey, Ann, and Mike had been calling.

Gerald explains to Mike what had happen to me. "She will be back to normal tomorrow, he tells Mike.

Christie girlfriend Tracey wanted to see how things were going in the Bahamas Island. She was thinking, "I will call her back now." Christie she calls Tracey. She said, "I had been feeling sick for a few days." She told her, "I am much better, now."

Tracey said, "That is good to hear. "You are by yourself on that Island Christie?" Tracey asks.

Christie said, "I have a Bodyguard who is somewhere spying on me." Oh, and I have met a handsome Policeman, and he works for the Coast guard. "I think he will be looking out for me whenever he can", I tell Tracey.

"That is wonderful it sounds like you are fond of this man," Tracey said.

"Yes, I am starting to have some feelings for him."

Tracey and I talked for a while. Then, I told Tracey that I had to go get some air. She steps outside on the terrace balcony to get a breath of fresh air. Then she calls Ann.

"Would you like to go some place, tonight? Ann asked. "There was a festival of some kind downtown, she said. "I am dressing casual. There will be food, drinks, and other activities. She asked Christie. "Have you been feeling good?"

Christie said, "No a doctor just left my suite." I had something called, "Heat Stroke, or the medical term" Deliria "I tell her.

"Oh, honey I am sorry I did not get that when I arrive here". Ann had stated.

The Doctor said, "This condition does not happen to everyone. It's just like "Sea Sickness," Christie explained.

"This does affect me and I carry pills with me," said Ann.

"I will be ready to go in two hours," Christie tells Ann.

Christie and Ann were waiting on the bus at the hotel, to go downtown. Christie saw Stephanie talking to her boyfriend. They were standing outside a building. They had not paid any attention to the other people. Christie had not done any Private Investigation in 24 hours. She observes them for a while. Then she and Ann went to the festival. Christie thought she saw Gerald. He was walking among the crowd.

He walks over to her and smiled. "I see you are feeling much better," he said to Christie.

"Yes, I am feeling much better, I replied. Thank you. I am back to normal". Christie hugged him.

"Oh, I am sorry I seem to have forgotten my manner". Christie smiled.

"This is my friend, Ann." "Ann I want you to meet Gerald." She had stated.

"How are you, dear?" Gerald said. He was looking at Christie.

Gerald was looking down at Christie's face. Then, he strokes his chin. Christie asked him, "Can I get a little personal?" "Yes", he said.

He started twisting his hair again. He had meditated for a minute. Like he thought I knew he had been following me around. He sighs.

"What are you doing here?" I asked him.

He had lost his thought. He had to come up with an answer that was discreet.

"It is such a lovely day, and I decided to come downtown, he stated to Christie. In addition to that, I am not working for the hotel today. Just bumming around, and I saw a pretty face".

Christie smile. Then she said, "Oh this woman right here she is quite beautiful."

"Not to mention, there are plenty of pretty faces on this Island," Christie added. Gerald smile. He shook his head. Then he responds, "No, I was not talking about this woman. I was speaking about you, darling". "Yes, you are beautiful," Gerald said to Ann.

"But, I am not interest in you. Forgive me, dear, he stated. Ann said, "I understand".

"I was referring to Carmella," he replies.

"I am nothing like these native women," Christie proclaimed.

He said, "I beg to differ darling." "You have something to offer as much as they do, dear." He stated, "You should not put yourself down". Christie did not respond.

"Thank you," she finally replied. "Well, I have to go", she said to Gerald.

THE ISLAND FESTIVITIES

He asked Christie "Where are you two ladies going?"

He was so striking to look at, too. He was smiling at me.

"Well, we were walking around to see the Festival", she stated.

"I have to be going too, I will check you out later". He stated.

"It is nice to have met you, Ann," Gerald says.

"Yes, it certainly is a pleasure to have met you too, "she tells him.

"As for you, "Island boy." She had paused. Christie had become affectionate towards him.

He was smiling, and looking down at her face. Especially when she made this remark:

"I will be seeing your handsome face repeatedly, while I am on this Island".

Christie felt embarrassed by her last remark. She thought it sounded too flirty.

"We will see each other another time. I am sure of that, dear, he replies.

"Well you have a nice day ladies". He said to them.

"You do the same thing, too," Christie replies.

He looks into her eyes and he had the warmest expression. He was smiling affectionately at her. He shook his head. He put his finger on his lip.

"I will give you a call, later," he tells Christie.

Christie walked around to the Festival. The native of Bahamas were expecting a huge turnout. They were providing live entertainment. There was a huge stage sitting outside. It was all lit up. They stay there for about 2 hours. Christie told Ann, "I have to go back to my suite".

"I was not going to mention this," Carmella, Ann stated. "I have asked someone to meet me down here." She said, "I hope you do not mind".

"No, that will not be a problem," I replied.

"I am going to take a cab back to the hotel." Will you be alright? Ann asked Christie.

"Yes, I will go back to my suite to work on my book." "I will talk to you, tomorrow". She hugs me.

I had told her a fabricated story. I hated to do this to my new friend. I really wanted to spend a romantic evening with Gerald. We could take a walk along the beach. We would talk about nothing in particular. Or, maybe we can go to his yacht and have a romantic dinner. Listen to some jams. I saw that he had a collection of nice music.

They were playing one of my favorite ballads. It was romantic. I wondered why he never shows any affection to me. He truly was a romantic man.

Christie falls for Gerald

On the six day, Gerald was standing at the window looking to see if she had gone to the shop. She was not downtown. He drove back to her hotel. He went inside to call her suite. She was not downtown and neither in her suite. She was not there, either. It was such a beautiful day. She was feeling normal again.

He thought he might see where she was at, now. He walks to the beach to see if she was there this morning. She was throwing pumpkin seeds to the flock of Flamingo birds. He just stood there watching her. He had his hands in his pocket. He was wearing a pair of Navy blue shorts and a matching, light blue Polo shirt. In addition, he was wearing a pair of sandals.

He saw her walking alone by herself. He smiles. In addition, he had caught up with her and he made a little poetic remark and a note of flirtation behind his statement.

He had stated to her. If the birds could only know what a pretty sight you are, they would be flocking around you night and day. I smile at him. I said to him. "Gerald, what are you doing here?" He was glaring into my eyes.

He was trying not to become affectionate with me. He was fighting temptation. He never held my hands.

I was walking in my bare feet. So I could feel the tingling of the sand between my toes. I use to do this every time I went to a beach. I was wearing a wrap around nylon skirt that had beautiful flowers designed, and a halter top that ties around my neck. Ah, ha! He exclaims. He said, "I have caught you giving me that look."

She had to laugh at him. What are you talking about, Gerald. He said, "I know you like me."

She replied to him. "There is no question about that," Gerald. I said, "Yes, I do very much."

He said, "If I can tear myself from the gruesome work that I am doing these days." "Will you go somewhere with me that is nice? He had asked me.

She said to him, "Sure you can call me at the hotel." He smiled. He said, "I will give you a call later."

Gerald becomes Affectionate to Christie

Gerald was walking beside me on the beach. I had stated to him, "You did not answer my question." He smiles. He said, "I can not stay away from you, darling."

"I keep seeing you in my mind," he stated. "I hear your voice calling my name, Gerald", he stated.

She asked him, "Is this the strange occurrence you were talking about earlier? "I keep hearing this beautiful music." She state to him.

He said, "That is our Jungle music." That is a sound that the African were accustoms to doing in one of their ritual, he stated. "We are close to Africa, than the other countries." """Some people say they cannot hear the sound, though." He had stated to me. This is a Cultural place to be, darling. My parents and grandparents knew a lot about this stuff. They would tell me some stories. He had stated to me.

It helps you to relax and give you a sense of peace. You are on Paradise Island.

He gets quiet. Then he said, to me, "You are getting me in trouble, girl."

She said, "Gerald, you are talking in circles."

He takes my hand, and pulls me close to him. "I had to promise myself that I would not become affectionate". He had stated to me. He started to give me a kiss, but he backs away. She asks him, "Why did you do that Gerald?" He said to me. "I am a Christian, and I assumed you are one too." I am trying to give you the utmost respect, darling. At that moment I thought that he was a monk. She had read that they never married. They live a life of Celibacy. Gerald he did not look like he was a "monk" I thought. He smiles.

Gerald asked her, "What are you going to do this afternoon?" She said, "I had thought about going downtown."

Christie said, "I am supposes to go out with my friend to a club." "I really am not a Club person," she stated. She said, "I love doing what I am doing," now. Walking, talking, feeding the birds, and enjoying the ambience of being in a beautiful place, she stated. He said, "I enjoy doing these things, too." Yet, I am adventurous. I like swimming, snorkeling, fishing on occasion, hiking by spell, and especially sailing on my Yacht. He had stated to me.

I like to go dancing when we have our festivity. He had said to me. I want to go swimming with the dolphins. I was thinking about tomorrow spending a whole day of doing adventurous things. He looks at his watch. I have to go. He said to me.

"Well, let me go about my business." He left me on the beach. I had gone back inside, later.

I had to take me a shower, and get dress to go downtown. I was supposed to be doing a PI on Stephanie and her boyfriend. In addition, to his company too. I put in my data information. I ask the data to tell me how to get to the village that was called,"Exuma Resort?" This was a resort. They draw me a map. I ask what kind of transportation will take me to this resort. They said a bus. You can take it from downtown Grand Bahamas, I rush to go take my shower, and gets dress. I had to hurry to get downtown. I had taken a cab. I got there just in time. The bus had arrived. I had gotten on, and paid my fare. It cost $3.00 in their currency. I had to get my money exchange when I had arrived there on Sunday.

Christie works on her Assignment

I had gotten downtown to where Stephanie was working inside a shop. She was modeling. I begin to look at the gown, that she was wearing today.

I asked the sales consultant, "How much is that gown that this model is wearing?" We are asking $5000. I was on my way walking out the door. Gerald, he was standing there. He smiled.

You might get some heads turn if you buy that one, dear. I had shaken my head.

Then, I had smiled. I had stated to him. They are asking for five grand. I reply. For that price, I want the president of the United States to invite me, to an affair at the White House. I had stated. He falls out laughing again.

I walk passes by him. He was standing in the doorway. I start to talk him.

He smiles. In addition, he said to her "You must have a hot date tonight."

No of course not. I am going to this Salsa Club that Ann has been begging me to go.

"Oh, it must be Ladies night out." He stated. He had put a trace out on me. He had found me, too. I had replied to his statement. I am seeing you, right. I had made the comment. He laughs. That is what I hope, darling. He said to me.

Christie said, "My friend has met a man and she might leave me all by myself."

He stated, "I am positive that will never happen." He stated, "You are a very pretty woman",

"Thank you I had said to him." Well, I have to go, I stated to him. I still had to go find me a gown.

"Check you out later," He stated. He was going to the Salsa Club.

Seeing Deon threatening someone

I was walking along when I had overheard a man conversation that someone was saying over the phone. I want my money that you owe me. I would hate for something bad to happen to you. You have 48 hours! In addition, I hope you will take heed to my warning. The man was, irate. He was frowning up, and his face had turns red.

He was wearing a white pin stripe suit, and a red designer shirt. In addition, he was wearing a pair of white "pat leather" shoes.

This man he was standing up against an old structure building, while he was talking on his cell phone. He flips the top shut, and straightens out his suit jacket. He frowns, and pinch his nose. He was annoyed about something.

I thought.

He was devastatingly, handsome. He had a dark tan. He has beautiful hair, and he looks like a foreigner. He did not look like was a Bahamian. He spoke in his native language. He was walking towards the shop.

I walk into another shop to be indispensable.

He had gone over to where Stephanie was working. He made a gesture with his hand. He gave her a little wink.

She cannot talk, to anyone while she was working. That was one of their Policies. What time will you be through working? He had pointed to the clock.

Stephanie was silent. But she understood what he wanted.

Gerald knew their rule at the shop. The models were not permitted, to speak to the customers.

He points to his arm. He was walking up and down each aisle. He begins to look around at the gowns. He had paid special attention to the designer gowns that she was modeling.

She was hoping he would like the gown she was wearing, now. She put up both hands. To make a gesture, in addition she was pointing to the clock on the wall. He nods his head. He was buying the dress she was wearing, now. He would get it, later. He smiles in approval.

He went outside to wait on her to finish working.

Christie had seen a cheaper gown somewhere else.

The man had stated to the woman. "This is like a dead-end street". Come on Steph. He stated, "Lighten up, darling." He put his arm around her waist. He had his own Van parked outside waiting on his company to come out of a Cigar Shop.

She said to him. Deon, "I do not want to go to your house right now." All you will be doing is handling business, she stated.

He looks around for his partners. They finally came out of the shop.

They both had a thin cigar in their mouth. I saw the expression on his facc. Hc looks very agitated. He looks down at his diamond, Rolex Watch. They were going to a party in Green Turtle Cay. One of his business associate had invited him to come. He had a beautiful home that was on the beach. He said that this man," He is quite wealthy and he was an African." He owns a share of his banking company. He had invested into Deon business. He is from Kenya Africa. He tells her this is an outdoor party. He said, "This man he gives the best parties." You can wear the gown I just bought you. Stephanie, I am exhausted. I want to go home to relax for a while. Listen to some Salsa music, have a little wine and cheese with some imported crackers that I just bought from the Market, he stated." You are giving me a headache. He sighs.

He had told her, she could not go anywhere by herself. He was very protective of Stephanie. He said, "It is not a good ideal for you to go carousing around this Island alone." She was always surrounded by Camera crews, Producers, and other staffs.

Christie had been observing their conversation for about 10 minutes from a distance. The bus had pulled around to where I was standing. Other people line up to get on the bus. It was a Tour bus that takes you around on all the Islands. I had a List of places I wanted to visit, too.

A person had ask me, do you hike?

"I said," No I have never hiked before, Christie stated."

This person said to her, "If you are Interested they have rock climbing lessons that will be at 1:00 to 3:00 p.m."

Christie had gotten back to her suite. She had change out of her clothes and put on a short set. First, I walk over to where I had kept my laptop sitting on the table. I needed to type in the data information that I had just heard with Stephanie and Deon.

As far as I could see, Deon was not a dangerous man. I saw he was a passionate man.

He knew how to treat this woman.

I needed to see Deon conducting his business. I had time to take a nap and relax for a little while.

I walk over to the glass sliding door in my suite. The drapes had been closed. I open it to get a view and I crack the glass sliding door to get a breath of fresh air. I was facing the Ocean side. I must have been asleep all night. The sun was rising like in the early morning. I figure I might have been tired from all that walking around in the hot sun.

Christie Goes to a Party at Green Turtle Cay

I remember overhearing Stephanie and her boyfriend conversation.

He said, "He was taking her to someone house tomorrow night to an elaborate outdoor party."

Christie had to find out if Gerald knew about this Village. I had his number on the night stand next to my bed.

He was back on his Yacht. He sounded like he was asleep. He answers the phone when he saw that it was me on his Caller ID. "Hello, babe what is up."

I had to laugh at myself. How do you know it is me? I had teased him.

He stated to me. "I recognize your suite number." How are you feeling, today? He asks me.

"I feel pretty good, "she had stated to him.

Is something wrong? He asks me.

"No I want to ask you a question", I had said to him. I want to ask you where is, "Green Turtle Cay?"

"Who wants to go there?" He asks me.

I said, "That I was just inquiring."

He said to me, "It is here at a small village in the Bahamas Island." He pauses for a moment. Wait a minute, he checks his calendar book. I see that I have been invited to a party. "It is in that Village," he stated to me. "Why do you ask about that village?" He asks me.

I just heard someone mention that Village in a conversation, I stated to him. I had told him a fabricated story.

He knew I was not being completely honest with him. "You want me to take you there?" He asks me. "I cannot deceive you," Gerald. I had stated.

"Yes I want to go there tomorrow," I had said to him. I really was not thinking about a party. "But, since you are invited perhaps I can join you." I had stated. Sure, I can bring anybody with me, he stated. Gerald said, "I know the man who is giving the party." He is also a friend of mines. He stated to me.

Are you going to go? I had asked him. He gets silent. He said, "I do not know yet." He said to me. He grabs his thin cigar, from off his nightstand. Then, he lights it. He was thinking of why I wanted to go to this party. He figures that this man daughter was going there. He knew that was why I was interested in going to this party. Well, let me check my scheduled. I will give you a call back in the morning. He stated to me. You and I have not gone out anywhere together. Do you have something to wear?

Christie said, "Yes I do."

After, he had hung up. Mike, he had called Gerald.

Gerald Resigns from working for Mike

This is Mike. He had told, Gerald.

He wanted to know how things were going with the Private Investigator. Hello, Gerald. He greets him, pleasant. He had become familiar with him. How is she feeling now? He asks him.

Gerald, he replies. "She is fine, Mike." Christie, she is out everyday trying to find information on your daughter.

"That is good to hear man." Mike said. She has sent me an e-mail, the three days since her arrival. Mike, he replies.

Gerald interrupts him.

Mike, a lot has happen since I started working on this job as a Bodyguard. In addition, I think I am not the right man for the job. He had stated to him.

Mr. McGuire asks him. "Why, is that?" Please call me, Mike. He added.

Well, it is of a personal matter, Gerald stated.

Mike he sighs. As he listen to Gerald.

He had dealt with this before in another assignment.

Gerald was still talking to him. You see, I like Ms. Christie. "In addition, I would like the opportunity to take her out without doing the job." He stated. I know that this will interfere in my work performance, he said in fact. This makes no sense to me. She is a Detective.

He then, added. She is capable of taking care of herself. Gerald was still speaking.

"I disagree with your point of view." Mike, he replies.

He was not surprise by this news. "This is not nothing new to me." Mike responded.

"She must be quite attractive." He added. Yes, she is beautiful. Gerald replies." Oh, I see." Mike stated to him. He was on his Website. He smiles. This happens every time I asked an employee to do something for me where a woman is concern. He had stated. He was using the Video Camera Recorder device that was attach to his computer.

Gerald saw what he looks like.

"You know, Gerald I have sent you $15,000 and when the job was finish, I was going to give you $15,000 more," he stated.

Gerald replies. "I will send you back your money". Wait a minute I am not angry! He was getting worried. He felt his hand was sweating. And the sweat was tickling, the back of his neck.

"I still think this woman needs your help." Mike stated.

"I will still be looking out for her, but not as a bodyguard." He stated to Mike.

"I am going to ask a few friends, if they could do me a favor. They work with the Police force, Coast guard, and Navy. He had, stated to him.

Nevertheless, we both know that she does not want anyone spying on her. Gerald stated. Yes, this is true. Mike replies. He gets quiet. This has trouble me from the start. Mike stated to him. I want to give her a chance to do this work alone.

Mike stated.

Gerald, he takes out a thin cigar. He lights it. He had been smoking a lot lately. In addition, he continues talking to this man.

You know that I am supposes to be accompanying her around the Island.

I am doing this job, for her protection. Gerald states. That is true. Mike said. I know how difficult this must be for you, Mike.

Yes this is causing me a hardship because now I am relying on someone else to make sure this woman is safe.

"However, because she is so observant, she will soon discover that you are her Bodyguard and will go after you in her fury." Mike had stated.

"You are so right." Gerald replies. I am glad I decided to quit this job.

There must be something; we can do to rectify this situation. He stated.

Gerald said," No I have made up mind." This will interfere in my trying to date this woman. Mike, he sighs. Then he speaks. Well, you have work for me the 3 days and that is your earnings. You can send me back the $8,000 and keep the rest.

Thank you. Gerald said. I will send you a check by certified mail." No, I want it transfer into my account." You have my information. Yes, I do. I will take care of that this afternoon.

May I ask you one more question? Mike asks Gerald.

Yes, you can ask me whatever, you desire. He had stated.

"Since, you are going to be seeing Christie will you tell her your real identity?"

You already told her that you hired me, right? Gerald asks him. He replies." Yes I did tell her that I was hiring a Bodyguard, who resides in the Bahamas." He stated. I will discuss everything with her, when I think it is at the appropriate time. Gerald stated to him. And he added. I hate deception. I have plans to see her tonight.

"Okay I guess you have to do what you have to do. Mike stated.

That is the end of this conversation, Mr. McGuire. He had said, "Good luck to you, young man. Gerald said to him, "I am sorry, for any inconvenience this might have caused you Mr. McGuire.

Mike McGuire had said, "This is no inconvenience I am a Businessman, I like doing things to help people." Especially I do things for people who are working under my employment. I will be calling you often if you do not mind. And please call me if there is anything, you are concern about or where they both are concerns.

I just wanted the woman who is working for me to be safe. He was agitated.

I understand that, Mike. Take care. Gerald replies.

You do the same, young man. Mike replies. He turns off his VCR. And he closed out of his Website.

Christie woke up at 6:00 p.m. and had to get dress. Gerald told her he would pick

She loves her new gown and she kept on looking at it in the closet. My gown was beautiful. It was pink made of nylon type material. It had diamond shoulder straps. It was cut in a V-line shape. It had tiny diamonds around the V-line. It came with a built-in-slip. It had a split going up one leg. She had her hair in curls.

She was wearing a pair of long diamond earrings, and a matching necklace. She put on an Island bracelet on both of her wrists. They were colorful with tiny diamonds. She had bought them at one of the Island shops. She put on her make-up, and she puts the things in her pink clutch bag. Gerald, he had rented a sports car. It was sharp. He told me it would take two hours to get to this Village. He had bought him a sharp Green suit, with a cream color shirt. He had matching leather shoes. He had his hair sticking up in his style he likes to wear. He had left his Yacht, to go to the rental car. I had gone to the elevator. I rode down to the main lobby. He had arrived just as I step off the elevator.

Ann, she had left me a messaged on my suite phone. She had apologized to me. I am so sorry, Carmella. She had stated to Christie. "There has been a change of plan. I am going to this party with my friend, James," she had stated. He had been begging me to go with him, for two days now, I hope you will not be angry with me. She stated. "I will call you tomorrow and we will do whatever you want," she said. So, she was not going anywhere with her girl friend. This party was strictly business for Christie. She had not thought about canceling her evening with Ann.

Gerald, he had parked his rental car. He had put on some music for the drive. He rocks as he drives. He had to drive the dead man curve. I needed to see Stephanie and Deon when they were not in public. I wanted to see how they act in another environment.

Chapter 7

This was the Seventh day, it was about 7:00 p.m. Gerald arrives at the hotel. He gets out of the car. He had the top down. He goes inside. He got a lot of attention. He looks around the lobby. He saw Christie standing by the window. He smiled and nods his head in approval. He walks over to me. He said to me, "You are beautiful, darling." Then he gave me a hug. "Thank you," I said to him. You look dashing in that suit, too, he stated to me. He thanks her. He held the door open for her to go outside. He smiles.

He made a cute comment. So, you want to see "Island boy" groove. I smiled. He put his hand across my back. He opens up the door, on the passenger side. I get inside, and he shut the door. In reference to what you said about the "groove thing". I hope you mean dancing. He laughs. He said, "I guess I am not that much for slang talk." I had stated. He smiled. He said, "I understand I sometimes think all black people talk the same way. He stated to me. If I said something you do not understand, just pull my arm and I will explain to you what I meant. He stated. She said, "Thank you."

You are quite welcome, darling. He drives off. "I am so glad that you call me yesterday to ask about the party," he stated. He said, "I had not had any time with you." It just happens, I love outdoor activities, he stated. He said something poetic and it was romantic. To see the moon making it first appearance, and to glare up at the stars that is giving it light and it is romantic, when you are with a woman. I had to say something to him. I had said, "You are very poetic Gerald. He laughs. Sometimes, I talk like that to people if I am trying to get a point across to them. He stated. "I will talk like that to any woman, only you darling", he stated.

This is a beautiful scenic drive. I said to him, "I do not have my camcorder." He stated to me, "You will just have to visualize with your beautiful eyes." He turns up the music. And he rocks to the beat. He looks at me for a second. It was dark anyway. "Do you like this tune?" He asks me. I said, "Yes I do very much it is quite jazzy." I rocks to the tune too.

Meeting Gerald's friend Manuel and Jamal

I sure wish I could have taken some pictures of the beautiful scenery.

They had gotten there to the party about 9:00 p.m. There were limousines, and fine vehicles.

I saw this stunning beach house. It had three floors with a deck on each one.

I had never seen anything like this in the world. They walk inside a gate.

He held my hand. He was looking for his friend, who had him invited to the party.

He heard his nick-name being called out. If it isn't the "Island boy" He smiled. He walks over to the man. He gave him a hug. His name was, Manuel. He had long braids that came down his back.

He was an African. Manuel, this is my lady Carmella. He hated to use this fake name. He was going to tell her the truth soon. He smiled. His friend gave her a kiss on the cheek. He used the word, Princess to her. He asked me. "How are you, princess?" This was an unusual sentiment he had called me. Gerald, hc just smiles with a funny expression on his face.

"I am fine." She said to him. Thank you for inviting us to your beautiful home, man. Gerald said to him. It is a pleasure to have you both as my guest. Let me get my wife, Lena. He said, "Whatever you want you can have it." I have all kind of food, drinks, and dancing to you drop. We will have the Limbo game, too. He said to us, "I think someone is getting ready to do the Island hustle." They had gathered in several lines. He pops his finger. Gerald, he smiles. He walks me out to the dancing area to a line. He dances in style with her to the music. He held my waist so that I could follow his step. He dances stylish and he was a terrific dancer. Christie smile trying to keep up with the dancers. He smile and told me that I was doing fine. I was glad that it was dark outside. She saw Stephanie, and Deon. They were dancing, together. Gerald, he twirls Christie around again. Gerald, heard his nickname, "Island boy" being called again. He looks around and saw that it was his close friend that he works with at the Coast Guard. He smiles. He went over to hug him. You have made it, my brother. Yes, he said. He still held Christie hand. This is my friend, Jamal. He was also striking in his looks. He had his hair cut short but it had some tiny curls. He had facial hair. He had on an African outfit. He had a cap on his head. He spoke in his Jamaican accent. He slaps Gerald hand. How are you darling? He had asked me. I said, "I am feeling fine." Jamal said, "This is good to hear or I will have to do something about this." He had hugs me, gently. Gerald laughs.

Gerald, did you tell your woman where you were born? His friend Manuel, he had asked him. He smiled. We both are natives of Kenya, Africa. My eyes had open up wide. Gerald, he looks at my facial expression. No, I have not had a chance to tell her about my cultural background. He tells his friend. Well, darling.

Your man is from Kenya, Africa. We call him "Jungle cat". Gerald, he shook his head. I had not been to my native country since I was a child. I will tell her about my history background, later. Are you hungry, darling? He had asked me. He had to get off this subject, too. Yes, the food does smell delicious. I had stated. I see some unusual bowls. They are called, "[calabash]" It means, "African bowl." Come on let me fix you a plate of something delicious. We have some soul food," [Sukuma Wiki],"in your language: Collard Greens. "[Ku Kuna Nazi]"—chicken with coconut Milk, and everyone favorite here on the Island, Stuff Oyster and last but not least. Kenya Beef in a mound of blended potatoes. There must have been 100 different types of food. Make room for my Red beans, and rice. And we have delicious desserts. Manuel, he is also a chef. He said, "My wife does all the cleaning." She was Gerald hairstylist. She owns a Hair Salon shop.

She was not surprise about where Gerald was born. He had gotten her a platter.

He fixes several dishes. They went to a table to sit down to eat. I am starving.

He told her. It is delicious. He fed some to her, like they would do in his culture.

So, when were you going to tell me you were born in Africa? She had asked him.

He had said, "I was waiting until we got to know each other better." I have lived here my whole life.

I want to go visit my sister who is residing in Gaborone, Botswana. She and I both have not seen each other in years.

I wanted to visit Africa, too. This was in some of her home Videos of places to see list. I thought about what Gerald had told me in their earlier conversation. He told her that, "he had been living in the jungle, and he did not think that he was ready to go to where people lives in a big City." She had asks him, if he had ever visit the United States. He replies. No very quickly. The men and women, they wear suits. In addition, men wearing shirts, ties, and fancy Alligator shoes. Carrying brief leather, cases. He stated. How do you know you would not like it, unless you visit? She had asks him. He stated, "I know how I am and I would have a phobia." He stated. Considering, the fact. He had said, "I hate being in crowded spaces like busses, and trains". Not to mention, "I like dressing casual."

He added. But, I know how to get cleaned. He meant dressing up. Christie said, "You are so smart Gerald." He smiles. She had stated to him, "You do not act like you are from Africa ". I guess I am a true black person—in spite of my culture and language."

He stated, "I read magazines all the time." She was laughing so hard at him. He said to me, "Not to mention I am a jungle cat." He said, "He was like a wild animal." A Lion, He said in particular. He stated, "I have not been tamed yet." "Were you born in July?" She had asks him. "Yes my darling. "He said. She had stated, "Then you are a Leo?" He stated, Yep that is my sign." He asks her, "What is your astrology, sign?" She said to him, "I am a Virgo". He said to her, smiling. "We have some things in common." She said," Yes I guess we do have ways alike." On the other hand, she was different. She thought.

He said, "She was the aggressive one and likes to do things on your own." He mentions that, too. He said something surprising, "She did not like being watch. Neither did she like to have someone look over her shoulder.

She nods head agreement. He was absolutely right about his astrology. He was looking in my eyes this was our first eye contact. I was distracted when I saw Ann there with a man. She calls my name, Carmella you are here. Gerald he left me along to go out front to use the cell phone in the rented car.

He was dressed in a sharp suit. It was wearing a royal blue suit with a cream color silk shirt. He was smoking a thin cigar.

He was talking on his cell phone. He had rented a white Convertible car with a white convertible top.

Gerald gets a call from the Coast Guard

He left his Yacht, sitting in the middle of the ocean. The water was a beautiful blue color. He had his speedboat, sitting in the back. He uses when he had a job, with the coast guard. He gets in the jeep and drives off.

Someone had said, "Did anyone hear that there is a storm approaching in our area?

The host said, not to worry. Everyone can come inside for the remaining of the party. Nobody has to go home.

You look beautiful, Carmella. Ann replies. That is a beautiful gown. Thank you. Christie said, "Thank you Ann."

She had said to Christie, "I hope you are not mad at me?" she said to her. I was feeling so guilty. Ann boyfriend he came over with some champagne. Hello, my people. Gerald had come back to the party. James he was black but he had an accent. He introduces himself.

I am James De'cor. He shook Gerald hand. I am Gerald Labrodereax, Carmella man. Christie she smiles. He was Stephanie advertising agent.

Ann gave me a hug. She said, "I am sorry that I had cancel our plans to go out together tonight, but James said there was this party that was supposed to be the best on the Island."

"Do not worry about this Ann.", Christie said to her. "We both are here and that is all that matters." She smiles. She said, "This is why I like this woman so much."

"I know you have works to do here." Ann stated. Christie did not say anything. James had asked me. "You are working here too."

"Carmella, she is a writer," Ann stated.

He congratulated me. "That is magnificent," dear. He gave me a hug.

Gerald, he had mention about another dance. He knew this was not of the truth. He had to quickly get me out of this line of communication. He had said to them, Hey I see someone is about to start a hustle." "Is anyone game?" He had asked them. They all said," Yes you bet we want to hustle. "They went to the dance area by the beach. Everyone had gone out to where there was dancing on the sandy beach. It was so beautiful, a light pale shade of pink. Some had taken off their shoes. This was the highlight of being on the Island. To see everyone smiling laughing, eating, drinking, and etc. Most of all to have a good time while in the moonlight. It was still quite warm outside.

Gerald, he took my hand. He put his arm around my waist to guide me. The music was on jam.

They were making a lot of noise. I was not familiar with this hustle. He told me to follow his lead. We had a good time. We stay until dawn. There was no storm. Christie bid Ann goodbye.

"I will talk to you, tomorrow Carmella." She said to me," You know I will be going home on Sunday." These are my last 2 days here. Ann stated.

She had asks me "How long are you going to be here?" I keep asking you for a reason. "I do not have that many friends and I would like to look you up when you get back to NY." "Oh, that is so sweet." Christie had replied. "I have a few more weeks," Christie stated. "When I get back home to LA, I am going to be calling you." Ann replies.

"That is so sweet". Christie stated. "I will do the same thing when I return home." They both smile.

I was getting tired of telling everyone a fabricated story. She had said something that made a lot of sense to me. She said, "She was glad to see a black woman that was determined to do something that was hard to do and she has accomplished it."

I had smiled with tears in my eyes. I had, reach over to give her a hug.

Ann said," It must be a reason or purpose for our meeting here on the Island." I remember that destiny that Gerald had told me about a couple of days ago. He mention about me finding my path, and being here on the Island. He added. I was so excited to finally meet someone who care about my well-being, and enjoy spending time with me. I was going to tell them the truth about my Identity. I was sort of worried about how Ann was going to take the news. I trust them both completely. Gerald, he had dropped me off at my hotel. I went up to my suite. I was very tired. I had to type in my data base, the information regarding seeing them at a party.

I told Mike that his daughter was having a good time at this party in, "Green Turtle Cay" Stephanie and Deon they acted like they were happy together." I had sent him a message.

Then, I had gone to bed. The next morning I had gone down stairs to go have some breakfast. They had a lovely buffet style bar. I had on a pair of stretch leggings and a tank top with a blouse that tied across my mid-drift. I had pins my hair up in a twisted ball. I had paid for my meal. They also had an outdoor seating. I really love the view of the

Ocean. I had fixed me plate, and I get a beverage. I had taken it outside.

I sat down at a table. Gerald, he was there working at the hotel. He stopped to get him some breakfast. He did not know I was inside the restaurant. He got his food, and went to find a table inside. He looks out the window, and saw me sitting down by myself. He took his tray and walks outside. He goes over to my table." May I join you?" He said to me. I look over at him. "Gerald, what are you talking about?" I had asked him. You do not need an invitation to sit with me. He laughs. "I am very courteous, some people like their privacy in the morning." He stated.

"Thank you, he replies". He smiled. He sat down across from me at the table. "What is on your agenda for today?" He asks me. Gerald I need to talk to you. This is not the place to discuss important matters. I will be free in about an hour. I will come up to your suite, unless, you have made other plans. He stated.

"No, I am sort of beat from all these traveling. Although, I do want to go see one other place before I leave the Island." I had stated to him.

Tomorrow, I am taking the day off to give my body a rest. He told me. I have something to talk to you about too.

Gerald Tells Christie some Shocking News

I was thinking about taking a ride on my Yacht and sit it in the middle of the Ocean. We can have a romantic dinner. I am going to clean up my place. He told me. I had to laugh. We ate our breakfast, he goes back to work. I went back up to my suite. Later, I went back downstairs to buy a magazine. I took a look out in the lobby.

Deon and his company were there without Stephanie. They were standing outside the Limousine. I had heard one of the men said, "Here he comes. Jerome had said to Deon.

Jerome, he goes to the front door. He always wore suits no matter how hot it was outside. He walks over to this man who was coming off the elevator. He was walking towards the front door. Jerome he grabs the man by his armpit. He said, "We want a word with you, my friend." "Take your hand from off of me!" He had exclaims. Nobody else had noticed this little scuffle. Christie was inside the gift shop observing from the window. Jerome, he had put his hand in his pocket. He replies. "I hate to make a scene." He put this object up against the man side. He follows him inside the limousine. They sat there for a few minutes, then drives off. I still had not gotten enough information on Deon friends. I paid for my magazine, and went back up to her suite. There was a news announcement that someone had got hurt. They had it on the television and radio station.

They did not disclose the persons name or the injury. I was surprised that they did not say the incident occurred at the hotel. The news said, "That further details will follow." Christie was wondering if this involves the scene earlier. She was waiting on Gerald to arrive. She had to tell him today about her identity while she had the nerves. She cracks her knuckles. He was still at the hotel. He finally took his break. He took the elevator up to her suite. He knocks on my door. She had changed her clothes. She had on a purple regular flower long dress with a pair of purple strapless pumps. She opens the door for him to come inside.

He smiles at me. You are looking pretty and refreshed. He had stated to me.

I had thanks for him for the compliment.

He had stated, "What is up, beautiful." He had called me this for the first time. She shows him the newspaper. He nods his head. "I have heard the news about this man getting hurt by a man today." This involved two other men. He added. He said. He went to sit down on the couch. I am glad that Stephanie was not around when this went down. He stated. "Gerald I was there when it started here at the hotel." She stated. He asks me, "What was it you had to tell me my love." I was trying not to cry. I said, "I think you are under the impression that I… She could not continue her sentence. It had gotten dark just that fast.

The First Tropical Storm

We both look out the window. The wind was blowing mighty strong. It was hissing, and I race to close the patio doors. The sky had darkens, and rain was coming down hard. I could not finish my sentence. I went to the television to turn on the news station. "They announce that a storm was approaching the area. Please find a safe place to protect yourself from the storm! They exclaims. I thought about my former job as a journalist-reporter for the newspaper station. "We had better find a corner to stay in until it cease." Gerald stated.

"I am so glad that you are here, instead of out there working on your other job." Christie stated.

"Yes, I am glad too. God is with me." He stated.

"I will go get some blankets" She stated. They had some extra linen and blankets in the closet, in case it got too cold with their air condition. This was the way to block off flying debris in case the glass break. They went to a corner. And they sat down.

They cover their heads and body with the blanket. She could not say anything to him, now. She hopes he would not ask me what I was going to tell him. I had lost my concentration.

This storm had lasted four hours. He had to go home to check on his boat, and bike.

I will see you tomorrow afternoon about 5:00 p.m. We will talk, too. There was no danger. I had to do my job if I wanted to get paid for my service. Ann, she had given me a call. She said that she wanted to see if we can go have a drink or a have a little something to eat somewhere before she leave to go back home.

I told her that I will meet her down in the lobby in 20 minutes. I was not dressing up. I just slipped on another Island wrap-around skirt with a blouse and I put on my low pumps.

Gerald, he had sensed that Christie was going to tell him something else too. But, we were distracted by the storm. He already knew she use to be a Reporter/ Journalist. And now she was a Private Eye. He was waiting on her to tell him the truth about her life. He was curious as to why she would never buy the expensive clothes. Mike he had gave her a large sum of money. He had pulled up her file and discovered that she was a wealthy black woman. Mike had already told him that his sister was her mother and they had money. He had sent him an obituary of his sister. Our dad was one of the men who had help built the railroad track. The government had finally decided to pay the men who had slaved and worked at this task for little or less pay. He said, "They had finally sent him our dad thousands of dollars for his job. He was able to live for a short while then he died. Gerald he was so surprised and in awe over this little history. Our family is wealthy. I am executor over the estate. Gerald he had laughed.

They had found a corner to sit in to protect them selves. She got them a blanket. They sat there for about 40 minutes. He said, "He had to go home to check on his boats. He had Insurance, though. He wanted a

Yacht like this his whole life. It was beautiful, and was huge. He had painted it his favorite color, green with white. It had his name on it in bold letter. Gerald, the "ISLAND BOY," Labrodereax.

He told her that he might see her later on if she wanted to go out tonight. However when he had gotten there, he received a message. He goes to check his message on his answering machine. He had to go to the Coast guard. They said to him, "A Cruise ship was coming in, today." He was happy that his boats did not get injured, neither his bike.

He was thinking about how Christie was looking before the storm had approached the area. She had tears in her eyes. She was glad that he found out her real identity. He just wanted to hear her tell him the truth. He did not mind using endearment. She likes to be called, darling. She would always smile.

He had already told her about his royal inheritance, too. They both kept secrets from each other. He was in the Rental jeep. It mine as well been his jeep. They kept giving him the same one. It had a blue convertible top. It was a stick shift.

Chapter 8

This was the 8th day. She was just relaxing at her hotel. She went around to where the ocean sat to walk along the sandy beach. She had on a blue jean skirt with a pretty yellow laces blouse. It was very pretty, and a cool summer outfit. She had a pair of flip flop shoes on, today. He was already at the hotel today doing his maintenance work. He could see her from the back lobby entrance. He smiles.

He had seen her in walking around the Island taking pictures of the birds, and the Island children. She was just having a good time by herself. She asks one of the children to take a picture with her, and they were smiling. She was asking them where they were from and what were their nationalities? How do you pronounce your names? She asks them what grades were they in, now. They were following her around on the beach.

Gerald, he was crazy about Christie. He looks at the clock to see what time he had a break. He had finish up and walks to the outside in the back. He walks towards her, and he touches her shoulder. He was tall, so she had to look up at him. She smiles. Gerald, what are you doing here? He stated. Why are you so surprised by my visits? He asks her. You know I work here whenever they need me. Yes, that is true. He takes her hand. He bid the children, bye. They ran along.

Come take a walk with me, darling. Are you thirsty? Yes. They had a Poolside bar sitting outside on the sand. They went to the bar. He said, "Let me take a wild guess what you want to drink. He had stated. She said, alright to him." He utters a name of a specialty fruit drink. They calls this their Island drink," Pine Colada, non-alcoholic. She smiles.

He takes out some money to pay the bartender. Keep the change, man. He stated to him. "Thank you, sir." The bartender stated. He bought himself a non-alcoholic, "Daiquiri" fruit drink." He could not drink any alcohol on the job.

Gerald had told Christie that he had a lending office downtown, and that he would not go to him for any money. She had written down that Deon had to leave the club early to go back to his house for some business. In addition, Stephanie was going to the resort. She types this into her computer. She was e-mailing Mike with the information she had discovered.

Then I had gone to put on my gown. A half an hour had not passed, before there was someone, knocking on my door. Christie thought it was her friend, Ann coming to tell me about her date with her new boyfriend. "Wait a minute, Ann." She had replies. He said, "This is Gerald darling. Christie told him to wait a minute.

She had forgotten that she had said to him, "He could come over anytime, if he just wanted to talk or have a "specialty coffee she could order from room service. She did not drink any alcohol. Neither, did she drink any wine after the midnight hour. She had put on her robe. "I am sorry, for coming back at this late hour." He said. "May I come in please?" He asks me. I open up the door for him. He had come inside. I had asks him. What is the matter there are no clubs open? He replies. "Yes plenty are still open." This is Bahamas, darling. He stated to me.

He was frowning up, now. I had never seen him, frowning. He said to me, "To put it blunt—there are some concerns that I need to straighten out, now." He stated. "

I am confused, Gerald." She had stated to him.

Gerald's Big Confession

Christie was surprise by his sudden change in mood. He was walking towards the patio door. He was holding my hand. We had step outside on the patio. He was acting different. He had a thin cigar in his hand. He threw it over the balcony. We were standing outside on the Terrace Balcony. He still held onto my hand. It was dark outside. The stars were shining bright. It was a beautiful view. I was facing the Atlantic Ocean. He was quiet for several minutes. Then, we came back inside. I ask him, "Why did you take me outside with you on the Terrace Balcony?" He replies. There is something I must say to you and I do not quite know if by stating this to you, this will quite be the same for us. I had to ponder, first. I do this quite often. He stated to me.

I had to ask God, if I am doing the right thing. I must get an answer from him. Gerald, you are confusing me. She had stated to him. Well, when I ask God for something I like to show him what or whom I am speaking about, because if I did not say a specific person or a particular thing. He may not give me the right person or thing that I want. I shook my head at him. "You have made a valid point, Gerald". I had stated to him. I was still confused about this "specific" word meaning. I did not understand what he was trying to tell me. And I did not want to correct him without making sure I was right. He was very smart. I said, "I wish I had a bible to back me up with this statement. "I have never received anything wrong from God." I said that God knows our heart and we do not have to be specific in asking him for anything. He gave me a warm smile. He was waiting on me to tell him this clarification. Christie had stated. He smiled and he takes out a bible from the desk drawer of the hotel suite. I was searching through the bible and still listening to him talk.

You have made an excellent explanation of something that I have been searching for an answer in my mind. He stated.

I was surprised.

“Christie said to him, “I am still do not understand your point of view, Gerald.

I will try to explain this to you as best I can darling. He stated,

“I am sorry for interrupting you. “ “It is alright.” He said to me.

Gerald states to Christie. “This is my version. I am not a bible scholar, and I may be wrong. Base on my personal walk with the savior, I have learned that if I am not particular or certain, of what I have asked. I may not receive the desire of my heart. This is what my father had taught me as a little boy.” He was a Minister. I will give you another example” You ask for a hat.” You know there are thousands of hats in the world. You receive a funny looking hat. The first thing you will have said, “this is not what I wanted,” So we need to be more specific.” He smiled and closed the bible book that was open.

Gerald becomes spiritual

Gerald said, “Let me tell you a little tale.” I saw this Yacht that I wanted desperately. I did not want to live in a house or an apartment. I walk over to the Yacht that I wanted. I said, “God this, is the one I want.” “If I am not asking too much, I pray that you grant me this Yacht.” I had closed my eyes. The dealer had given me a call that week. He said, “Although you did not offer the right amount I am going to let you finance this one and it will be yours. This was all I needed to hear from that dealer. So, you see if you asked for anything and not be particular you could get just what you asked for. I said to him, "I am not that good with the bible but I read it quite often." I wish I had my bible. He goes to the desk drawer and takes out a bible. I had told him, "The savior knows our heart and we do not have to show him what we want. I have a long way to go to get there. She had said to him. I do not know a lot about everything. She had stated to him. He thanks me for sharing that with him. He had stated, "I will be happy to teach you what I know," darling. He said, "This makes sense too. " He smiled. That is a beautiful testimony what you have told me Gerald. I had exclaimed. He smiles. I had given him a hug, with tears in my eyes.

I must get right to the point! He had exclaims. He goes back to his earlier conversation. Forgive me for being so blunt He had stated. We had sat down on the couch. You are terrible distraction to me. I cannot stop thinking about you. He frowns again.

There is something, I must tell you, Christie. He stated. He did that on purpose. This must not go any further. I was in shock, he knew my real name. I could not say a word. He looks at my expression on my face. He went to get me a bottle of water. He opens it. He hands it to me. He continues talking to me. I cannot keep going on with this charade. I have let it gone too far, and I am getting tired of keeping secrets. I hate deceiving people. I said nothing. I was not in a daze this time. I was crying. He stated. I will begin by stating this thing," I know everything about you and your Journey, here to the Bahamas Island. It has nothing to do with a book, you are publishing. I was still in shock. There is a man that sent you here by the name of, Mr. Mike McGuire. He hires us both.

He was looking down at my face. He had to see my reaction. She was pondering. How come I did not expects him to be my Bodyguard; he was a Police Officer, and a Coast Guard. Then, she thought again. He was handsome, and charming. He was fun to be with, too.

He tells me what he knows about my assignment. Mr. McGuire, he is trying to get some information on his daughter that is here with a man we have been talking about earlier. I was stunned. He said to me, "You are quite specious—if I had not been hired by your employer then I would have believe you were just here to write a book." She smiled.

You are a Private Investigator or should I say "Eye spy." He smiled. I had come back to reality. I was daydreaming about this man who was sitting in my suite.

I knew my surrounding and I saw him in my future. This was like looking into a crystal ball. He had appeared to be mysterious. Yet, he is very caring and understanding. I really owe him a great deal. I had to be honest for the first time tonight.

I said to him. "No, I prefer to be called PI." He looks at my face, hard. Then, he smile. He had stated. I should say beautiful PI. I was smiling. I had to thank him.

Now, for whom I am. I was hire by this man to watch you. I cover my mouth.

Then, I stand up to put my hands on my waist. You are my bodyguard! I said in an outburst. I was getting ready to explode. Then, I had thought. I was going to tell him the truth, anyway. I had calm down. He answers me. He said, "Yes, I am your bodyguard.

He replies. He was speaking soft. You do not have to worry. He stated. I have end, my employment with him. I told him, "I could not do this anymore because of my personal attachment for you." Then you are pretending to be a maintenance man? I had asks him. He shook his head. No I am really a maintenance man. He stated. He stated to me. "I like fixing things." I still do all of my other jobs. He added. This is very surprising news, Gerald. Or is that your real name? She asks him.

"It is, darling and shielding my real name is not something I would do." He stated. I am no, spy. She smiles. He continues talking. "This is what I have become since your arrival." He stated. "I have been watching you, for 9 days. " I told Mr. McGuire that I was giving him my resignation. In addition, giving him back his money he paid me.

I ask him. "Will this cause you a financial hardship?" He smiles. He shook his head.

He stated. "I just like to help people who are in a difficult situation." That is why I have become a Bodyguard. I am register with the Police department. As well as I am an officer. He stated. I am not destitute. I will not be destitute for a long time. I know you found out that I am from Kenya, Africa. Yes, I was waiting on you to tell me about that when you were ready. I had stated to him. Well, I am the ancestor of a Royal family. My great-grandmother is not a native of Africa. She is of British descendant. Her parents were royalty. She was a Princess. I believe that I am considers a Prince. My great-grandfather he was from the African tribe. He left Africa, and took his journey to Great Britain. Where he met, and fell in love with my great grandmother. I felt myself hitting the floor. I had fainted. He stops smiling. He went to pick me up. He carries me to the couch. I could not hear anything he had said after this news. He takes some water to put it in his hands. He rubs my face with the water. I came back around. He asks me, are you alright? I shook my head. Did you say that you are a Prince? He was crying now. "Yes darling I am of a royal family. I had promise my parents not to tell a soul. I asked him, "But why Gerald?" They felt that I might be in danger, if people knew who I was on this Island. So you decided to tell me. Yes, I am relieved. The only person who knows this about me is my friend, Manuel." His family knew my parents they both lives in Africa and he felt like I needed to tell you the truth.

He smiles. He stated, "Therefore you see why I am not worry about money."" I have my money in a secret trust fund in a British Bank Account. I have never touched any of it." He stated, "That is the least of my worry." I still have my other jobs, he stated I wanted to work and make money of my own. She felt the same way. And I have saved it my adult life. I have a long way to go before, I am desperate for money. He stated.

Mike, he is very worry about your safety here. I reassured him that I was going to keep an eye on you even more, he had stated.

Now, I need to know does this change the way you feel about me. He stated to me.

She stated to him. "I am in shock, Gerald however I am glad you told me the truth." She said with sadness. She had not told him about her money yet. She was relieved. "I really am quite fond of you, and I would be crazy to stop seeing you because of this situation." She had stated.

I am glad you said that to me. He smiles. He replies. "That is all I needed to hear." He said, "Nothing else matters to me, except that you are safe."

She said, "I have been here for almost two weeks." Why are you telling me this now? She asks him. He frowns. I hate to deceive people.

Right now, I want you, darling. He stated to me. I mean I want you apart of my life, he had stated. Are you proposing to me? She asks him. He falls out laughing. I thought he was going to roll over on the floor. He held his stomach. He could not stop laughing. She had utters something humorous. She said, "Not today, huh?" I had replies. I have answers my own question. He was still laughing at me.

He pulls himself together. He takes my hand. And he said, "Not right, this minute, Christie. He had stated, "I feel something deep for you too, darling."

Gerald wanted her to quit the Assignment.

There is so much you need to learn about me, my cultural background. She asked him, "Do you have another wife?" He shook his head. He said, "That is the old tradition I am not married." I did not come here to find a wife. This is where my parents came from Africa. They just told me to make sure she is the right woman. They told me the story about "Samson and Delilah. " She had read that story in the bible and saw it on television when they made a movie from the story. He looks at me serious. Getting back to what you had said before, "I just meant that I wanted us to be together here on the Island." I will give you some time to think about it. He stated. What do you mean here on the Island? I had asked him. He said, "I want you to move here to the Bahamas Island." She stated, "What about my PI job here?" He said, "I want you to be happy with your career." I will not try to stop you from your work." She sighs. He stated, "I will allow you to think about this some more."

I smile at him. "I could give you your answer, now." She replies. Let us wait until we go out on the town. He replies. All, right. She replies.

He had stated. "I know you are working on this case, and that is more important to you." She nods her head. She stated, "Yes this is my first case and Mike he is paying me a great deal of money." This is a fact. She had added. She had on some music. It was some beautiful Island music.

She had to change the subject. Gerald, where is this music coming from? He replies. Well, we have some music coming from Jamaica, England, and France. And even in the United States. He had stated.

It is beautiful. She had replies.

Yes indeed, he stated.

Gerald said, "I listen to the music all day myself. He stated, "It makes me want to dance." Then I had smiled.

Can we get back to our original discussions? He asks her.

"Yes, of course I am sorry for interrupting you." She replies. No, apologies needed my darling. He replies.

Gerald Tells Christie that she is not PI material.

This last statement is important to me. He added. "I will not be working for Mr. McGuire." He said, "I want to continue watching your back, from a distance."

She had added. "Gerald I am a Detective, too." He nods his head. He said, "Yes I am aware of your training as a Detective." He stated, "I know everything about you, darling." "I have talked to Mike for a long time. He said, "You have a temper, when you can not have your own way and are in a disagreement." Or, someone said something to make you annoy.

That is one of your characteristic; I am willing to work with during my quest for knowledge on what make you tick. He stated. He was smiling, now. I have to be frank with you, Christie.

In my honest opinion, you are not quite experience enough to do this job. He stated.

This man is a notorious, businessperson. That means he deals in a criminal way.

If you do not pay him back on time, he will have someone come hurt you. How do you know about him, Gerald? I am a Police officer, too. He has been arrested numerous times. He always gets out on bail. I have never come in contact with him, personally. I must know, Gerald. Is Mr. McGuire daughter in any danger? I had asks him. I do not think so. He replies. I think that he really cares for her, and will not allow anything bad to happen to her long as she treats him right. In addition, she stays out of his private affairs. He had stated to me. I still think that she should be with someone else. I had stated. That has to be her decision. He stated. I had asks him.

Christie wanted to get closer to Stephanie

Should I get personal with this woman? He said, "No that is not very wise decision." Her boyfriend he is traveling with tough characters. For you to suddenly become a friend of Mike daughter, he might become suspicious. And he will try to find out your real connection with this woman. He is smart, darling. He stated to me. This is not something new for him. I mean he has been doing this thing for years. We just have not caught him in the act. He was speaking from a police point of view. He had stated. I hate to have to hurt someone out here. He said to me, "there is only one person who I care about right now."

I think Mike will agree with me that it is best, you should resigns. He had stated. I was about to explode. I felt my throat getting dry. My voice was about to crack.

I was getting another flashback of John and I conflicting. I had to express my opinion. I said you listen to me, Gerald. For your information I am a good Private Eye, and this is something I wanted to do for a long time. I am very capable of taking care of myself. I do not care what you and Mike agrees where I am concern.

I am not going to stop being a Private Eye, because you two seems to think that this line of work is too dangerous for me. I turn my face away from him. He stood up.

He said to me. The last thing I wanted to do was make you upset. I will go to allow you to cool down for a while. We both are very tired. And we might say the wrong things to each other. I will bid you goodbye, and give you a call in the morning. He sounded sort of bitter. I was very tired. I did not stop him from leaving my suite. He let himself out. This was our first time disagreeing with each other. He took the elevator, and went down to the lobby. He went to his rental jeep. He saw that it was after 1:00 a.m. in the morning. He drives back to his Yacht. He would forget their conflict.

He was quite fond of her, and this was a touchy subject for her now.

I had felt bad about the way I spoke to Gerald. I could not sleep. I waited until I thought he had made it to his boat. I ring his phone. He finally took the call.

I said, "I am deeply sorry for my outburst." I do not want to argue with you, Gerald. I had stated. He was pleased for the way I had called to apologize. You are something special to me, darling. I am thinking I might have been too hasty in what I had said to you at the suite. I have no right to force you to do anything; you are not ready to do when it comes to your career. He had stated to me. I was crying.

He would say nothing else to me about resigning from my assignment.

I told you this bit of Information in hopes, it will encourage you to end this assignment as soon as possible.

I had to choose my words carefully. She said, "I appreciate your concern for my well-being. I will tell you what I told my former boss.

If I am going to succeed in this business I will have to take risks, and that may be a little tough at times. She had stated to him. Before you told me your real identity, I had this envision of this Bodyguard following me around the Island. He was still listening to me. Every time I thought about him, I felt like exploding. I made this promise to Mike that I would not ask him to release this man from the assignment. Or he would find someone else to do the job. She had stated to him. He was dozing off. Then he said to me. Darling, I am getting very tired. We will talk in the morning. He stated. I corrected him. This is in the morning. He said, "It is way passes your bedtime". I am going to bid you a pleasant night of rest.

We had strong passion for each other. I could not stay angry with him. I was glad that I have spoken my peace. He had stated his opinion. And it was the end of that conversation. I get ready to go to bed. I slept until later in the afternoon. I had to go out to gather some more information on Stephanie boyfriend and his company.

I thought about what Gerald had said to me in the suite. This gave me an ideal.

He is smart and will eventually start observing people that are always around him.

This is why we need to be together. I was not acting like a spy. I had to do this without anyone noticing that I was around. I should be under surveillance but discreet. They had taught me at the College. If you want to become indispensable, you should do things from a distance. Like duck around a corner, or sitting in a car behind a building.

Perhaps, sitting up high looking out a window from where that person may be standing. I did have some binoculars. I did not have a hearing device. I went to my laptop to go on line to the HSN. I saw some items that they said were good for law officers. I had not gotten my badge yet. They told me it would take 90 days to receive it from the Federal building at the NYC. I made the order using my credit card. They said it would take a week. I had to give them my license number. I said to the man, "I am a Private Investigator". The female it sounded like she had fainted. He apologizes to me for giving me a hard time. He said good luck with your career. I had thanks him.

Gerald asked some of his friends to watch Christie

Gerald had gotten a call from his friend, Roger who was a Coast guard, too. I think the little lady is getting way over her head. He had said to me. I ask him, "What do you mean?" He was from Dominic Republic. He spoke in an accent. Well, I am watching this fine lady holding a binocular. She is standing behind this building, and watching two men coming out of a shop. I said to him, "that is not wise." I think I will go find her and try to convince her that this is not a game. Thanks, Roger. I owe you a big one. He stated to him. You are quite welcome, my friend.

He was finishing up at the hotel as a Maintenance man. He rushes to his bike. He takes off in a hurry. He drove downtown. He was looking for Christie.

Gerald, he had spotted Christie going into a Restroom. She was at the Coral Beach.

She wanted to wash the sweat off her face and neck. Then buy a cold drink to take on the bus back to my hotel. It was 95 degrees. But, it felt like 111 in the sun. I took me some paper towels and wet them. She wipes her face and neck off. Then she went back outside to go to the Oceanside bar. I take out a $20 bill, and was standing there to buy me a cold drink. I felt a hand touch my shoulder. I look around, and it was Gerald. I ask him. What are you doing here?

He smiled. He said, "I was looking for you darling." I will buy that drink for you. And I will give you a lift back to your hotel. I want to talk to you in private." He stated. He looks serious. I said to him. Alright, I am feeling very hot.

I think I am not feeling too well. Come on let us sit down for a few moments. I told him what I wanted to drink. He bought it for me. We went to a stump by the edge of the Ocean. It was cooler sitting at this spot. I felt a breeze.

I am quite worry about you, Christie. He had not called me by that name before.

"I do not think you realized what you are doing here on this Island." I beg your pardon? I did not want to hear this same conversation again. I said to him, "I thought we were through discussing this last night." He shook his head.

He stated, "This is not the movies and I can not sit back and watch you get hurt." He stated. Let me explain something to you, Gerald. When I was in NYC I had to take on tough assignments. I was a Weather Journalist-reporter. I had to tell a former worker, from NYC. He thought that I should sit back and watch while he did all the work. I was fighting back anger, but I was frustrated. I crack my knuckle. I can not understand why I have to explain this to every man that comes my way. I felt a tear fall from my eyes.

He gets quiet. Then, he said to me. "I know this is your first experience and you are a woman and this is exciting for you." Let me put it to you as delicate as I can, darling. He stated. "You might be educated, and have the tactic to handle a tough situation. In all, honesty you have not gone out into the real world. You have not come up against fierce people. You need more experience working with a

Detective. You will be dead on the street like those other helpless women. You are handling this job, dangerously." He had stated to me. Being a spy is terribly dangerous. I am asking for all my friends to look out for you. Some are working with the Navy too. Christie was in shock. He looks at her face. Yes, that is right. "I am ready to push the panic button." He added. Mike he is climbing the walls in NYC. He takes out a thin cigar and lights it. I was trying not to get angry again. I spoke calmly. I have seen plenty of television shows. Yes, that is the trouble. You have not been out in the real world.

I am perfectly capable of handling a situation. I had stated. Oh, you mean the Firearm you have in your possession.

I was shock. Yes, I do have a pistol on me. She replies. In addition, to my other tactics I can use. He was not smiling at her now. I had pull up your file, and it is in the system at the Police headquarter here. You have forgotten that I am a Police officer, and I have been for 17 years.

You sound just like Mike. I had told him. He is right. Gerald stated.

What I am doing will be free of charge. In addition to that, I have a personal Interest in you as well as whatever you do here on the Island. Do you object? He asks me.

No. I shake my head. I had said," no of course not." He gave me a hug. I have to get back to my Yacht. I will drop you off right now. The tides were coming in, and he had his Yacht in the middle of the Ocean. He takes my hand. My bike is up against the building. He parked it there so he could walk to the beach. He was still talking to me as we went to his bike. I have to clarify this to you, Christie.

The Bahamas Island is not that big as NYC. You will wind up at the same place, frequently. He replies. I must sound like an idiot. He laughs. No. "This is a new surrounding and you are not familiar to the

Island." I do not mind you asking me question. He stated. I see nothing wrong with your being inquisitive, darling. That is what Mike told me. I must put the information that you gave me into my database. He said something she had never heard him, uttered. He said, "Squash that information—that is further from my mind! He wanted to pull her closer to him, but he just said, "I will see you tomorrow." What is on your agenda tomorrow?

Christie Gets the True facts about Deon

"I want to go swimming with the dolphins and drive to the Lagoon Island". He gave Christie a kiss on the forehead. "You get some rest." Christie told him. He looked very tired. He agrees. "Yes, I am exhausted. I may take me a few days off."

I went up to my suite to type in the data on what Gerald had told me on the beach. It was after 9:00 p.m. I had not listens to any music all day. So, I turn on the radio in my bedroom. I was daydreaming. I was somewhere far away. I put my laptop away on the table in the front room I went to go lie down on the bed. I was not feeling that well. I had closed my eyes for a while. My phone rings. I had forgotten where I was at right now. Who is this, Tracey? No, this is Gerald.

He stated I had gotten back to my Yacht, and I said to myself; I have not done anything fun and the night is still young. I thought you were tired. I am a little bit. I want to take you out somewhere. Are you feeling up to getting dress? Yes, I supposed. I will pick you up in an hour. Put on something real pretty. I will find somewhere for us to go. He had stated.

She went to her closet to find one of her gowns she had bought from one of the shops here. She forgot to ask him where they were going. She went to get wash up. She puts on a Pink nylon gown it was sleeveless. It had a spaghetti strap across the shoulder. She had a pair of pink strapless pumps.

She fixes her hair so that it could hang down her shoulder. Then she put on her make-up and earrings set. She had to change her clutch bag to match her dress. She put all her cosmetic things inside, and her key to get back inside her suite. She had her credit card and other credentials too. She left her suite to go to the elevator. She rides it down to the main lobby. Gerald, he had rented the jeep this time. He gets out to opens the door for her. He had his hair in the style sticking up that the men wore on the Island.

Where are we going? I had asks him. He stated. I read in the newspaper that there was something that was going on in Freeport Bahamas. He looks at his watch. I think they have live entertainment. I feel like dancing. Moreover, you really do not want me to go there by myself. She smiles. It was an hour drive from the Bahamas Island.

You are teasing me. He smiles. Yes. He replies. Don't you think that I am charming?

"You are very charming as well as devastatingly handsome." She stated.

He smiles. He gave me a gentle hug.

However, I was getting ready to go to bed. She had stated to him.

"You were not sleeping." He stated.

"You are right." She stated.

He stated to me. "Once again I am right."

She replies. I do not professed to be right about everything, Gerald. On the other hand, you are smarter than me, he laughs. Hey, I was just making a joke. He hugs me. I am in a good mood. We will not talk about my work, neither yours. Is that a deal? He asks me.

I said, "Yes I am here for business as well as pleasure." I had stated to him.

"Now, you are thinking like me." He stated to me.

He drove me to a clubhouse; where they had a live entertainment and dancing. He had to pay the cover charge to get inside. A hostess she seats us at a table.

He pulls the chair out for me, and I sat down. He scoots it under the table. The hostess said, "A server will be here to take your order. Enjoy the evening. We both said, "Thank you." He takes out a thin cigar and lights it. He begins to dance to the music from his seat. They were playing Island love songs. Are you in the mood for dancing, darling? Yes, if it will keep me awake. I had stated to him. He smiles. He stood up to hold out his hand. I took it, and we went to the dance floor. To my surprise, a beautiful woman came in the front door. She had gotten a lot of attention. Gerald, he was not paying any attention to her. He held my waist, and we were dancing slowed to the music. Stephanie she had arrived at this same Clubhouse. This beautiful woman was Stephanie. She was by herself.

See a Different Side of Stephanie

We were having a good time tonight. The performer was sensational. It was a very romantic atmosphere. To my surprised, Stephanie was there alone.

She was not dressed the way she normally dress in designer gowns. She had on a silver mini short sequin dress. It was silver gray. She had on some pretty pumps that had sequins, too. She had told Deon she was going to the resort to go to bed. She was on the dance floor dancing with other people by herself. Men were surrounding her at the club. She appears to be having fun. She looks over and saw me walking with Gerald back to our table.

"Hey! There is my new friend." She said to me. I spoke to her nicely, "How is it going?" She said, "It is just terrific, I am alone to do my own thing. Oh, I have forgotten my manner. My name is Stephanie McGuire." Gerald, smiles. He introduces himself to her, too. Hello dear, I am Gerald Labrodereax. She held her hand out to shake it. Then, she put her arm around my neck. She looks like she had been drinking somewhere else before she got here. She had this glossy look in her eyes. She said to us, "I am glad someone has a man that can give her attention. They both had smile. You must be this woman, boyfriend. She said to him. He smiles. He nods his head. Let me buy you two a drink. She threw her arm up in the air to get the server attention. She must have had one too many. I was thinking to myself. I will come over to your table. She follows us to our table. And she plops down in a chair. She looks around the room, and shook her head in disgust. Deon partners had come inside the Club. She told the server to get whatever we wanted, to put it on my tab. She goes over to Jerome. She Pulls on his arm. He was shock to see her in the condition that she was in, now. Dance with me, Jerome. He supports her waist. He always dresses sharp. He takes her over to a table. No, I want to dance. She exclaims. Alright, only one danced. He had stated to her, He takes her to the dance floor. He pops his finger, and dances with her to the music. Curtis, he had made a call to Deon. We have found your woman, she is at the club. I will be there in a little while. He thanks, Curtis. She and Jerome were still dancing together.

He finally told her that she needed to sit down for a while. She was getting drunk.

Chapter 9

This is the tenth day. I had still needed to find out some things about Deon business. I was asked to go out to this place that had a Casino inside, and a Night Club inside. Ann, she said that this was her last day here on the Island. She said, we have to do one more thing together. We might not see each other in a long time.

I had agreed to go out, tonight. She said I am renting me a car tonight. I will meet you in the lobby at 8:00 p.m. I said to her, "Aright but I am tired from last night. I want to get me a little nap. And I needed to do some more work on Stephanie boyfriend.

I had not spoken to Gerald, yet. He was asked to report to the Coast Guard head quarter. I had wanted to have some lunch with him, today. I still had not told him the truth about my trust fund. He already knew I was a PI and he thought I needed the money. It looks like every time I get ready to tell him the truth, something always distracts our attention.

It was a lovely breeze. I open up my screen, and turn off the air conditioner.

I had put on a short set to take a nap. I had the front desk to give me a wake-up call.

I got my call at 7:00 p.m. I went to take me a shower. I was wearing my red sequin gown that had tiny flowers. It had a spaghetti strap. It had a split going up one side.

I had put on my red sequin high heels. I drape a white shawl across my shoulder. I had my ear piece device behind my left ear. I place this tiny microphone inside my gown. My recorder was in my red clutch bag that came with a shoulder chain strap.

They had told me in the instruction booklet, that I could shield the thin cord inside my purse or pocket.

I had not been able to contact Gerald at all tonight. He was not answering his page or his cell phone. Neither his phone on his Yacht. So, I left to go to the Club with Ann. I had told Ann that she looks beautiful. She had on one of my favorite color.

She wore a Yellow strapless gown. It was sheer. She had her hair hanging down her back. It was beautiful, and a designer gown. I think a few men had whistle at us.

A valet man he had brought her car to the front entrance. He opens the door for us.

Ann, she tips him. He said to her, "Thank you darling". I sure wish I can go with you two lovely ladies. We both, smiles. She drives off. We have to drive to Nassau, Bahamas.

Gerald, he had finally answers his page. He had to go to the Coast Guard boat to watch a ship that was coming in, tonight. He had to use his binocular to observe the passengers when they got ready to dock. They had to make sure that it was not an Illegal ship. They called them, "Pirate Ships". He smokes a thin cigar. He answers his cell phone. This is Gerald. He replies. It was his friend who was working with the Navy in Nassau Bahamas. He was going to pay him some money but he said he did not want his money. He was his friend and went to the same church he attended as a boy. Your lady is here in Nassau, and they are headed towards the Casino place. Thank you, Kenny. I owe you a big one. He clicks off. He continues to do his job. He could not go to this place, tonight.

Deon was speaking to Stephanie at the Night club. He said, "I heard how you have been carrying on in front of people and that I associate with in my business.

I have heard how you have shown out at this place. I am appalled at you, telling strangers that I have been neglecting you. He put his head down, sadly. He grips her arm. She was staggering. She was drunk. Now, let's go to home because I am getting tired. He was very in a passive mood. It was like he did not care about anything right now. She did not want to go home. She walk over to someone else table. She plops down in a chair. Deon, he just looks at her behavior.

He walks over to the stranger table, and he apologizes for her intruding on their privacy. He made a gesture with his neck to Curtis, who was his driver. He stood up

and walk to get the car. She had her head dropped down to her chest. He lifts her up and drapes her over his shoulder. Jerome, he left some money at the bar. He said, "This is for any trouble we have caused here tonight." He held the door open for Deon as he carries his woman to the Van. He had driven in another car.

Jerome he held the door open in the Van. Deon, he put her into the back seat of the Van. He shut the door. I want to ride with her to the house. He tells Jerome I want you to take my keys to the car that I had driven here, and brings it back to my house. Curtis, he was waiting on him to get inside. He put Stephanie in the van and he sits up front. Curtis drives off. Jerome, he had gotten into Deon other car.

He drives off to the house too. This was the first time that Christie had seen her at this way. She knew that this woman was deeply trouble. She had to go put it in her data base that she had seen Stephanie tonight at a club. She was not going to tell her dad what kind of shape that she was in, tonight.

Christie and Ann had arrived back at the hotel. They were both tired. I will see you tomorrow. She gives her a hug and they went to their different floors.

Christie she was anxious to talk to Gerald. She had to ask him this puzzling question. She goes to her phone to call him on his Yacht.

He took the call. How was your evening out with Ann? He had asked her.

She said, "We had a nice time together." Gerald I want to ask you a question. Do you remember our earlier conversation about Destiny?

He said, "Yes I do remember that conversation."

Well, "If this is Stephanie destiny that you have spoken to me about earlier, I am curious as to why she is going through so much hurt and pain? How come she is so miserable? She stated.

He rubs his eyes and sat up in his bed. He was trying not to yarn. He stated. What do you mean, darling? He asks her. Then he yarns anyway. Well, sometimes you think a person has it all. Yet on the exterior they are no better than the rest of us who are striving to get to where she has already arrive to her destination. She stated to him. He just said, "She has chosen the wrong path. It has nothing to do with the career. But it is the man she is with that has pulled her away from her true happiness. He had stated. I have to go get me some shut-eye. I will see you tomorrow, darling.

Christie decides to do Detective work on Deon two Partners. She had put out a detective search about their past work experience. They had taught her this at the College. You should do a thorough investigation if you want to be effective in your work.

She had left an e-mail on, Mike website. He was asleep. He did not check his e-mail right away until much later. He had slept for several hours. I had gotten up to go have some breakfast downtown. I had taken a shower, and put on my dress that was Yellow with flowers.

It has a thin spaghetti strap on each shoulder. I had on low pumps. I had my Hair pin up with a hair clamp. I wore my expensive gold loops earrings. I had put on two bracelets for each wrist. I had made it downstairs to catch the early bus.

Gerald he was still sleeping. His alarm had not sounded off, yet.

He had no ideal that she was planning on finding out more on Deon partners. His phone rings. He reaches over to pick it up off his night stand.

She was on her way to where Jerome lives. He lives in a village that was located in Free Port, Bahamas. He also lives in a Resort. She found out that he was a Bodyguard.

Gerald, he finally answers his phone. Hello, this is Gerald. He said. Hey, Mike. What is up? He asked him. Have you spoken to Christie, today? He asks him. No, I have not seen her since last night. Why, is something the matter? He asks him.

Not that I am aware of, but I am a little concern. He stated to Gerald. I have received an e-mail this morning.

She is planning on finding out more on my daughter boyfriend. She was saying, "Something about I have to become indispensable. "She said, "I have to go to some of the places where he frequents to conduct his business." Gerald, he jumps up and grab his white long pants. He puts them on and takes a shirt from off the chair. I have to go, Mike. He had said to him. I will talk to you later. Bye. He puts on his Coast guard shirt, and white shoes. He takes his keys off his table. That was the key to his bike. He left the Yacht. He gets on his bike, and drives down the road to go downtown. Christie, she had found a Café that Stephanie and Deon were having breakfast. It was in "Cora Beach Hotel. " He had to put out a trace on Christie.

He had asked his friend who was a Coast guard to do him a favor. He had asked him, "What gives with this woman of yours man? He was using his head-set and was speaking into a microphone attached to his shirt. He said, "I want you to look out for this woman she is a PI, and a Detective." He tells his friend. I know what you are thinking. He had stated. Just keep an eye on the PI. I will owe you a big one. He was using his binoculars. He said, "You know I have your back". He had been friends with Gerald for a long time. They were both born in the same country. He had asked him to look out for her when he was on Patrol. He had sent him a picture of Christie. "If you spot her "Malik", that was his nick-name too. Please page me." He was worried about his woman. He had told him. She is here in Coral Beach at a café, man. I see her using a binocular. She is quite pretty, too. He smiles. Thank you, man. I owe you a big one. Yes, $50,000 in big bills. He laughs.

He had an ear piece device behind his ear too. So, he did not have to use his hands.

Gerald, he was page from the Coast Guard. He was asks to report to their Head quarter office. What is happening? He asks his boss. A cruise ship is coming, and we have to make sure there are plenty of officers on sea, and land. He has been working with them at the coast guard for many years. Christie she had asked for a table in the back. A woman server had given me a middle table. I thank her. The server she gives me a menu. I will be back to take your order. She stated. She left me alone. I was trying to hear Stephanie and Deon, conversation from a distance.

I had not eaten any breakfast yet. I was hungry. I did not want them to recognize me being at the same place. I was being discreet. I had just purchase this Detective device. I had a tiny microphone attached inside my top, and an ear piece attached behind my ear. The dealer said, "That is the best on the market." She kept the recorder in her clutch bag. I had seen it on, HSN. She had bought her a Coffee maker set that came with four mugs from this same company. They said it was very effective, and you could hear anything from within a half a centimeter radius. They would not sell it to me, unless I gave them my license number. I had disagreed with the man. I told him, "That was not true what he told me about them getting into trouble." I am not ignorant but for the sake of keeping peace and I would like to have this device. I had just given him my license number.

They ask me to, "Please be careful with this device". The manager of the HSN said to me, "This little device could lead you into a world of trouble, if it is caught on your possession, young lady. "He stated.

I am a Private Eye—and Detective. They were in shock. I think the woman sales consultant had fainted. She hand the phone to a man. They sent it to right away. I had to go down to the front desk to pick it up. I had just started using it. This device cost me $2,000. A server greets me. Are you ready to order your food, miss? The server, she spoke English.

I will have some coffee, now. I will have your Belgium waffle breakfast with one scramble eggs, and two slices of bacon. I had stated. Yes, ma'am. She replies. I glance back over at Stephanie and Deon sitting at their table. He was looking into her eyes, as they were engrossed in their conversation.

He tells Stephanie that he was going, to go to Cuba, today. He was frustrated. He had pinch his nose. I notice he did that when he was agitated about something. She was pouting, now.

This is personal family business, darling. I will be gone for just two weeks. I am going to leave you some money into your account. He smiles. Now, you have to promise me that you will not give my partners any hard time. I want them to go everywhere with you. She frowns up.

Do I have a choice? Now, you are sulking. You can still have fun. I am going to leave Jerome and Curtis here to handle, things for me. I want you to behave yourself. He tells her. She stated. How can I have fun when you are going to be somewhere else, for two weeks? She had asks him.

How come I never get a chance to travel with you on your trips? He shook his head. You will be a distraction. He stated. This is not a pleasure, trip. I told you that this is family business. I promise we will go somewhere else when I get back. He stated. It depends on your being a good girl. He smiles. He was handsome. He made the remark. I do not take bad girls, anywhere with me. He stated. You will take me to Paris, France? He laughs. You are funny this morning, darling. I was thinking that to some other nearby Islands. He stated.

He sighs. He smiles at Stephanie. I was just teasing, darling. Long as it we're not going to the United States. She hugs him. She was happy with this news. Christie, she orders some breakfast after they had left.

Stephanie was going on a trip. She was going to tell her dad, after she finds out more on Deon business. She was ready to do some Detective work. She follows Deon to his office. She had taken a bus to the Village where Stephanie had lived. Deon, he had gone inside his office. I had to do a FBI search, on how to find Deon office. The data base told her where his office was located. He was right downtown, in Grand Bahamas. I was about to go into a shop. I had stopped, when I saw a man who was about to enter Deon office. He was very agitated. He was sweating, profusely. He went inside.

Finding about Jerome is a Bodyguard

Jerome and another man grab his collar. He was talking in his language. I have your money, man! Jerome, he reaches into the man pockets. He takes out an envelope. He counts the money. He tells Deon that is all here, man. Deon, smiles.

You are lucky, my friend. I was getting ready to ask these men to take you somewhere that is not pleasant. Have a nice day. The man rushes out of the shop. He was flying down the street in a hurry. She had to find out something on this Jerome. He had a tough side. He was standing outside. He smokes a cigar. He checks his pager. He had met a woman on the Island.

She waited a half an hour in the shop, until he had left the area. She had heard the other man, name too. Curtis you will be coming to Nassau, Bahamas, too. Deon, he had said something to him at the Restaurant. He went to get his car. She had to find out what his name was too.

She went back to her hotel. To types in what she had seen earlier. She was sending it to him, later. She mention that Stephanie is planning on leaving the Island to go to Paris, France. I will find out the date she plans to leave. She said she is happy with the news and I think she is not in any danger. She put on some music. She was going to relax for a while.

She wanted to see Gerald. He was at work. He could not get away. It was later when he had called her at the suite. He asks her.

"Would you like to come for a visit on my houseboat, and have a change of pace?"

I will fix us some lunch, and we can just listen to music or watch home movies. He had stated to me. Yes, I had applies to him. Okay. He said to her.

He told her that he would be there in an hour. To dress in casual, wear.

A Horrible Storm had Approach the Island.

She saw Gerald, later. He said a severe storm was approaching the Island. The sky had darkened, and a treacherous breeze sprang up. The mango trees were swaying side to side in the direction of the tides, coming in from the ocean.

The storm is here! He exclaims. He had driven his moped bike over to the hotel to pick her up. He had on his jogging suit, now. He was speeding to find somewhere to hide. This was the worst storm that they had in a long time. He could not get to his Yacht, now. He was glad he had pulled it to the Shore. He had covered the Yacht with a huge plastic bag.

He had heard on his radio scanner that a storm was heading in their area. He had sand bags on the land. His boat was sitting on the dock. He had it secured with heavy hooks. She gets off his bike. She was holding on tight to his waist. I have never had to take anyone to this place we are going right now. He had stated to her.

She was puzzled. Do not be afraid, now. He had stated. We must hurry to this place.

It was not in a restaurant, or inside a building. Our lives are in danger.

We have to find shelter at once! He tells her. He held her hand, and they begin to run fast. Where are we going? To the Island, "Light House Center" that is located, nearby." This was near his resident. He opens up a door, and they were inside. He locks the door. Nobody else was inside, now. They do allow visitors daily. He told her we will hide underneath this stairwell. He told her if you are a believer, you should pray now. Our lives are in his hands. They said, "This was a Category 3 storm". It was one of the worse storms that have ever struck the Island. It could be a total disaster for Bahamas. The siren was sounding off. That meant everyone had to find some shelter. He had put his arms around her, and they held each other in a sitting position. They could hear the wind hissing, and beating against the brick Lighthouse. It was sturdy so that it could block the wind, and rain.

He said," The tide is coming to shore." We will stay here until it had calmed down. This was one of the smallest villages on the Island. After the storm was over we went inside this Clubhouse. He identified himself. He said, "I am officer, Gerald Labrodereax." He had asked them, "How is everyone doing here?" He had spoken the Bahamian language to some who could not understand the English. They said, "We have been praying." He smiled. "So have we, "he replies. He introduces Christie to them. I wave my hand, because I did not know their language. They were friendly. They were hugging each other. He said, "You can all go back to doing whatever you were doing." We had left and walk to an outdoor outside Café.

"I do not know about you, I am starved." He told me. We sat at a table. A server had walk over to them, after being in the Clubhouse. "What would you two like to have?" She asks us. "We would like to see your menu," he stated.

"Yes of course," the server replies to him. She said, "I will bring it to you, now." They had a cooking area where they did their cooking of the Island food. She came back with two menus. Can I get you something to drink? He smiles.

I will order for the lady. She wants the Island fruit drink," Pina Colada." To make hers non-alcohol and mines too. I will have the Strawberry Daiquiri, non-alcohol. He had stated to the server.

"I would like to go to a church here," Gerald. Christie had stated.

"I will take you wherever you like to go," darling, he stated. He held my hand. "I will take you to where my dad used to be an Associate Minister," he had stated. I am off on Sunday. He had added. We will go for the Morning Service.

He takes out a thin cigar, and a lighter. He lights it. He was so handsome. He had his hair braided again. He had told me, "It was too curly to braid, so she twists it." And she puts a tiny rubber band on the end, he stated. I had smile. I guess your sister is quite beautiful and has that beautiful hair too. Yes, she had cut her hair short and was wearing the curly styled the last time I spoke to her over the phone.

He smiles. "Yes, indeed she is beautiful." He replies. "One day I want to go visit her," he stated. "I have not taken a vacation in years." He had stated.

That is ridiculous. Christie had stated.

I want to hear about your African heritage, she had stated to him.

He smiles. "I am apart of a Warrior tribe, too. I guess this is why I know how to handle myself and I am so committed to protecting people."

He had stated to her.

We called ourselves, "Samurai Tribe." In Addition, to my being call a "Prince, from my great-grandmother side of the family. I have not ever visit Great Britain.

Will you ever leave the Bahamas Island? I had asks him. He said," No this is my home." This is a beautiful place to live. He had stated. "I had agreed with him, it never gets cold here." I did not mean to move anywhere else." He sighs. Then, he laughed.

I like to see him laugh. I smile at him.

"I afraid you were going to ask me to move to New York City." He had stated.

"No, way it is perfect here". Christie replies. It is freezing there in the winter season, and you would probably get sick. I had stated to him.

"I have not gotten sick here, he stated.

"Are you serious?" She had asked him.

"Yes, I have never gone to a hospital." But I will have allergies and cold symptoms, he stated. Just like you all do in your climate. As a matter of fact, "I had a cold before you came here and I stayed on my Yacht to recovers. "We could take a sick leave, anytime." He had stated.

Christie explains to him what she meant. "I mean to take a trip to some other place." I had stated.

He smiles. Like where will I be going? He had asked me.

She had stated to him, "I was thinking we can go to Africa and perhaps Britain." He shook his head but he started laughing. He said, "I will only go to Africa, if I was going anywhere now." "It is too far away to travel to British." He had stated. You should see where your heritage is, Gerald. They have Castles. "Your family may have their Castles still there." She had stated.

"Now, that is an ideal." He stated.

Will you think about it? She asked him.

He said," Yes I will let you know my answers before you leave."

He said, "I would like to go to Africa to visit my native homeland." "I have not gone since I was a small boy," he stated.

You would visit Africa! She exclaims. She gets excited. She asks him again.

"Yes, I have a sister who is residing there, and I haven't seen her in years." He shows her a picture of his sister. She was beautiful just as she had pictures her. He smiles.

I have a niece and brother-in-law I haven't met yet. Do you talk to each other often?

Yes, but I have been so busy. She wants me to come for a visit. He replies. You ought

to go. I have never taken a trip on a plane or a ship by myself. He stated. She asks him. You would go if someone else went with you? He smiles. Who might that someone be if I may ask you? He had stated to me. I had replies. I would love to go to Africa. He laughs hard.

Would you rather go with someone else? I had asks him. He pulls me closer to him. I am seeing you, right? He looks into my eyes. He gave me a kiss. That is wonderful!

I had said to him. When are we going to leave? I had asks him. He said to me. "Hold on a minute." What about your Private Investigation job? He asks me. We can go when I have gathered some more information on Deon partners. He looks at me hard.

What kind of information? He asks me. If I am going to be successful at this job, I must gather the tough part too. He shook his head. That could be dangerous. I am a detective. I had told him the truth.

You are serious, darling. I will have to arrange my vacation time. For all these

trips I am taking. I smiles at him. He was still laughing at me. You said that you have not gone anywhere in years. This is very true. I had no ideal that I was going to be going this year. I will see what I can do, darling. He stated. We left the boat.

Later, Deon was getting ready to take his trip. He was at the airport. He said aloud, "Now, behave your self while I am gone my pet." He gave her a kiss. Will you bring me something back? She asks him. Yes, of course. If you will, behave. I do not buy things for bad girls. He smiles. I am leaving you in good hands with Jerome, and Curtis. Stephanie bid him goodbye. She walks towards the window so she could see him take off in the plane. He waves at them as he walks to the ramp.

His company bid him goodbye. A car was waiting on them.

She told them she was going to the site, first. She had to do a shooting for her modeling job. Then she was going to a shop to model. Christie, she would go to one of the shops where Stephanie is working. When she arrives, a man hand held her waist. She was in shock. Hello, dear. He said. It is James Décors. How are you? She replies. I am fine. It is will be different when Ann is gone. He stated. Yes, I will miss her, too. She had said to him.

Christie she was distracted when there was a disturbance on the street. It had involves three men who were having a shuffle on the streets of the Bahamas Island.

A man was protesting that he be left alone. It was two of Deon partners. He had hired them to be his bodyguards. And to help him with things that were difficult.

Jerome, he held his pistol to the man side. You can come with us quietly, or we have other measures. Christie, she had her pistol in her purse. And she was wearing her hearing device behind her ear. She was carrying her tape recorder in her purse. It was the latest technology. This resembles a compact mirror. It was silver gray. She was prepared to handle herself for any trouble. She continues talking to James. It is nice seeing you again. He put his arm around her waist to give her a hug. You take care, darling.

The man was speaking in rage. Get your hands off of me! I do not have anything you are looking for here. They had ignores his outburst. They held him pin to the building outside by a shop.

He tries to snatch from their grips. Jerome, he takes out a pistol. He put it at his side. "I have what you want!" He said to the two men. "Wait a minute!" I have the money! "Can you meet me back at my suite in thirty minutes?" They both started to laughs. "It only takes 10 minutes to get to the airport from here." Jerome stated. He was smiling. He was handsome too. He looks familiar. He was tall and had his hair in finger waves but it was brushed forward to his face. She thought.

She was trying to remember where have she seen this man before besides the Island? Christie, notice him at the club several times with Deon and Stephanie.

She and Ann had gone there one night. After, she felt better from her sickness.

He was handsome, too. He speaks firm. "No! Wait! The man had cried. We want the money right now! He had exclaims. Jerome, he reaches into the man pocket to take out the Yellow Envelope that looks like it came from a Bank. It was $30,000. It was in stacks of $1,000 dollars bill. "Please let me go!" He cries. Jerome said, "You are short of

$20,000 my friend." "I will sell my boat and other possession! The man was shouting at them. "I have a wife, and children! Can we talk?" They help him into the Limousine. "Let us go for a little ride." Jerome stated. Christie, she felt sorry for the man. If he could not get all their money she did not know what would happen to him.

They drove off with the man. James, he shook his head. There is trouble everywhere these days. James replies. "What did you say?" "I was paying attention, to what they were doing over there across the street." She stated to him. That little incident we just saw a few minutes ago. "Oh, yes." She replies. She nods her head.

"So where is the man who has swept you away from us at the party?" He had asked her.

"He is at work I suppose." She replies.

It has been good seeing you. I had told him. If you see Ann before I do, tell her I said hello and I am thinking about her. I said to him. He said, "I will tell her I saw you, darling." He walks away.

She had to go back to her suite to do a detective search on Jerome. She got back to her hotel. She rushes back to her suite. She goes inside, and turns on her laptop computer.

She enters his name, and put in Bahamas Island. His name had pops up on the screen. The data said that he lives in a Village called, "Harbour's Beach Resort," in the Nassau Bahamas. He had moved from the other location in, West Bay End. They said that he was born in Key West, Florida. He had live in New York City. He had been in the Bahamas Island for 7 years. Stephanie had ask him, "How come he could not find another job." The data had put down that he uses to be a Bookkeeper/ Accountant. Christie noticed that he knew how to count money very fast.

Making plans to go to Africa

Christie had gone downtown again. She wanted to go inside to see what Stephanie was doing. She was there modeling clothes.

What is the price on that one this model is wearing? She had asks the Sales consultant. She was looking at this other gown that another model was wearing now.

The sales consultant she replies. It is $3,800 for this gown. Thank you. She had replies.

Can I try that white one on please? She had asks the sales consultant.

Yes, what is your size, miss? I wear a size seven in petite. Yes, of course. The sales consultant tells me.

She was still looking at another cheaper gown. I had asks her again.

What is the price of this yellow gown? We have a sale on that one too. $1200 is the price of both gowns, ma'am. She smiles.

Then, I want to try on the white and aqua gowns. A familiar voice said you ought to buy the blue nylon one. Christie had to smile. He had walk inside the shop. It was Gerald. She said to him, "Only if I am going some place special." Tonight it will be that occasion. He tells me. You have to make some tough decision. He had said to me. I was puzzled by his remark.

"Oh, excuse me." I had stated to him. I had to speak to the sales consultant. She had said, "May I help you, miss?" I only wanted one gown. The cheapest one you have in here, please.

It was the White nylon gown with an attach slip. It had a spaghetti strap. I had stated to the sales consultant. Gerald shook his head. He did not want me to buy that one. He said," I want you to try on the beautiful aqua gown." He had told me. I had to smile and shook my head. That one cost $3,800, Gerald. He laughs. He already knew I had more money. We have a misunderstanding here. He tells the sales consultant. I had smiles. I had gone into the fitting room. She went to find the gown Gerald wanted me to try on for him. The sales consultant brought me the blue gown and the white gown too. "Christie, please hurry up". Gerald had stated to me. "We have somewhere to go". He had stated. Alright, give me a few minutes. I try on the aqua gown. He wanted to see how I look in the gown. I had come outside of the fitting room. He smiles. I smiles, too. It is beautiful. He had stated. "It is perfect for where I am taking you tonight. I am going to buy them both for you. Hurry to take it off so I can purchase it." Gerald had stated.

Gerald replies. He smiles. I went back inside the fitting room. I took the gown off. The sales consultant took them both to the cash register. I had put back on my same clothes. I came out of the fitting room. I had look at him strange. That gown cost $3,800. "I said to him, "You still have time to change your mind." He was smiling. He said, "I am not worry about a price darling."

I have to be somewhere else. He had taken out a credit card. She rings up the bill of sale for the two gowns. She hand him back his credit card. She put the gowns in a garment bag. We were walking towards the door. I said, "I can still turn back around and get only the cheaper one. He laughs. He had asked me, "Do I look like I am a cheap man?" I shook my head.

. He said to me, "I am never going to change my mind when it comes to buying you things. " Oh, Gerald. I put my arms around his neck. He was holding my bag.

I gave him a hug in the shop. He said to me, "I have some good news to tell you.

"I ask him, "What was the news he had to tell me?" He said to me, "I will tell you the news when we leavc this shop.

Alright I guess I can wait. She replies.

Chapter 10

The sales consultant had put the gown in a garment bag. We had left the shop. He had told me that he spends thousands of dollars on things he wanted with his credit card. He had put a large down payment on the purchased of his Yacht using his credit card. They walk out of the shop. He tells her the good news.

I have arranged for my vacation. He tells her. That is wonderful. She said. Where are we going? He smiles. I want to go to only one Continent, darling. Kenya, Africa. "First we will go to where I was born, and then we will go see my sister." She was so happy.

"You did not really expect me to go to Great Britain?" He had asks her.

She shook her head. "No, not really I am just glad you will go to Africa." She replies. "When will we be leaving?" She asks him.

"In a week if you are able to leave." He had stated to me.

She stated to him. "You know I am going with you."

He smiles. Then he asked me, "How will you be able to go while working on the Assignment?" She had gotten silent. I remember the conversation about his Royalty. He had told me he had so much money from his inheritance. He would not be destitute in many years to come.

He had bought me two gowns. I want you to look beautiful when we go out to dinner, or hit a club here. "When we get to Africa, you will wear some of your new apparels," he stated. He wanted to take me someplace special.

So Christie had to go back to the suite to change her clothes. He was already dress to go out. I had tears in my eyes. I had said, "You are everything I ever wanted in my life."

He smiles. He had felt a tear fall from his eyes, too.

"If you are going to become my wife, you will have to be honest." That is all I ask for in my mate. He had stated.

You are a true officer, Gerald. I had told him.

Yes, because of the way I was raised. He stated.

She said, "I want to establish a reputation for being a good Investigator."

"Other wise it will be useless for me to be here," she stated. He shakes his head. And he stated. "I would not say that," darling. "It is a good thing you are here," he stated. He smiles. He looks into my eyes. "You would not have met me," he stated. "If you had not came here to work on an assignment." He stated.

I had smile at him. That is true, Gerald. I remember the conversation about the destiny. He gave me a kiss. Even though, we both knew our standards. He said, "We must control ourselves in these kinds of moments." He steps backward. This was different from the other times. He said, "I am saving myself for our wedding night."

I had to laugh at him. I did not hear his remark about becoming his wife.

Soon as I get back… I had shortens my sentence. I look at him hard. What did you say to me, Gerald? He repeats it.

"There is so much you have to learn about me, first," he stated.

I held his neck. "I most definitely want to become your wife." I had stated to him.

He smiles. He strokes my cheek. "There might be something you can do here from the Island." He stated.

He was ready to take me back to my hotel. We had gone to a lovely secluded area where they had romantic music and quite talks. We were dancing under the stars.

It is getting later in the evening. I will take you back to your hotel. I will see you tomorrow. We will go somewhere else romantic. You get a good night rest. He kiss me goodnight. He left the hotel.

The next evening he had called me to say he was coming to pick me up in 3 hours.

They had to get ready to go out tonight. The weather had turn back beautiful. It was fill with sunshine and a cool breeze. I had to go find a Salon on the Island.

I winded up going to the salon where Gerald goes to get his hair braided. Or, twisted he calls it. His hair was so beautiful to me. I took a cab to the village where the salon was located. I had walks inside the salon. It was an African-Jamaican establishment. Hello, my name is Christie. I was referred to come in here by a man name Gerald Labrodereax. She had stated to the woman.

Oh, yes I know this man very well. She had an accent, and she was pretty. The hairstylist said to me. I am a good friend of Gerald. My name is Lena. It is a pleasure to meet you, dear, she stated. I do not know if you remember me at the Party where we were that night? She had asked me. No, I can not recollect. Well, I am the wife of Manuel. That was our house where you all came for the party. She said to me. Oh, yes I do remember. I said to the woman. You have a beautiful home. Thank you. She said to me. Gerald, "he tells me a lot about you. " She said to me, "he is so happy" Before you came here he was a loner. I can not imagine Gerald being a loner. I had said to this woman. Yes, he hardly ever go anywhere-all he does is work. Or, he stays on his Yacht. This can not be the same Gerald. I thought. Yes, he was quite sad. He would not even go to church. You have change things for him, Christie. We were going to get married.

He had wanted me to quit my job. He made that statement about finding something to do on the Island. I wanted to be his wife. I had taken out my laptop, and type a message to Mike. I think I am going to resign from this job. There is so much happening in my life. I do not want the rest of your money. As far as I can see, your daughter she is safe. Her boyfriend he is in some kind of trouble. I appreciate everything you have done for me. I wish you the best in your endeavor. I will be praying for you. I sign my name. I had sent it to him. He was not at home to get my message.

Christie tells Ann the truth

It was 5:00 p.m. in the afternoon. Ann was leaving in the evening. I had asked her to meet me in the hotel bar. I must tell you something about me. Ann, she said that she would be down there in ten minutes. I had gone down to the lobby. I walk over to the Outside Pool bar. I had gotten me a table that sat by the Ocean. Ann, she walks over to me smiling. She looks sad, too. She gave me a hug. She sits down. I sure hate to leave this Island. She tells me. I am sure going to miss you, Carmella. I had frowns up. There is something I must tell you, Ann. Before you hear, it from someone else. My real name is Christie

Higgins. I am not a writer that is working on a book to be Publish. I am a Private Investigator and I am here to do an Investigation on someone here. A female Private eye, who is black? She had stated to me. Yes. I had replies. I am also a Detective. Are you kidding me? She asks me.

No. I take out my identification. Why did you have to deceive me? She asks me.

I am working undercover, dear. It was for my safety, and the person who I am PI, here. I had stated to her. I will understand if you are angry. I had stated. She shook her head. I am just surprised. That is fascinating to hear. I like you, Christie. I want us to be friends. She had stated. I want that, too. I hug her. I will give you my number, and my website. I had made some business card from here. She smiles. I have one, too. She stated.

I will be moving here to the Bahamas in a few months. OH, my stars! She cries. You have found love. She exclaims. Yes. So, have I. I am going to get married to a wonderful man. His name is Gerald Labrodereax. I had stated with tears in my eyes. I want to come to your wedding. Ann, she said to me. I will send you an Invitation. I was wiping my eyes. I am so glad you are not angry with me, Ann.

We hug each other again. I have met that handsome, man at the party. Oh, yes I almost forgot about that night. I am so happy for you, Christie. I have fallen in love with someone, too. Ann said to me. Let me guess, James. She laughs. I want to come to your wedding. I said to her. It will be in Paris, France. That is where he lives.

We had talked to each other for a while. I told her that I had to go find someone to put some braids in my hair. Gerald said to me. You should call, Lena. She had started to do my hair but a storm was approaching the Island. So, she closed up her salon. She wanted to give me a wet set.

She said it will last longer. But, the wind was blowing hard and beating up against her window. It had gotten dark outside. I had stayed in there until Gerald he came to pick me up. I was going out with Gerald. I will miss you. I will miss you, too. She said to me.

I had gotten up to walk away. I had tears in my eyes. I was going to miss, Ann.

It was 8:00 p.m. and Gerald was on his way to pick me up. I had found a salon to put some braids in my hair. I had grown my hair longer. It was still Auburn. I had put on the gown and my matching aqua high heels shoes. I walk down to the elevator.

I had to go down to the lobby. I get on the elevator, and I ride it down to the lobby.

Gerald was standing there by the door. He had a jeep. He smiles at me. I walk over to him. He gave me a kiss. I can not describe how beautiful you are to me, Christie. He said to me. Thank you. I had stated to him. He had on an aqua color suit. It was sharp. He supports my back, and let me walk out the door first.

She walks to the Jeep. You have rented a jeep again. He shook his head. No, it is mines. I just bought it tonight. He was smiling. I told the rental agent that it mines as well be mines. I had to laugh. I paid him cash. I said to him, I can not have my wife riding on the back of a bike. I was not sure if you were going to said that to me.

Christie gets proposed to at the Restaurant

I had stated to him. Gerald he looks at his watch. He held the door open on her side. I get inside the jeep. He shut the door. He walks around to the driver side.

We are going to this place that has a Casino, night club, and a Restaurant. I had made reservation for us to dine at the Sky View Inn. It is on the roof.

He drives off. They arrive at the Grand's International Casino Hotel. He had a Valet park his Jeep. They had gone inside. I walk to the elevator with him. He pushes the button to go up to the Sky View Inn. The ride was magnificent. I could see the ocean looking down. He said something else to me. "I have another surprise for you." I have changed my mind. I am confused, now. He smiles. Come on let us go to our table. He gives his name to the woman at the booth. Gerald Labrodereax and fiancée Christie Higgins. I was smiling. He was calling me his fiancée. We were escorted to a table.

He had a bottle of champagne on the table. With a bouquet of, flowers in a vase.

He smiles. You have told me something that made a lot of sense. He had stated.

I have said so many things to you, Gerald. I had stated. I have no right to ask you to stop doing something that you loved. I am a very reasonable man. I touch his hand.

I have resigned from being a Private Investigator for Mike. I have sent him an e-mail tonight. He is not home, so he had not responded to my message. I am so happy. Gerald, he was crying. I am going to make this up to you, darling. I have kept something else from you, too. He pours me a glass of champagne. I am not destitute. I hope not for many years to come.

I have a trust fund that was set up from my parents that I hardly touch, and also I sold my grandparents house. I am not a Millionaire. But, I am well off. He laughs. He reaches over to hugs me. We have so much to discuss about each other, and make plans for our wedding. I was wiping my eyes with my fingers. He hand me a handkerchief. I wipe my eyes with his handkerchief. He takes out a Velvet black case. What is this, Gerald? He hand it to me. There is one way to find out, darling. Wait a minute before you open the black velvet case. I have to do something, first. He stood up, and get down on one knee. He held my hand. I look around the room. All eyes were on him. I said, "Gerald what are you doing?' He smiles.

"Will you do me the honor of becoming my wife, Ms. Christie Higgins?" I was smiling with tears in my eyes. I said, "Yes with all my heart. I will become your wife." He stood up, and gave me a kiss. Now, open up that case. They were clapping for us.

I had opened up the velvet case to stare at a huge rock that was so brilliant that the light from it was bouncing off the wall in the Restaurant. The color of the room was a pretty aqua blue and the glimmer from the chandelier had sparkles around the room. He said, "Let me put it on your finger, darling." It was a beautiful aqua diamond ring. I said you must have been very busy tonight. He sat back down at the table. "You have no idea. First, I went to buy my Jeep. Then I stopped at a Jeweler to see about picking out a ring.

I had to rush back to the Yacht to go get clean up for our night out on the town.

I am sort of tired, but I am going to have a splendid evening with you tonight."

He had stated. "I have something else to tell you, too. Well, I had spoken to a traveler agent who has booked us to Great Britain. I have not flown anywhere this far, so I did not know how long it would take. They said that we could get there in one day.

Like if we left from Africa we could get there in 24 hours. I told them that is where we were going in a week." He stated. "Now, I have to ask you a question.

Which place would you like to get married at, darling?" He was smiling. "Let me check to see if I heard you right?" Christie asked. He smiles. "I have to tell my sister Adrianna so she can set thing up for us, there. Or, tell them at the Great Britain that we are getting married there. Which ever you decide is what we will do." He stated. "I have to know, now. I have already told my sister we were going to get married. She is hoping we can have it there in Africa." Christie began to cry. "I rather get married in Africa." Christie said. He was smiling. "I have to call her, right now." He said, "Right this very minute." I had exclaims. "Yes." He replies. "There is going to be a big celebration. They will have an African style dancing celebration outdoors. We will have to go straight to Kenya, where she will meet us there with her husband, and my niece." I stood up. I have to go to the restroom. I went to the restroom crying. He tells people I am overwhelm.

An Island woman came inside to make sure I was alright. She hugs me. This is wonderful, "I am happy for you, both." She said to me. "Thank you." I said to her. I came back to our table. I smiled.

He calls his sister long distance. She was crying, too. "I will set things up for you two when you have arrived. I have not gone to Kenya in a while." She had stated.

I cannot wait to see you both. I will be there next week. Bye. He said to his sister.

It is all set, darling. I do not know what to said, Gerald. He held my hand. You have said, yes to become my wife. He had stated to me. There was no dry eye in the Restaurant. The server came over to take our order.

Then, we went out on the dance floor. He turns me around, and we dance to a beautiful jazzy song. I was smiling.

I could not believe I was going to become his wife, and getting a trip to two continents. I had to notify my friends, Tracey and to call Ann. Not to forget John, and his wife. I must send an invitation to my former boss Mr. Walter White, and his wife, Judy. He must have read my mind. You can invite your friends from NYC. He had stated. I had to laugh. We had a beautiful romantic night. I was so happy. I almost forgot we were on an Island.

They had a festivity going on, until dawn. It will start at 11: 30 a.m. and there were live entertainment. He asks me did I want to go walk around to the Island, Festival? I said," Yes I am not ready to go back to the hotel." That is not going to happen, darling. The Night is still young. He stated.

I had almost forgotten to tell you that a performing artist is going to be here tonight. He is one of our favorite performers. I get excited. He and I said we like the same song. Gerald, he had taken off tonight. He told them not to call him during no circumstances. He saw some of his friends who were Police officers. They were trying to make the crowd move so that they could bring out the performer.

They were saying to the crowd. Please disperse! Please disperse! They kept saying this in their language. They had told the people to move in an orderly fashion or they would be force to shut down the event. Gerald, he held my hand. We walk to the area to stand and watch the Performer. They had this event on the beachfront. It was very crowded. There were free food, and drinks too set up in booths. Gerald, he nods his head at his friend. He was off duty and happy he was able to be at the event. Two ships had arrived at the same time. Some people wanted to dance.

In about 10 minutes a Master of Ceremony comes out onto the sandy beach. He held a microphone in his hand. He said, "Will you put your hands together to help me welcome one of my favorite performers of all time. They are from the Paradise Island.

These men had performed all over the world. They had back-up singers with them. We all claps and some had whistle. Gerald he whistles too.

The Polices had finally convinced the people to move in an orderly fashion.

They had to make sure the crowd leave without any problems.

The ship they had to be back on board by midnight or they would sail off without them. They were running to the docks. Gerald, he takes my hand. And he takes me out to dance.

He smiles, and he does a dance. He pops his fingers, and twirls me around. I was smiling. I was dancing with him. He twirls me around again. I was so happy. He could really dance, too. He did not really look like he was an African. He said that he was Mix with two cultures. We had stayed out until dawn.

I could not keep my eyes open. He drops me back off at my hotel. He had to take me up to my suite. I hope you can handle this delicate manner by yourself. He had stated. I am leaving, now! I had promise my parents, I would save myself until I got married. He had stated to me. I told him, "I will make it fine. He did not even kiss me goodnight. He rushes out of the suite in a hurry. I had to grin at him. He had shut the door so fast I could hear him rushing to the elevator. He rode it down to the main lobby.

I put on a pair of shorts with a tee shirt. I was too sleepy to put on a night gown. I climb into my bed. I had gone to sleep. Gerald, he had gotten to his Yacht. He did not hang up anything.

He tosses everything to the chair. He dives into his bed. We both had slept all day.

I had to make sure that Stephanie was alright. This was the end of my Assignment. Mike, he had received his e-mail. He was not surprised. He was relieved to hear the news about my getting married to Gerald. I had said that they we were going to get married in Africa. He was supposed to be going to Hong Kong. He wanted to meet the both of us when he comes there to see his daughter.

He had told me that he was coming there on Monday. I want to see you both. I should be there on Monday in the afternoon. I had left a message on Gerald answering service. I said, I am going downtown to have some breakfast at the Café.

I will not be down there for too long. I will see you, later. I had stated. I get dress and went to take a Shuttle bus that was out front.

I had gotten downtown to the Cafe and saw Stephanie.

I was not wearing, my hearing device that came with a head-set and micro recorder. I was asked where I wanted to sit down. It does not matter. I had stated to the server. I was looking around to see Stephanie if she was with her company.

The two men were at the table. She was not happy with them being there.

I was surprised when a hand was on my shoulder. I look around, and saw that it was

Gerald. He leans down to give me a kiss. I am sorry about last night. He was laughing. I had to get out of there, expeditiously. I understand, Gerald. He goes to sit at the seat across from me. He takes my hand. I had loved my diamond ring. I could not believe I was getting married.

He interrupts my thought. He smiled.

"I have received your message. You forgot to tell me which Café. That is alright."

I am here, anyway. He stated.

I was looking at my beautiful engagement ring on my finger. I see you have gotten down here fast. Christie had stated. Yes. There were so many people down here today. I thought they were going to asked me to report to work. I took the day off again. He replies.

How did you rest? He asks me. I said, "It was just wonderful." Last night was truly an excitement for me, and I am on cloud 20. He laughs. He said to me, "Believe it or not I feel the same way." He had stated to me.

You have made me feel pretty special in asking me to marry you in that way. Christie stated. He smiled.

A server greets us. Are you ready to order, darling? He asks me. I said, "Yes I think I want your Pancake breakfast with bacon. He said, "He wanted the big breakfast." It came with everything. He smiles. What would you two like to drink? I think I want some coffee, and orange juice. I had stated. He said, "I want the same thing."

Are you working with the coast guard, today? I had asked him. Yes, unfortunately I have to be there tonight. I am working with the Police this morning. He had stated. I ask him what about the Maintenance job? He said, "I am resigning from that job." Why, Gerald? I ask him. I want to spend more time with you, and it really makes me very tired. He had on his Police uniform. You love doing that work, Gerald. I had stated to him. Yes, I do. He replies. I do not want to go into anybody else suite except yours. He had stated. I understand how you feel. I had stated.

He takes out a thin cigar, and lights it. He touches my hand. What are you going to do the rest of the day? He asks me. I still have my Itinerary where I can go look at different sites. The bus will be departing for give a Tour of the different Islands.

I am catching it right after we finish eating. I had stated to him. Good. I will not be able to see you tonight. He had stated.

Mike is coming to the Bahamas Island

Oh, I almost forgot to tell you this news. I had stated to him. Mike is coming here on Monday. He wants to meet us both. I told him everything that is happening with us. I had stated to him. He smiles. That is nice. I really like him, too. He had stated to me.

I had gone back to my hotel. I turn on the television. They said that two men had gotten into a brawl at a Night Club. And they both had been arrested. They mention the two men name Deon Gonzales and a lawyer name Alphonzo Ricci. They said that," Nobody was injured."

They had been arrested for destruction of property. They are waiting on their arraignment.

The news anchorman said, "That an argument got out of control and they were swinging their fists at each other. They knock over a fish aquarium and broke some valuable things that were in the club.

I wanted to find out who is this Alphonzo Ricci character was so I could see if he was a criminal. I had type in his name, and put in Bahamas as to where he was living and his occupation. The data said that he was a lawyer, this was odd.

They had put down what he specialized in and discovers that he dealt with shady business people and was a prosecutor. I had put two and two together. I had discovers that he must have wanted to prosecute Deon for something he was doing illegally. But, why would he be fighting him at a club? This did not add up. I was thinking. I could not wait for the news media to tell the story that was soon to be out tomorrow.

I sat there all night listening to the news. They were not discussing anything else.

I did not make it to breakfast that morning. Gerald, call and said he was very busy and would check on me later. He stated. I had told him the news. He said, "He had heard it on the Coast guard ship. He said he was on the dock. I had not gone to the dock, yet. What are you doing, now? I had asked him. He said, "I have to make sure that everyone gets on his or her ship for departure without any problem. They were all discussing the news. I had told him. He said that he could not finish talking to me. I said I understood. I will talk to him tonight. I was still listening to the news.

They said that both men were charge for destruction of personal property. Their bail was post at $500,000.

I had thought about Stephanie, now. I was not on the assignment anymore. I was her cousin. This had made me happy.

But, I was going to still tell Mike the news. I had e-mail him. He thanks me. I appreciate your looking out for my daughter, your cousin. He had stated. I cannot wait to meet you, Christie. "You do not know how happy and relieved that I have finally told you the truth." I want to meet you, too. I had stated to him. I am alone without a family. "That is not true," dear.

He said, "I believe that I have some other family on my side are out there somewhere, but I have not been able to look anybody up. I had gone to turn on her shower water so she could go downstairs to the Restaurant for dinner. I could have order room service. I had taken out a wrap around skirt and a halter blouse that tie around my neck. I had a thin blazer in case it was cold in the restaurant. I had my hair down in curls. I had pins my hair up to take a shower. Then, I get dress. I head out to the restaurant. I had found out about this lawyer. He specializes in nailing criminal doing shady business. I had called Gerald while he was out working by the docks. I had told him what I had found out. He said to me, "This is what I heard, too." He yarns. He was tired. I could tell it in his voice. He has been putting in more work on his other jobs.

I do not understand why he gets into a fight with Deon. That news will come out. He tells me. I am going to go back to my boat to take a shower and go to bed.

Call me later before you go to sleep. He had stated to me. I said, okay.

Gerald said he was not going anywhere else tonight. I understood. He was exhausted. I had gone to the Restaurant. I was not ready to go back to my suite.

Christie still had the desire to be a PI

Maybe Stephanie will be hanging around town. She had taken me a cab to go downtown. She had gone to the resort where Stephanie resides. Christie was not planning on buying anything else. She was just walking along taking pictures. She saw Stephanie walking by herself. She had not seen since the club when she had gotten in a drunken manner. She looks like she had been crying. I wanted to know what was wrong with her now. I walk over to where she was standing. I said," hello do you remember me? "

She said, "Yes I do remember seeing you." I am Christie. I told her my real name.

Wait a minute. I had heard that name, before. I talked to my dad, and he told me that there was a woman here that I should get to know. Is there some place where we can talk in private? I had asked her. "Well,

I had told my boyfriend company that I am not going anywhere." She said, "There is a nice Café right here." It is quite delicious and expensive. "She said, "We can go have some dessert, and coffee. Alright, I said to her. I follow her to the Café. We got a table together. She asked me, "Who are you, Christie?""

Are you sure that nobody is coming to join you?"

I had asked her. She said, "My boyfriend he is waiting to be arraigned. "

He will not be joining me. I am sure that you have heard the news. And his partners are conducting business in his absence. She put her head down in her arm.

I had touched her shoulder. I understand your pain, Stephanie. She looks up at me,

She asked me again. Who are you? I have been hired by your dad to PI you, and your boyfriend, as well as his company. What is it you want to know about me? She asks me, "I have resigned from this assignment. I am just here as your friend. I really like you, Stephanie." I had stated to her. "I wanted to make sure you were alright."

"I am angry, and disappointed." She said to me. "I am tired of this relationship. I am about ready to dump this man I think I can find me somebody else." I know you can, Stephanie. I had stated to her. I gave her a little hug.

I wanted to see you before I left the Island. The man you have seen me with, we are getting married. We are going to Africa for our wedding. I had stated. Congratulation, honey I am happy for you both. She had stated to me. I am glad someone has found happiness.

Thank you. I had stated. You will, too Stephanie. Give it some time. Will you send me an invitation too? You want to come to the Wedding in Africa?

"You bet I do, I need to get away from here." My dad he is coming here next week. She stated.

Yes, I know.

I had to get back to my hotel before it gotten late. Someone had whistle at me for the first time. I smiles. A man walks over to me, smiling. He said, "I have had my eyes on you the first day you have arrived here." I was stunned by who this man is, he was Jerome. I said to him I had not even noticed you. He said, "How could you when you are with that man everyday."

I smile. He is my Fiancée. Now, I know I will have to stay clear of you. I am not ready to go that route. He said to me.

I ask him what route is this, you are speaking about? He said, "Getting married again." I am happy, now.

"I had no ideal that he had been married." He was trying to make conversation. Well, darling it has been nice chatting with you.

I held out my hand. He shook it gently. Jerome said, "And you will be careful, now." Christie said, "I will and you do the same." I had stated to him. I was so surprised that I would meet this man. I had gone up to my hotel suite.

I went straight to the telephone to call Tracey from New York City. I told her to go get her husband, so he could hear the news at the same time. "I am getting married in Africa to a man, who has turned out to be my secret Bodyguard." I could hear her screaming for her husband Horace. He came to the telephone. What is happening? I told them both the news together. She was laughing and listening to me. We had become such two pitiful women with all that crying we had done two weeks ago. I told them that he had been trailing behind me from day one, and we fell in love with each other. He is an African and British descendant. He is from a Royal family! I had screamed in their ears. They were both laughing. I had stated.

Do not ask me to explain about his heritage? I am still confused about that, myself. Anyway, we are leaving for the city of Gaborone Botswana. That was in the country of Africa. That was where his sister resides. I will meet his sister, and her husband, their little girl. She is arranging for a Traditional wedding Ceremony that is supposed to be big. I wish you two can come see me walk down the aisle. Tracey said I am coming! Horace, said to his wife, "not without me". I had to cry. You two are the closest people to me. Walter and John they are dear to me, too.

I will have to call them, too. We will need all the details, honey. I am going to go get some invitation cards. Soon as I get my information, I will send it to you. I had stated. We are so happy for you, Christie. I cannot wait to meet your new Husband.

Tracey, she had stated. You will get that chance. He is wonderful. I have to get off of here to make another call. I had said to her. I will talk to you real soon.

I was about to go take off my clothes and watch some television in my suite. There was a knock on the door. I said, "Just a minute. Who is it? It was Gerald. I open up the door for him. He came inside, and he gave me a hug. I thought you had gone back to the Yacht. I wanted to see my beautiful fiancée. I feel like asking you to pack your things, and move into my Yacht. But, that would be wrong. I can sleep on the couch. He laughs. No, darling. That is temptation for me. I had better keep things static quo, if you know what I mean? He had stated to me. Yes, I do understand.

Were you on your way out somewhere? He asks me. I said," No I had just came back from downtown where Stephanie resides. "He had gotten the news from his friend. I could not tell him a lie anymore. He was not angry.

Where did you go, Christie? I wanted to see how Stephanie was doing. So I went out to her Resort. He shook his head. I knew it. My buddy told me he saw you tonight.

What were you doing visiting Stephanie? I had to make sure she was alright. She is miserable. I think she is going to break up with her boyfriend. That is good. He stated. She will be happier without him. He had stated. I told her who I was, and she is glad I told her my real identity. I am relieved, too. Stephanie wants to come to our wedding too. Gerald, he takes my hand. And he walks me to the couch. I have told my friends from New York that we are getting married in Africa. He smiles. They are coming to our wedding. Do you mind? No, this is not a problem for me. He stated to me. Whatever makes you happy, will make me happy. I put my arms around his neck. You are supposes to be sleeping. I have enough rest until in the morning. I came to tell you that we are to be at the church before 11:00 a.m. for their Sunday morning worship service.

Gerald takes Christie to church

I will pick you up about 10:00 a.m. We might have time to have a bite to eat before we go to church. He stated. Gerald, he was wearing his green suit and a cream color shirt. He was wearing his green leather shoes. His hair was standing up in the curly look. Christie, she was going to bed early. She had laid out a Yellow flower dress with a white wide belt. It had flairs out with lots of ruffles. I had made me a cup of coffee, in my suite. I was looking at my laptop; I was not erasing my program, just yet. Gerald. He told me that he did not have a problem with my working as a Private Eye. He just did not want me to do this job here in the Bahamas Island. He stated it was too dangerous.

I had gone out to find me a Yellow page directory. I wanted to see if there was a Section on PI agencies. Maybe they needed someone to do a PI in a secret manner.

She was not ready to quit her business. Mike, he had told her, if all went well with him when he returns home. He would try to get her a job working in Washington, DC. He was coming there on Monday.

I had almost forgotten that I had done a job for Timothy Wade. I had given him my Website to contact me if he needed another job. He was a divorce lawyer.

I did not really want to work with him, this was always so sad. I had thought.

I could find something else I would like to do. I was not moving here right away. I had to go home to handle things. Or convince Gerald to let me keep my PI business and Loft in NYC. Gerald, he had called me up.

You can come down to the lobby, baby. I will be there in 15 minutes. He had stated. I had put on my make-up, and earrings set. I had grab my purse, and key.

I walk out of my suite. I walk to the elevator. I rode it down to the main lobby.

I still kept my laptop on all the time. I keep it on all day and night.

I was walking to the lobby. They had a complimentary Continental breakfast. I went to get me a bagel, and Orange juice. I put some cream cheese on it. I had gone to sit down at a table. I was not trying to meet any more friends, yet. However,

I spoke to this woman who was looking at the Bahamas Newspaper. I said, "Is there something interesting in there today? She said, "It most certainly is here see for yourself"

Chapter 11

Christie she meets Stephanie mother and Mike wife

She gave me her newspaper. It said, "That there is a Missing Child report."

It has been learned that this child is somewhere here in the Bahamas Island. They would pay $100,000 to anyone who can locate this child and give them the information. In returns, that person will get a check for that amount. Christie, she takes out a pen and pad. She writes down the name. Thank you. She hand the paper back to the woman. You can have that page. Thank you, said Christie. My name is Christie Higgins. I had stated. I am Wynona McGuire. I was stunned by her last name. I had just arrived here last night. I have been away from a long time. I had been living in other parts of the world. I am just here in the hopes of finding my long lost daughter. I was interested in hearing her story. She may not want to see me. I was very young, and I was not ready to be a mother. I had a wonderful career.

So, I gave her up to my husband to Raised. How old is your daughter? I had to ask this woman. She said to me," I believe Stephanie she is 32 years old now. I cover my mouth. I was paying attention to the front entrance.

Gerald, he should be here soon. This was Stephanie mother. The woman looks very sad, I do not know if my husband will forgive me. She was still married to Mike. Mike did not mention to me that he was married. He just told me about his daughter. I said to this woman, "You will never know until you face them both. How long will you be here? Indefinite, or at least until I find out if they wants me in their lives again. I gave her a hug. I wish you the best, honey.

Maybe, I will see you again. Yes, I will be around. I am on my way to church.

Gerald, he had arrived at the hotel. He gets out of his Jeep. He walks to the front door. He opens it, and went inside. I am here, darling. I have to go this is my fiancée, Gerald Labrodereax. He smiles.

Honey, this is Mrs. Wynona McGuire. He stood back in shock, too. He smiles. And he spoke to the woman. It is a pleasure to meet you dear. He supports my back, and leads me out the door. I get inside his jeep.

Tell me she did not say her last name is, Mrs. McGuire. He had stated.

"Yes, she is Stephanie mother. She is also the wife of Mike McGuire." I know you have found out some information on this woman." He had stated.

"I was just listening to her story. She had given up her daughter when she was younger to travel all over the world." He was driving away, and listening to me speaks about this strange woman.

"She is very remorseful, and wants them both to forgive her for this terrible thing.

I told her to just be honest, and to face them both." I had stated.

"That is good advice, darling." He held my hand, to kiss it.

I told him, "Yesterday I would have been bitter about having someone who had deserted their child." I wipe my eyes. "I do not have a mother anymore." I had taken out a Kleenex. "I have compassion for people now." He sniffs too. He looks at me. "That is wonderful I want things to work out for Mike." "I wonder how it will turn out."

"I will be praying for them." I had told, Gerald.

I will most definitely be praying for them. He had stated. I like Mike. "I think he should be happy." I am so grateful to him for bringing you here. "He had stated to me.

I had gotten in touch with my friend who has been attending my late Father church.

His name is Kenny. He said, "We will be having dinner at his house." I see you have been eating bagel with cream cheese. He had stated. I am sorry I did not bring you one. I had stated. I am fine. They arrive at the church. It was a Modern building.

I was surprised. He had parked his Jeep on their lot.

I was still trying to find out more information on Deon and this Lawyer. I wanted to save this Newspaper to read it later. She had gotten a glimpse of the news line heading. They had said that an owner of a Lending company and a lawyer who is a prosecutor for the D.A. office. The witnesses had said the owner of the lending company walk over to the lawyer at his table and said something ugly about him being at the same place where he was at. The lawyer said, "He had a right to be wherever he chooses." The first thing he was going to do was put him out of business, then behind bars. He told the news media this man decks him at the table. They begin to fight destroying the club. The lawyer admits he was at fought to fight him, being a lawyer and officer for the court. He paid his fine, and was released. As for the other man he was let out on bail, and has a court date pending. I had put the newspaper in the back seat.

They were getting ready to go inside to the church. Gerald, he gets out to walk around on my side of the jeep. He held out his hand. And she takes his hand. She steps out of the Jeep. He gave her a warm hug. They walk up the steps to go inside. The Pastor was standing there, greeting people. He looks over at Gerald, and gave him a bear hug. It has been a long time, brother Labrodereax! He exclaims. Gerald, smiles with tears in his eyes. Yes, I have been so busy with all my jobs. I was smiling at him with tears in my eyes, too. I am very sorry, darling. The lady beside me is my fiancée. Ms. Christie Higgins. Welcome to my church, dear. How are you?

We had stayed until the service was over. We had to take a rain check on the dinner invitation. Gerald had to go to work.

Christie Goes To a Bridal Shop

I walk over to the shop to browse around for a while. He had gone back to work. I walk inside this Beautiful Wedding Gown shop. A sales consultant she walks over to me. She said to me," you are getting married." She looks at my hand. I had a huge diamond ring on my finger. I said, "Yes I am getting married." I was just browsing around to see what kind of gowns you have in here. There was a beautiful gown that was in displayed behind a glass case. It was nothing I could ever describe to a person. It came with this very long train. She said to me. That design is from Paris, France. You ought to try it on, dear. She had stated to me. I ask her how much does it cost. She said to me, "When a woman is getting married she does not worry about a price. I had stated to her, "I do pay attention to prices." She apologizes to me. I keep forgetting that everybody cannot afford these gowns. "Perhaps I can show you a cheaper one on the racks." She had stated. I had stated, "It will not hurt anything." She unlocks this door. "She asks me what was my dress size? "I told her I was wearing a size 7. She went to get the gown. I will assist you in getting dress. She walks me to a fitting room. Just let me know when you are ready to try on the gown. She locks the door. I had change out of my outfit I was wearing. I call the sales consultant. I told her I was ready to try on the gown. She came inside. She helps me slipped it on from the bottom. Then she zips me up. Come step out to take a look in our large mirror. She held the train. I was crying. It was the most beautiful gown I had ever seen. I had my hair still in braids. This is just perfect for you, dear. I had to ask her one more time. How much does this gown cost? She said, "$50,000" I was racing to get back to the fitting room. If you change your mind I will hold this gown for you. I will give you my card. I thank her, and she helps me get out of the gown. I had put back on my clothes.

Christie had to go Downtown Bahamas

I still had some errands to do this afternoon. I needed to go buy some Invitation cards. But, I still wanted to find out what was happening with Deon friends.

He replies. Oh, I see. I put the newspaper under my purse. Stephanie and Deon had arrived at the Café. I was kind of hungry. I was surprised to see them together. Stephanie she was going to tell him she wanted out of their relationship. I was a Detective, and if he put his hand on her I would step in to intervene. I did not want anybody to hurt me or any woman. I sat at the back by the ocean. I felt a cool breeze. I pick up my menu. They had some stuff Oyster. I had them at the party. It was delicious. I wanted to hear their conversation. I had put back on my hearing device. I had my microphone attached to my purse. I was listening to them talked.

Stephanie, she was crying. Deon, I cannot keep going on this way. You have treated me so wonderful, and you are such a handsome man. I think it will be best if we went our separate way. I am sure you will find somebody else. He said nothing. Then he stated, "You are dumping me, darling?" He asked her. She lowers her head.

"Yes, and we both know that this would happen one day." She stated.

He nods his head. "You know I felt this was going to happen by the way you are constantly sulking whenever we are together."

You know I am not happy with your Friends, who follow us around. He said nothing to that remark. They are my business partners, and they look out for my well-being. Yes, I know they are your bodyguards. Stephanie had said to him. Christie, she knew just how Stephanie felt about that situation. I will come over to your house to pick up my things. And to return to you all the gowns that you have bought me, the jewelries, as well as other things. He said, alright. I will be expecting your arrival.

Stephanie, she got up to leave the Café. Deon, he sat there looking sad. He took out a cigar, and lights it. He told the server he wanted a bottle of whiskey. She asked him did he want a shot. He said, "No I want the whole, blasted bottle." He exclaims. He was very upset. He stayed there for a half an hour then he left. He could not get into anymore trouble. So, he was not going to make a scene with Stephanie. He takes out his cell phone. He calls up his partner, Jerome. He said, "I am expecting Stephanie to come out to the house." She and I have broken up. I do not want you to harm her. Let her be. This is over,

Jerome." He had stated. "If you said so, boss. Do you want me to come pick you up?"

"No, I am going to the office." He hangs up. Deon stated. The server gave him a bill.

He left $100 bill on the table. He walks out of the Café. He goes to the Limousine.

Ann Bids Her Farewell

When Christie got back to the Hotel she had receive a message from Ann.

Ann said, "She was leaving tonight." Do you want to meet me at the Oceanside bar for a drink? My flight leaves at 9:45 p.m. She asks me. I will be downstairs in the lobby in 15 minutes. Okay Christie. This was the first time she had heard her name mention by Ann. She had all her bags downstairs in the holding area. I had to go freshen up and put on something cool. The sun had gone down. I had this green lounging apparel set. She had not worn it out of her suite. I put it on and slip on my high heel slippers. I had put on my make-up, too. I had twisted my braids in a pony tail. I had gone downstairs to the lobby, and she walks outside to where the ocean set. I walk over to a Bar to find a table. Ann, she had waves at me from the back entrance. She walks over to join me at the table. We had order our drinks. I wanted mines to be non-alcohol.

Ann and I discussed our Wedding Plans

We talk for a long time about our plans of getting married to the men of our dream.

I have to get your invitation sent out to your house in Malibu, California. I will send it to you right away. Gerald and I are planning on taking our trip next week. Will you be able to take another trip of this kind? Oh, yes. I am the owner of the Boutique remember? Yes, I had almost forgotten with so much going on in my life.

"I have spoken to James and he said he wanted to come on this trip." He said, "That is closer to him than LA." He lives in Paris, France.

I will send him an invitation too. Christie stated.

"No, that will not be necessary, just send it to me Christie." Ann stated.

We had stayed outside at the Bar for almost 2 hours then Ann said she had to go get her bags to head out to the airport. A cab was waiting outside for her to come out with her baggage. I gave her a hug. I will call you soon as I get home. I said, "Please be careful. I will say a prayer for your safety. Then I had left to go back to my suite.

When I had gotten back to my suite there was a message on my phone.

I thought it was Gerald. But, it was Mr. McGuire. Christie, she had forgotten to tell Mike about Deon. I had promised him I would still give him free information. He probably heard about it there in NY. That was not the reason for his visit there.

Christie tells Mike about Stephanie break up with Deon

I had returns his phone call. This is Christie. He greets me pleasant. How are you, dear? He stated.

I am fine. I had stated to him. "He asks me how was things there?"

It is very fascinating and I am finding out more things on your daughter boyfriend. I had replies. Oh, I have heard that he was out on bail last night. How is my daughter doing? He asks me. Well, she seems to be dissatisfied with this man. I had said to him. "I think this is the drawing point of their relationship. I had talked to her for a little while. She had broken up with him."

He sounded happy. That is good news to me. You do not have to worry about her anymore. He is not going to harm her.

She is going to get her things from his house, and return everything he bought her.

I knew she would be smart enough to let that man go. He had stated to me.

"Your daughter she is very smart, and knows what she wants in a man." I had stated to him. "I believe that she is going to be alright." He sounded like he had been crying. His voice was cracking.

"I am so glad that you said that to me, Christie. This is all that matters to me.

He had stated to me. I hate to see her unhappy and that make me very unhappy.

I have spoken to her on several occasions. She is a beautiful young, lady. He smiles.

Thank you.

I want to come there next week in the attempt to see her before I go to the Island of Hong Kong. Mike had stated.

Chapter 12

Mike tells Christie the truth about his Illness

"Christie I must tell you something about us." I do not want anybody else to tell you this but me. He gets silent. I want to say for the most part, I think you have done a tremendous job for a first time being a Private Eye. I appreciate your hard effort and I think one day you will become a top notch and Private Investigator Detective. Christie, I have kept something from you too. I am your Uncle on your mother side. Your mom was my sister, and she was a McGuire. I came around when you were real young but I left because I was so grief stricken over my sister. You come from a Wealthy family. My dad, your grandfather help build the railroad tracks. It was later when they started paying him for his hard work. I know that you had something in a trust fund from both parents, but you also had something extra from your mother too.

I had put it in a Swiss bank account until I thought it was the right time. I have actually given some of it to you for working for me. There is still some of it left.

He stated. I really could not find you when you were growing up. I think there must have been hundreds of Higgins in NYC or in the United

States. It was later when I decided to hire a PI to do an Investigation on my daughter, your cousin. You are right around the same age as my Stephanie. "I know what you must think of me, dear. I have some issues too and my mind, have been pre-occupied." He stated.

Christie was crying hard.

"This man is of a criminal sort. I rather you not get any deeper involve in his affairs. I am sure a trial is coming up soon and he will be the main topic around town." He stated.

"Yes you are right he does have a trial coming up soon. I have heard this from Gerald. He is ready for us to be out of the country. You know that we are getting married in Africa." She had stated to him.

"I had no ideal. I am happy for you both." He stated.

Thank you. She replies. I wanted to send you an invitation, too. But since you will be here next week I think I will just give it to you in person.

"Please do so that I can buy you two a gift." He stated.

That will not be necessary, Mike. She stated.

I insist Christie. I am putting into your account the remaining money I owe you for this assignment. Mike stated.

"Mike, I do not want that money." Christie stated.

"I have already made the transaction, dear. Accept it graciously. You have done a tremendous job. He stated.

I had started to cry. Thank you. "I would have done better, but other circumstances occurred in my life." She had stated.

"I will put the rest of the money into your account today before it slips my mind. Oh, I want to meet you in person. I wonder if we could have dinner when I arrived there on Monday. I know that you want to include Gerald. After all he is your Fiancée." He stated.

"Yes, you are right."

"Well, it is settled. I will make arrangement for dinner on Monday. There is this Eloquent Restaurant everyone here is talking about in NYC. They said, "It is underground at the bottom of the ocean." You could see the sea creatures swim while you are dining. He said, "I am going to call to make Reservation. I had frowns up. I did not care too much about going underground anymore. I had gone with Gerald to the Aquarium Center. He had stated. I will make it for 5:00 p.m. on Monday. I am supposed to be arriving at the Grand Bahamas Hotel by 3:00 p.m. I will have enough time to relax before having dinner.

Mike had to tell Christie a fact

Mike he wanted Christie to be aware that she was not handling things by her self even though Gerald had quit the assignment. I want to know do think that nobody knows what you are doing there on the Island? I had to come up with a logical answer. I had said, "I am sure that the Police are looking out for my safety here in the Bahamas Island. Christie stated.

I know it is for sure that Gerald has been very busy working on his other two jobs.

I hate to break this to you dear. I have been talking to Gerald almost every night.

He has asked his friends to keep an eye on you that work with the Police Department and also with the Coast guard. And even the Navy too. We both knew that this job would not be that easy for you to do, considering that you are an inexperience Private Eye, and Detective. He had stated. I am not your friend, but an ex-employer. I do not think you were able to handle this job on your own. Please hear me out before you explode.

He asks me. You have never seen a real crime scene. And you are a Detective until you have actually worked on cases.

"If that is what you really want to do, then you should be sleeping on the FBI doorstep. I would ask them to give me a chance.

"In all honesty they may say yes, because it is against the law to turn a woman down if she is qualified to do a job."

I know about discrimination, Mike. She stated.

"I am one of their biggest Advocate supporters in this discrimination constitution." I did not call here to get on your worse side. I know that this is something you wanted to do because I had given you a chance. She was wiping her eyes. I have a conscience, Christie. I could not live with myself if something bad was to happen to you. I love you as much as I love my daughter. I know that my daughter is in the hand of the Savior. And I know he is watching over whether I am around or not. He sniffs. I am not a cold heartless man who will send an inexperience woman out to do a job, when there are hundreds of Private Investigators all over the country. He had stated to me. I was talking to a close friend of mines who is a FBI Lieutenant in Washington, DC. He said he is starting a new program for Women who want to be Detectives and they already had their training. What he is going to do is send these women out to work on a real life case under the supervision of a man. He will pay you women a salary while you are under an Internship program that will take 3 months. You will have to stay at one of their housing units until you complete the program. After your completion you will get a Certificate and be place wherever you desire to work. Or, they will replace you at one of their location. I do not want to go back to school anymore.

I had stated. Let me tell you this again, "You will be in a program that will allow you to work on an actual case with the Detectives who are already certified.

He said, "Nobody in this country will hired you to go out on a case without prior work experience. He said, "I will put your name down for an apartment where you will share with another female. They will pay for everything. All you need is your money for spending. He stated. That mean you can use your money for whatever.

I have to know your answer soon as possible. You can talk it over with Gerald.

This is a great opportunity. Do not pass this up because of your stubbornness.

He had stated to her. Incidentally you will get paid a six figure salary once you are actually working in this career. He had mentioned this to me. I do not care about the money now. I was going to be well taken care with Gerald money and mines. I had stated to Mike. I understand. Well, I hope I did not upset you too bad. He had stated. I am not upset, just a little surprised in this news. I will talk to Gerald and get back to you with my answer. Thank you, Mike.

I will have to think about this for a while, Mike. I had stated to him.

This call was to tell her to stop Investigating on Deon partners. She was still taking down data on them.

She needed to get some air and collect her thoughts about going to a Program in Washington, DC for 3 months. She was tired of going to school. She put on her a pair of Capri orange color pants set that had some beads at the tail of her top and also at the bottom of her Capri. She put on a pair of sandals that were orange.

She grabs her key and her purse that had a shoulder strap. She left her suite and takes the elevator down to the lobby. She walks out of the hotel.

Mike he felt that he needed to put his mind at ease. He was a dying man. He had gone back to the doctor for the last time. And they had given him a month to live.

He could not keep asking her to go out to investigate on his daughter boyfriend, partner. He was relieved to hear that his daughter had broken up with this man.

He tells her. I have to put you her in order, if this involves his money. He had gotten angry. When she told him she did not want him to call her everyday. It is my job and concern as a parent. I have to know everything about my daughter whereabouts. You really are inexperience in this Business. He stated. You were so busy being distracted by this bodyguard that you forgot to call me to say how things were going last night. She gets silent. I was going to e-mail you this morning. I was with my friend who I met here. She is leaving to go back home.

Mike takes his Frustration out on Christie

You told me that you were going to tell me some information even though you are not working on the assignment anymore Christie. I was depending on you for that information. He had stated. I had gone downtown. And I spoke to her at a Café. She was very sad about her situation with her boyfriend. She spoke about him being in jail and was waiting on his release. She is fed up with this man. She was not upset about this man going to jail. I could tell that she was more concern about her own relationship, Mike. She had stated. Oh, really. He had replies. He asked Christie. How did she look? She had stated, “Stephanie looks beautiful and does not look happy right now.” She stated. Christie was upset and a bit nervous by the tone in Mike voice. I made the comment about how I can imagine how she felt. He sounded harsh, "You can imagine how she felt." He stated. "What about me I am here climbing the walls." He did not have on his Video of him this time. He said, "I am not feeling the best these days." If I am sound too harsh. It is because so much is on my mind." Mike, I am sorry I have been wrapped up into the ambience of being here in the Bahamas Island. "Not to mention, I fell in love with this man, Gerald. " She stated. I had tears at the corner of my eyes. He was now sympathetic. I understand about falling in love, Christie. But a job or commitment should be your number one priority. You are my only source of communication by way of phone or e-mail. I cannot see what my daughter is doing. I would have been calling off the hook if I was a Private Investigator. This is vital news and I am not angry at you Christie. I am just frustrated about my own personal issues. I was trying to fight back the tears that had drop down my cheek. My voice had quivers too. I wipe my cheek with my finger. I wanted to crack my knuckle.

I guess you will not refer me to someone else. She said to him. He felt her sorrow.

Yes, I had promise you that when you finish this Assignment. She smiles.

She wipes her eyes. He was more pleasant. He stated. I was going to tell you at dinner about the man who I had contact for you. This man he is the head of the FBI Agency in Washington DC. He will be calling you in a few weeks. But, I had to tell you now. I have so much to do before I get to the Bahamas Island. The doctor had told him to handle all his affairs. He said with a little bit of sadness.

He stated. I have to get to Hong Kong right away and I have to see my daughter.

I do not know when I will be able to see her again. He stated. This sounds very serious. She stated. Yes, it is very serious. He replies. That was why I hired you to

Give me a report on all her activities there in the Bahamas. And to see whom she is keeping company with over there. He said with a low voice. She could barely hear him speaking.

"I have some health issues and I want to see a specialist there who can help me Prolong my life." He stated. She replies. I am so sorry, Mike. She wipes her eyes. She was crying out loud. Please do not cry, baby. He said to her. My main concern is for my precious daughter to be happy and as well as my only niece. I am so happy for you right now. He hesitated stating this part of his sentence. He said, "If I am

going to leave this place, I want to leave knowing that she is well taken care of and will be alright." Christie could hear him sniffing. "This is the only thing that matters to me, right now." He had stated to me.

His voice quivers. "Sometimes I think the medical science do not know everything.

They are not God, and can be quite wrong in their diagnosis. I question them all the time. I said, "How do you know this is an accurate prognosis?" The doctors get so angry with me, they tosses me some pamphlets. This is to shut my mouth, or rush me out of their office. I am not a harsh person, but when you are talking about the fate of whether I am to live or die. I tend to get angry. I will apologize when I am wrong." He had stated to me. "I am not a brilliant person. However, I am quite smart. I have acquired a Law degree while I was just trying to keep my head on straight. I had also stumbled onto the Medical Terminology Course. I have gotten a certificate of completion. I have gone to school just to keep my mind from wandering, while raising my daughter." He said to me, "I have lived a good life."

I have everything I could possibly want in this life. I have prayed that I can see my daughter one more time. I am hoping that if I see this, Specialist. In addition, if he is able to prolong my life." I may be able to use you for other assignments or point you in the right direction to someone else. I just want to say this to you, Christie. "I am so proud of you for doing something that is virtually impossible in this world." He smiles. He said to me, "You remind me of myself, dear." I am glad I was the one that was able to help you." And I know that my sister, your mother would have been proud of you too." He had told her that her mother was a McGuire. He had stated to me. His dad was one of the men who had built the railroad track, and later the government decided to pay him the right amount of money he deserves. It was thousands of dollars. He said, "He was name the executor of the estate and he has some money that belongs to you." "Christie I really did try to find you but I could not remember your grandfather first name. There must have been hundreds of Higgins in the NYC area. I never gave up hope. I finally found you when you had started your own business." He was wiping his eyes. "You were just 11 years old when I last saw you at that funeral." She was crying too. Anyway, you are wealthy dear. I want to transfer the rest into your account to use at your own discretion. He had stated.

My eyes were turning red from crying so hard. I had gone to my bathroom sink to wet a face cloth. I was talking to him on my cell phone. I told him, "I have to be able to move around." He said, "I understand." I was in my hotel suite. He continues to tell me this sad news. He stated to me, "If by chance this visit to Hong Kong does not work for me. "I do not want you to ever give up on your dream." His voice was breaking up again. I had swallows a lump in my throat. He started to coughs. He takes a sip of his glass of water. I could hear him gulping. They must have given him some bad news. He was talking different.

He had finishes his last statement. I was crying so hard that my head begins to hurt. I thought I could not say anything else to him. I had managed to say one more thing. I said to him, "Mike I have to go." But, I have been praying for you to be healed." I believe in miracles. He was crying aloud. I was wiping my eyes on my face cloth. "Wait a minute," dear. He stated to me. He had to tell me something else. He had stated to me. I must say this one last thing. I have a large corporation and sometimes I may want to do an employees PI search. This is not illegal. He had stated to me. "I have heard of this at College." I had stated to him. "I may be able to use your service. This will be kept confidential." I was smiling. He said, "If all goes well with this trip I am taking next week." He did not want to get off the phone. I was thinking.

"Since this is what you like doing I may keep you on my payroll." He stated. If this visit is a success and I can resume my normal life. Then I will call you to see if you are interested in doing an assignment with your new husband, permission of course. I hesitated before asking him this last painful and heartbreaking question. I knew I did not want to hear his answer. Mike, are you dying? I had asked him. He gets silent. He was never this blunt. He said, "Not today, I hope." He said in a different tone. I was crying, even harder.

My doctors here are pumping me up with a bunch of medicine. That is why I am seeking some other help. I have some excellent health coverage. This will allowed me to travel out of the country to see a Top notch specialist in my condition. I will call you on Monday when I arrive if that is alright? He said to me, "It is all right." I will be here at the hotel most of the day. I had stated. Since I am finish with my assignment. Christie, I still want you to keep check on my daughter. I like her, anyway and she is my only cousin. I had replies. I will keep an eye on her for as long as I can. I had stated to him. He sniffs. Thank you, Christie. He replies. I have to go, Mike. He stated. I do not feel very good right now.

I was feeling my uncle pain, and I just wanted to be his strength. He was the one who pave the way for me to get started in this business of mine. I went to wet another face cloth. That other one was soiled. I drop it on the floor for the housekeeper to take to the laundry room. I had hung up. I was wonder if it was too late for him. He sounded so sad. I could not stop crying. He told me not to worry about him. I had gone to my bed to bawl for as long as I can stand it. He was the one who had made a liar out of the devil. "I am going to run this race to the beginning to the end."" In addition, I will win the Prize." This was a quote my Professor, he uses at the College. I am going to do just what I wanted to do. I am thinking to myself. I had thought of some terrible things when he thought I should stop working on this assignment here. Now, I realize that he was just looking out for my well being.

I thought I was going to be sick. I had not known him for a very long time. I felt like I knew him my whole adult life, and now he is dying. I felt so terrible. I just wanted to walk around the suite crying. Why did he tell me this news earlier? Gerald, he was knocking hard on my door. I had gone to answer it. I fell into his arms. He held my waist. I know you have spoken to Mike. He stated to me. I was still crying hard. Was he very hard on you? He asks me. He had put me in my place, Gerald. Calm down, darling. He tells me. He shut the door to my suite. He walks me to a chair. He helps me to sit down. I was covering my eyes. It is going to be okay. He tells me.

It is something else he has told me that made me this upset.

He went to get me a face cloth to wet my face. He hand me a few Kleenex tissues. I blow my nose again. I finally speak to him. I feel so bad for the way I have talked to him. He was only caring about my well being. I was trying to act tough. He was so right. This is my very first assignment. I had stated. You did nothing wrong. It is partially my fault, too. Gerald stated. I have found someone that I was attracted to, and forgot the purpose for my being here. I failed to do my job. This man he is paying me a great deal of money. He nods his head. I had said something cruel to him in my anger. I said, "I do not want you to call me everyday asking me about my job. " I will notify you by e-mail or via phone. He said to me, "he has never dealt with anybody in that way. He said to me. I am a Lawyer, and you do not know what you are talking about. I am paying you for a Service that you are rendering to me. I can call you 24/7. He had said once, "I want my money back that I have given you if this is the way you are conducting business." He was not serious when he said that Christie. He just wanted you to think for a minute. Gerald stated. I had apologizes for my remark. He apologizes for his anger. He went on to tell me a sob story about his health condition. "Do you feel like talking to me about it?" He asks me. Not really. I had replies. I will try to tell you, Gerald. I had stated to him.

I appreciate your being honest with me about your feeling. He had stated. That goes double for me. He added.

I know I am not experience enough. I had stated. He said. Practice makes perfect, dear. Gerald takes out a thin cigar. He lights it. What else did he tell you, Christie? He has health issues and probably is dying. He is going to see a top specialist in Hong Kong. He does not know if he will be returning back home. I was still crying. He wanted to make sure his daughter, was going to be alright. I had to shake my head. He said if he has to "go", he wants to make sure she is going to be okay without him. Gerald, he was crying now. He likes him, too. They held each other.

Why he did not tell me about a health problem before I had accepted this PI assignment. I had asked Gerald. It was a sentimental feeling that came over me since the conversation with Mike. I thought something was the matter when

Oh, he told me that I was his niece too. I had added. Gerald sighs. I came over to tell you this tonight. He had call me this morning, crying. He sounded different. He asks me how you were doing. Then he asks about his daughter. I was not going to tell him anything. It was not place to say anything, darling.

However, I mention it. I told him about her boyfriend getting into trouble. I would never come up against you where your job is concern. He had stated.

"But I have been carrying around this man secret for two weeks." I was shocked. I told him he had 24 hours to tell you who he was to you or I was going to tell you myself. "Secrets and lies do something to me." He stated. I have been in this police business for 17 years, darling. He had stated to me. "I quit one job and go right back to another thing. They call me crazy, Island boy. "I do not care what they call me." He stated to me.

"I care about people safety. In addition, to what goes on here in the Bahamas."

"Yes, it is beautiful here in the Bahamas Island." "I do not blame you for caring." I had stated. "He made a statement he had never said to me before when they were discussing things about this Island. We have things going on here that the travelers may not be aware of because we keep it behind close doors. And we want to get the tourists, and travelers to come back again. I am not saying that there is imminent dangerous. Danger lies here and everywhere. Because we are an Island, unlike other countries we have a different custom. We are acceptable to hide or cover up things. I understood what he meant.

"I just ask a few police officers who were my friend and while on duty to keep an eye on you. They worked for the Coast Guard and Navy too. He stated.

He was hoping I would not be angry at him. I didn't pay them anything just gives them a free dinner or a night on the town with his wife. He stated. Mike had pleaded with me to quit trying to gather more information on those men. He is right, darling. He said, "He is coming here on Monday, and wants to see us for Dinner. He said, "We will be dining at an eloquent restaurant that is underground where you can see the sea creatures while you dine. That is nice. Gerald stated. He laughs at me. I had changed the sad conversation by telling him about my fear of going to the bottom of the sea. Now, you will have more time for me. In addition, I can relax a little bit. She gets a bottle of water off the coffee table. She needed some ice but she drank it warm. He sat down. She sat next to him. We will talk about him anymore dear. We have a wedding and trip to plan. She was not crying anymore. He holds her hand. I want to know if you want a traditional wedding or a more upscale wedding with the whole works. He had brought along with him a disc to show her a film of how they do their weddings in his country. She covers her eyes with her hand. She was so emotional now. He put his arm around her waist. Do not start that up again, darling. He hand her a wet cloth. Her eyes were red from crying so much. It is going to be alright with us. And I have the faith that your uncle is going to be fine. He will be your uncle too. She stated. You are absolutely right, Christie. We will hope for the best. I want to go to church again, Gerald. She stated. You want to go tonight? He asked her. No, tomorrow if there is a service. She had stated. Yes, that will be fine. I will call Kenny and he will know what is happening at the church. He stood up to put a disc in the DVD to show the wedding ceremonies they had in Africa.

He had told her about his dad church. I was planning on taking you on Sunday but we could go on Saturday. She forgot today was Friday. Do you wish to go to one tomorrow? He asks her.

"I do not know, I guess I could wait." She said. They have prayer and worship service tonight too. I will check the time. We can go tonight if you like. He replies. He gets out a yellow page book. He looks for the name of his dad church. He turns the page. And they had a prayer and worship service. Tonight they will have two services. One was in the afternoon and another in the evening at 7:00 to 9:00 p.m. A friend of mines is now the Minister at my dad church. He saw his name in the Yellow Page book. I use to frequent the Church when I get a chance to go. I am getting hungry. I really came over to see if you were interested in having dinner with me. I stood up and said I need to get away from this suite.

Even though, it was beautiful hotel. We can look at this later. He smiles. He was so handsome. I felt like I was the luckiest woman alive. How soon can you get dress? He asks me. Now, I had replies. He laughs. I had said it so fast. I mean in a jiffy. I was ready to get a breath of fresh air after going through an emotional moment. I had gone to my bedroom. He said, "Make sure that door is closed. I had to laugh at him. She shut the door. She went to change her clothes, she found a pretty

White and Yellow Sundress has big pockets and a wide belt to wear around her waist. She slips it over her head and then put on her strapless pumps. She freshens up her make-up.

I had picked up my gold pair of earring. I had come out of the bedroom.

He smiles. You are one of the prettiest PI I have ever seen. He said to her. She Thanks him.

They left the suite. Christie said, "I want to ask you something, Gerald." He smiles. He said, "I think I know what is coming out of that pretty mouth of yours."

"Let me finish." She replies. He said, "Okay I am sorry."

"Why have you not tried to make your move on me?" He laughs hard. I knew it! He had stated, "There is a little story I think I have already told you." My dad was a Minister.

"I have made a promise to him, that I would wait until I was married before getting in any kind of relationship with a woman." "It is hard when you are romantic involve with a beautiful woman." He was smiling. "Not to mention, I am a true romantic person."

Christie ask him, "Are you serious?" He said, "Yes I am not kidding." He was laughing though. She was smiling. He said, "I must take you back to my houseboat so you can see the pictures of my parents for one last time. "My mom would smack me on the back of my neck when I look at a girl the wrong way."

She laughs. She said, "Here in the Bahamas are some of the most beautiful women I have ever seen. She asked him, "How come you never married anyone?"

He said, "I was not in a big rush." "Plus I was saving myself for the right woman to come along." You must be in your early 30's. He shook his head, and made a funny sound. "I wish I were still in my thirties." He replies. "No, I am in my early 40's." Get out of here! I had exclaims in unbelief. He laughs. He shows me his driver license.

He was taking me out to dinner on his mo'ped motorcycle. He loves his bike too. "This is my baby and I could not have made it without this bike when I needed to get around the Island, Christie." He said. Moreover, it is easy and a fun ride to get to my Yacht. You can even pick it up. He said. He said, "It weighs about 100 pounds." He tells me to swing my legs over, and hop up in the back and hold onto my waist. It is a very enjoyable ride, and quite exciting to look at the Scenery while you are riding. He had stated to me. Put your feet on the stump. I let him get on first. I hop up on the back seat behind him, doing as he has Instruct me to do, while I held onto his waist tight. This was my first motorcycle bike ride.

We arrive back at the Village where he lives, "PORT LACAYA RESORT & YACHT CLUB." He had made sure I had gotten off his bike, before he gets off. He hooks his bike to a pole. He had a kick stand he uses too. He points to his Yacht. There goes my baby. If it is not too late I may let you take a look inside for one last time. He had stressed this again. I was curious as to why he put emphasis on this "one last time." He had it in the middle of the Ocean. I had asked him. How do we get out there, "swim"? He fell out laughing. He had stated to me. No, I have a speed boat that is sitting by the dock. I had shaken my head. I have seen those ski boats in movies. I said, "I can not ride one of those things." He smiles. I will go bring my boat to shore. It looks like the tides may come out, anyway. He had stated to me. I want to move my boat anyway.

They had music, and dancing at the Restaurant. A server seats us. A band was setting up. It was pretty inside at night. He had told me that he could not come here by himself. I like the atmosphere here because you can eat and observe the ocean from behind us. And you can see my houseboat that is sitting in the middle of the ocean. He said, "He had woke up earlier this morning and move it out to the center.

You can see it, if you look out their window. He had stated to me. You are sitting on the water here you know. He had told me. Yes, it was so beautiful tonight. I felt like I needed it to be somewhere else. We stay at the restaurant for about an hour. He told me to wait while he go get his speedboat at the dock so he can get to his Yacht. I saw him turning the Yacht around to come back to the shore. It was a beautiful Yacht. He had pulled it to the shore. He gets off the Yacht smiling. He held out his hand to me. I took his hand. He helps me get on the Yacht. He had some bad music playing inside. He said, "If it should storm I will already be near the land. He had sand bags too. " I walk downstairs to go to his living room. He smiles. He had already taken out the picture of his parents. He said, "Do not let their happy faces fool you. I had to laugh. I knew what he meant. I said, "They have taught you well." Christie was rushed out of there so fast before she had a chance to sit down. He was walking her back upstairs to the ramp to go to his bike. He said, "You have seen enough of Island boy for one night. I am going to have to take you to church on Sunday. I said, "This will be fine." He gets back on his bike and I climb behind him.

He drove me back to the hotel. I know you think I am crazy, darling. I said, "Yes you are quite insane. He laughs. I know about fighting temptation. And I have to beat it with a brick every time I am near you. I gave him a hug. You say the most wonderful things to me, Gerald. I just tell it as I see it, darling. I told him to go home to get some rest. He said, "I will see you in the morning. I have to check my schedule. I will give you a call. He was rushing out of the hotel like lightning. She said out loud. Goodnight "My Island boy. " He had turn around to look at her and he smiled. He put his finger on his lips. And he touches the glass door. He was gone.

She felt like she was on cloud nine with him. She did not want to leave this wonderful place to go back home to handle things. She had not discussed about the Loft to him yet. She went back to her suite. She felt much better being away for a while. She had missed Ann already. She could not wait to go to Africa with her fiancée and meet his sister, her new brother-in-law, and niece. Gerald drove back home and he was ready to turn in for tonight. So he thought. He got a call from the Coast guard. They needed some guards to come in to observe a ship that was arriving shortly. It was 9:30 p.m. Gerald, can you come on out to the head quarter?

Sure. They paid the bill for his Yacht, bike, and other things he needed. He had to get change to put on his uniform again. He never said, "No to them." He made thousands of dollars for working with the Coast guard and the Police. He went to his bike to drive to the head quarter. They all knew that he was getting married. We know you are romancing a beautiful woman. He just laughed. He takes out a thin cigar and lights it. He went to the ship and did his duty for the length of time.

He had gotten a cup of coffee too. The ship had arrived. Everyone was getting off at the dock. They told him he could go home to get some sleep. He drove his bike back to the Yacht. He tosses his clothes in a laundry basket. He had to wash tomorrow at the Clubhouse. And clean up his Yacht. He had it looking very nice inside like a mobile home. He did not want to hire a maid service. He had a bar installed. He has a kitchenette, bathroom, a storage room, a living room, and a bedroom. The deck was upstairs. He put on some music so he could go to sleep. He check to make sure that there was no storm approaching the Island.

He put his photo album away. He went to put on his pajamas because it had turn cooler at night.

Christie remembers his sister name is Adrianna and her husband name was Brad. She is a doctor in Africa. She lives in Gaborone Botswana. She never travels because of her patients she cares for over there. He has told her that we are coming there next week. She was excited. She could not wait to meet them. They both were called doctors. He works at the University of Botswana. That was how she met him, Gerald said to her. They have one child. He said, "I have a niece she might be six.

The yacht was shaking a little bit. There were some tides but Gerald he slept right through it until in the morning. He was exhausted. He slept like a baby. He was glad that he had moved his houseboat to shore. And he had just bought some more sand bags from downtown. There were no storms approaching tonight. Christie she remembers doing some weather tracking of storms. She listens to the news for a while before dozing off, too. There is a lot she needed to know about caring for a boat too. She was going to be living on it too. He told her he had a book and videos to walk her through it step by step.

Chapter 13

The next morning she did not have anything to do so she thought she would go find Stephanie. And see if she wanted to have some breakfast with her at a luxury restaurant or cafe.

She went to find her an outfit to wear and takes her shower. She was dressed and downstairs to wait on a bus to arrive. She walks to the bus stop and was getting on the bus. They were talking about a storm was heading in the area. She decided to turn right back around to go to her suite to turn on the television again. When she got there, Gerald had left a message on her phone. He said, "A storm is approaching the area babe and you should not try to go anywhere for a while. I am working with the maintenance because they needed someone to do an on-call and I have been loyal to them for years. He said, "He was 5 minutes from her and might pop in for a quick hello. She wanted to see him, anyway. The sky was getting dark and the wind was blowing heavy up against the windows and glass sliding door. She went to turn off the air conditioner. She turns off the lights too. She knew what to do if it approaches the area. She heard a knock on her door. She went to ask who it was at the door. Gerald replies," It is me darling." She opens up the door for him. He smiled and gave her a kiss. I will only stay for a few minutes. I have to get home to check on my Yacht. I don't think you ought to drive anywhere else right now. She had stated to him. He was shock by her putting it to him that way. He understood what she meant. He smiles. He said, "I think you are right in your assumption. It is dangerous to be outside. He stated. But I will make it home. She was not satisfied with that statement. I insist that you stay here for a while. He smiles. She said to him. You can sleep on my couch or sit up and watch the news. That is not so wise. He stated. She replies. I insist, Gerald. He said. Nothing is going to happen to me. He smiles. That is an understatement. She said.

We are not looking for anything here to happen either. I will get you a blanket, and pillow. He smiles. You are tough.

I smiles. Yes. I guess after all I have been through these last four years.

They get ready to travel to Africa

The wind was shaking his bike. He looks out the window. He replies.

I think you are right. The storm is here. He had locked his bike. It was in the afternoon time. The 11:00 o'clock a.m. news was on television. He stayed there listening to the weather until they said it was safe to resume their normal activity. He left to go to his bike. He told her that he would see her later on when he was ready to go to somewhere for the evening. He went to his bike and drove it to his Yacht. They were announcing another storm now. There was a tropical storm heading in the area. They said it was a Category 1 and it could do some damages. He had insurance on his bike, and boat. He was praying that nothing would happen to his boat. She was worry about him. She calls him on the Yacht. You know you should have stay here longer. I will be fine, darling. Remember I am an Island boy and I am use to these kinds of things. I appreciate your concern. I will see you tonight. You just be careful. I will Gerald. She hangs up and went to order some room service for her lunch. She had made a pot of coffee herself. They told her it would be forty-five minutes before they brought her food. She thanks them. The storm had passed over and everybody was happy. It was just a tropical storm. She had taken a nap. Gerald had worked for the Coast guard all day and he was ready to go out with Christie. He had to go over to wash out his things first. They stayed open 24 hours. He checks the Internet to see if he had any messages. He went to changes his clothes, and head out to go to the hotel. Later that evening she got dress and went to have some dinner with him. She was thinking about going to Africa with him. He had wires his sister telling her of his arrival.

He had wired his sister to tell her what day he would be arriving and who was coming with him. I look forward to seeing you soon. She wires him back. I am so excited, Gerald! He laughs. He wires her back saying, "He will be taking an airplane." He had not flown anywhere outside of the Bahamas Island. He was given some the information on a flight arrival, and a hotel accommodation. The ticket agent had said to him, "You cannot get into that part of the country without taking a train." You will have to stay on the airplane for another 8 or 9 hours. He was feeling some emotion. He wipes his eyes. He purchased two tickets for both of the transportation. He took a lunch break and calls Christie. She was not in her suite. He left a message on her cell phone then he decided to leave a message. She wanted to go to church today. He would tell her today. She misses her friend, Ann. She had not met anybody else. She had gone to the board walk that was downtown. She watches the crowd walking around the Island. It was getting close to the time for Gerald to take her to the service. She saw his message and he was coming to get her to the afternoon service. She had to find her a dress and heels. He was already on his boat changing into a dress slacks and a shirt.

Chapter 14

Christie goes to Church

He put on a suit jacket and dress shoes. He had bought a jeep. I will be there in a half an hour to pick up my jeep. He head for the airport. He drives to the dealer.

He drives away to go to the hotel suite.

She was in the lobby. He gets out and walks inside. Hey, is that you outside? She said to him. He shook his head. He said," No but it is a loaner." He replies.

Come on. She follows him outside, and he opens the door. How come you did not drive your bike? She had asked him. He replies. I still do not trust this weather. I rather have you inside a vehicle in case, it should start up again. Thank you. She replies. That is very considerate of you, Gerald. She stated. Good. They arrive at the big church. She was surprised. It was beautiful. He parks on the lot. A Minister was standing at the front door in a robe. He was shaking and hugging people as they were getting ready to come inside the church. He had a handsome face. He was in his forties.

He spoke with an accent. "I greet you all of God people ". Welcome to my church.

He had shaken my hand, gently. He put his hand on Gerald shoulder. Aw, you have not been here for a long time, my brother. The Minister had said to him. Gerald, he had to laugh. Yes, I know it has been a while. I will be coming more often. Gerald stated.

I have brought my fiancée who wanted to come to your Prayer & Praise Service.

That is wonderful. He held out his hand. I held his hand, too. He said to me, "I am so glad to have you here, dear. He had asked me, "Are you a tourist?" I said to him, "Yes, so to speak." Whatever your reason for being here on the Island, I am please you chose to come here." The choir was lining up outside. They had on choir robes. They were getting ready to March into the church. We went inside the sanctuary. We found a seat in the back of the pew. We were told to stand to receive the choir. The minister he walks in front of the choir. The Musician was playing the music.

Everybody was clapping as the Director was directing them.

They were marching to a familiar song they sang at a church she had gone to in New York a few times. "I'm Glad to be In the Service One More Time". We had to wait before they went to their seats. We had to remain standing up for the Pastor to come to the pulpit. He said a prayer, "then he thanks us." He made a gesture with his hands. We could be seated. He had stated. We are going to have a selection from our choir, then get into our service. We will hear from a man who has been truly blessed. This soloist came to the podium. Gerald, he smiles. This was his friend. He was handsome, too. He was not a Native of Bahamas. He had given his testimony to the church. He said, "I have been here for 17 years." I was in the Navy in Hawaii. When I had finished my active duty I decided to make Bahamas my home. It just so happen that what I was trained to do in the Navy. They needed me to come do the same work here. This song is a testimony because I can think of all the places I could have gone, and where I would be if my Savior were not by my side. And something my grandmother use to said to me. Kenny, make sure you are ready." That day will soon come." They clap.

Some said, Hallelujah. Wave their hand. He smiles. I am going to sing, When We All Get to Heaven / We Will Shout Hallelujahs and Said Thank You Jesus. Amen. The choir rocks side to side. He had a nice voice. He held up his hand as he sang. Tears fall from her eyes. This was a friend of Gerald. He smiles. And shook his head. She stood up with the others. And they were shouting. Christie, held up her arm. It was a beautiful ballad. The director of the choir was dynamic. They sat down in their seats. Gerald gave her a hug. The Pastor he said, "If you have a special prayer to come to the altar.

Christie she had gone down to the altar. Gerald he came down with her too. They held each other hands.

The service was beautiful. Some had beautiful testimonies. Gerald, went over to his Friend Kenny after the service was over. He slaps his hand, and gave him a hug. They were laughing. Gerald, he introduces me to his friend. He gave me a hug. He said to me, "Welcome to the Bahamas Island, dear." I should have known that it would take a woman to bring this man back to church. He had stated to Gerald.

Actually, I did not stay there long after signing up for the service. How do you like living here? She asks him. I love it. He replies. He has a beautiful home it was build from the ground up. How can you remember what my house looks like? He had stated to him. He was messing with Gerald. He smiles. He had his hair cut short in a style. He wore a Yellow suit with matching yellow shoes.

You have not been over to my house in a while I am surprise you remember it.

Gerald laughs. He was about to comment on him not visiting his Yacht, either. A Teenager boy he comes over to them. Dad, are you ready to go? Christie asks him. You are a father? He said to me, "Yes I have a wife with 3 children." Where is Delana? Gerald asks him. He said to me, "I told her she could rest in this afternoon. I would see to the children going to church. His wife is an Elementary school teacher. A 6-year-old little boy came from out of the children room. He was holding the hand of a 2-year-old toddler girl. He smiles. He said to Christie "These are my children. You have beautiful children. Thank you. He picks up the toddler girl. He had two boys and one girl. We have been truly, blessed. He tells Christie. Yes, I can see. She stated. So is this the last time you are going to see me, man? Kenny had stated. No of course not. Gerald stated. Good. Come on over for dinner tonight. He stated. Are you kidding me? Gerald asks him. No. I will call my wife to tell her I am bringing over some company for dinner. Kenny, he had stated.

Christie tried to protest. That might be imposing. She stated. No, my wife loves entertaining company. She has plenty of food. We had gone to his house. We were eating and talking to each other outside on the patio. We had finished eating our dinner. His wife pours Ice tea for everyone. At our home we drink after we finish eating. Joy had stated to Christie. "I think I understand that custom," said Christie. The children drank their drinks. "Can we be excuse, mom and dad?"

Their son asks them. "Yes take the children to their rooms." Junior took the children hand and walks them into the house. He had a computer and his own phone. He was very smart, too. "He told the small children to go somewhere to play." Not in his room. They had heard what he said, because the windows were open. We just smiles. He wanted his privacy.

"They are adorable." Christie replies. Thank you, they both responded to her.

Joy, she stood up to go take the food and plates inside. Christie she went to help Kenny wife. She thanks her. Christie, she likes Joy. She asked her, "Where do you go to get your hair done like this, Joy?" She said," Whenever I just want someone else to do my hair I go to the Salon." "I will give you my hairstylist business card," she stated. "I was also curious as to where you get that name from?" Christie had stated. She smiles. She begins to tell me her tale. "My parents are very religious. I have to tell you a little story. She had put her dishes in the sink so that she could put them in the dishwasher. She stops working. She said, "My parents thought that they were not ever going to have any children. I was a miracle baby.

It happens on a Christmas morning at 1:00 a.m. at a Navy hospital in Hawaii base. She explains. My dad was in the service too. My mother was over there to be near him. This story could go on for ever, but I will say this to you. "I came out of my mother wound and she was filled with Joy. Christie was wiping her eyes. Gerald and Kenny were crying too. All my relatives were so excited. My mother said to the family. "I am going to name this baby, Joy." I had to hug her. She was a beautiful person too. She was always smiling. I said, "That is a wonderful tale." I was asking her about her teaching.

"What grade do you teach?" Christie asks her. "I teach kindergarteners" She replies. We had gone back outside to be with the men.

Kenny, he tells me how he had met Gerald. I met Gerald as I was coming out of the Coast Guard and Navy Head quarter. I told him I was so glad to be out of the service. He asked me where I was going to reside when I had got release from the service. I said I hope right here in the Bahamas. He and I work with each other. I am now a recruiter Officer for the Navy. And on occasion I may have to do my Airman duty on the jet. "You fly a navy jet?" She had asked him. That is why we never see each other.

I have other jobs. Gerald had stated.

How come you couldn't call each other? She had asked them. They smiles. That is hard to do when you don't be at home to answer a phone. Kenny had stated to me.

I am glad you decided to come to church for a visit, man. Kenny stated.

"I was amazed by the way you all have service here." She stated.

Oh, it is Universal. We have some of the best Ministers and choirs in the world. Tomorrow morning we are having our angels and youth Service. A what? Here we have our youth put on a program. Our son is going to be the MC. He has worked hard to put this program together. They will do everything the Adults do during our Worship Service. They will have singing, and Praise dancing. I wish you could come out to see them. It is amazing what they can do. Joy stated.

I would love to come but I have to see what Gerald has to do. Christie stated.

I will check my schedule, dear. He replies.

The day after tomorrow she was seeing Mike for the first time. That was on Monday.

"So is everything going alright with you, Gerald?" Kenny asked him.

"Everything is fine I can't complain. God is good to me."

We have to get together more often. Kenny stated.

"That is a must. I am going to work hard to do that, my friend. The dinner was delicious." Gerald stated.

Wait I have some dessert. I have two whole pies in the refrigerator.

One is a lemon-lime pie, and the other is a sweet potato pie. Joy stated to us.

Should I go get the children? Kenny asked his wife.

No. I will save them some for a snack later. I will make us some coffee. She stated.

She left us outside. I said, "You are right she does loves to have company". Christie stated.

Kenny he laughs. "We both are homebodies and this is all we do here." He stated.

Christie had asked her about the school. They work her hard at the school. She said, "Here we have school 6 days a week, a half a day. Just one day off on Sunday." Why, I had to ask her? Christie said.

"Because we live on the Island we have to keep up with the US school system."

"We have one College and University here, too. "So many people come from all over the world to attend our college, and University." "Our son wants to be an Astronaut. Right now he is being trained for this career. When he graduates we are sending him to Houston, Texas to the Astronaut Center. He has to go to their College and when he graduates he will become an Astronaut."

Wow. Christie had stated. "Has he ever left Bahamas?" "Oh, yes." She replies.

"I went to see my parents during the Thanksgivings Holiday." They live in Brazil. If I do not go then, we send our son. Christie did not know what her nationality was but she spoke with an accent too. She was born in Brazil.

"We send him there for Thanksgiving and he come back the day before Christmas."

"How exciting this must be for a young man to travel alone." Christie stated.

"Yes, indeed." They had both replies. "He cannot wait for the holiday season. We think he has some girlfriends over there, too." Joy stated. She continues, telling about the school. "Here the children have 2 months off for their break. And they have to return to the school at the end of December. They get one day off for the New Year. I had kept her from bringing out the dessert from asking her so many questions. "She comes out with the two pies and she had put the other part for the children to snack on later. She brought out saucers and mugs. Kenny, help her with the tray. He sat it on the table. She pours us some coffee. She hand me a knife to cut her pie. I cut the first slice and a slice for Gerald. He thanks me.

"I am so fascinated with the life here in the Bahamas Island." She smiles.

She said, "Oh, really." "When Gerald and I get married we will make this our home." She laughs. She said, "I thought Gerald was going to leave Bahamas."

He said, "No way, dear it is the other way around."

Kenny he smiles. He said, "I am glad to hear that man."

"Perhaps, you two can come to Africa for our wedding. I have your invitation here in my bag." Christie stated.

"That is something to think about, Christie. Kenny and I will discuss that later. If we are not able to attend we will get you two a gift." She had stated. We ate their dessert. Gerald, look at his watch.

He said, "As much as we are enjoying ourselves we do have to go." I have some work to do in the morning.

What time do you have to be at work? Kenny asks Gerald.

Gerald said, "8:00 a.m."

Kenny said, "Our Wednesday service starts at 12:00 noon. And we have a night service at 6:00 p.m."

"If I can get finish with my job I might be able to bring her to week night service on Wednesday." We have some packing to do for our trip. Gerald stated.

Yes of course. We do understand. Kenny stated.

Christie visited the Children School and go on field trip

"Oh, Christie I am taking my students to the Library for a field trip. If you are not doing anything you should come with us. I will have bag lunches. We might go to other sites." Joy stated.

What day will this be? Christie asked her.

I would like for this to happen tomorrow morning, at 9:00 a.m. Just come out to the school. I will save you a seat on the bus. Joy stated.

"Thank you and I will give you a call in the morning." She said.

Joy hugs her.

"I will see you at the school tomorrow for that field trip in the morning." Christie stated. She wanted to do some more exploring and sight-seeing. She had to bring her camera too.

"You are welcome in our home anytime." They both stated to Christie. "We will be praying for you, dear." They had stated to her and Gerald. "Thank you." We both replied. We walk to where his Rental Jeep was parked.

Chapter 15

Gerald takes Christie to Africa

Gerald and I were asked to come to his sister and brother-in-law, home. They live in Gaborone, Botswana. This was South Africa. It reminded me of New York City. This was an urban renewal area. They both were waiting anxious to see us get married in Kenya, Africa. They had planned a huge wedding ceremony. All their colleagues were coming to the wedding. Their daughter was a part of the wedding party. This was a beautiful country. I had ridden on a train with him. We had to take a train to get to their community.

We had learned that this was where they had discovered of diamonds.

His sister she works at a hospital as a Primary Physician in the morning. While her husband Bradley he works at a University as a Professor until in the evening. She had arrived home to pick up her daughter from the baby sitter, who picks her up after school.

Her husband he was trying to get home. They were supposed to be leaving tomorrow for Kenya, Africa. All of Gerald friends, and Christie were coming to the Wedding. Some said, "They would arrive on the day of the Wedding. They heard her Van pulls up in the drive-way. They live in a

Townhouse Apartment. They were going to buy a house in another location, later. The babysitter had opens the door for them to enter their home. Gerald, he had rented a luxury car, He was crying when he saw his sister face. He held out his arms. She ran to them. It has been so long, baby. She was crying, too.

I am so happy to see you at this wonderful occasion. This is my fiancée Christie. I am Adrianna. That is a pretty name. Thank you. It is a pleasure to meet you, dear.

She hugs her, tenderly. I know you two must be thirsty. Yes, a little. He said to his sister. Let me get you some cold beverages. I will just take bottle water. Christie stated. What about you, brother dear? She asks him. "I will take a cold Root beer soda if you have it, dear." "Yes, we do." She replies. "We have root beer, coke, Pepsi, Strawberry, Orange, and Grape." "I have some Papaya juice, too." I had not drunk that in years." Christie stated. We have it here. "I would like some of that, please." "It was so hot that it did not feel like any air was blowing." Men, women, children wore shorts with tee shirts.

They dress in suits with ties. Or dress pants with a white shirt, and tie. They dress urban renewal style. The women had on halter top with a wrap around skirt with a bandana on their head or scarves. They had cabs, too. Some rode bikes.

They had a two car garage. I was quite surprised. They had two cars, but her husband he prefer to take a train instead of driving. She went to her kitchen.

Their place was very modern. They stayed inside because it was scorching hot outside. Gerald tried to play with his niece. She had held onto her mom dress tail.

Our daughter she is very shy, and she does not speak English. Oh, they both said.

My husband he only taught her to speak our native language. Gerald, he speaks to her in their language. The child laughs. She went over to him. He picks her up.

I had smile. He told her that I was going to be her Aunt. We were getting married in a few days. She went over to hug me. She was adorable. I had told Adrianna to go ahead and pick out a gown for their daughter. I was going to go shopping today to find me a gown. We sat and talk for about two hours. Then, we heard the door open.

It was Adrianna husband. He smiles. He was also African. He went over to hug, Gerald. He spoke English, too. How are you, dear? He went over to hug me, too. I am Brad. I want to welcome you to the family. Christie said, "Thank you." I had asked Gerald what was their last name. He said, "Their last named were Livingston." I know you all must be starving, now." No, it is too hot to eat."

Gerald replies. He laughs. I hear what you are saying. We have the air on high. We will eat here in a little bit. Then, the rest of the evening we can do as we please.

We can not do too much, honey. Adrianna had uttered. Christie and I have to the Mall.

Adrianna said, "We have to find her a beautiful gown not an African attired."

Brad said, "Aw, most definitely, will you need a Tux, Gerald?" Gerald said, "No, I am going the old traditional way." Christie and I agree. Good.

He was wearing an African attired. Brad said, "There is a shop right close to home that has fine apparels for Men." "We can drive there in a while, man." "I want to take off my stuffy suit, and get comfortable." Brad stated. "Will you excuse me, brother-in-law? He went upstairs to their bedroom.

His daughter she likes to follow him around the house. She stands by the door. He said, "I will be out in a few minute, Muffin." He calls her. He gave her a kiss. Christie and Gerald had checked into a Lovely hotel that was right downtown. But, for their wedding night they were staying at the Hilton Nairobi International Hotel. They had just built it in the last 10 years. It was very modern, and a high rise hotel.

It was very expensive and had Four Star Restaurants. The food and drinks were sky high. Gerald, he had charge everything to his credit card. They had built a new road, and sidewalks. They were leaving in the morning. They had to take a train to Kenya.

Chapter 16

Once they arrive at the hotel. Then, they were getting ready for the Wedding Ceremony. They were going to put on an African show for them the night before the wedding. This was considers the main attraction.

They asked Gerald if he wanted to participate in the dance recital. He was honored. He had to go to rehearsal. They wanted to go to the Safari Trail. Christie, she loves Elephants. She had elephant figurines around her Lofts. There was a bus that takes you on a tour of the Safari trail, Kenya National Park.

Well, since nobody is hungry. Christie and I can go to the Mall. Come on, sweetheart. She said to her daughter." Mommy has not seen you all day." She takes her hand. "I have very cold air in my Van." She tells Christie. Gerald, smiles. He gave his fiancée a kiss. He said, "Hurry back my love." Christie smile. We had left the cold townhouse to go out in the humid sunny air. Adrianna said, "It gets cooler at night." "We will sit outside to get a breath of fresh air." Adrianna said, to us. Sometimes we get a cool breeze. I have mosquito repellant, and poles to ward them blood hounds from biting the crap out of you." She had stated. Christie laughs. "You have to forgive my slang." She had stated. Christie said, "I like it, and appreciate what you are saying." I like her, too.

"So do you love it here, in Botswana?" I ask her. "Yes, with all my heart." She replies. "I care for the under privilege children and Adults." This is why I never travel anywhere else except here in Africa. We take our daughter to the Safari Trail twice a year. She is so excited. She wants to go to this big wedding, too. "

Christie smiles at her. I had gone out to find a long gown just for her to wear. I will show you tonight. I have to hide it, because she will try it on over and over again." She stated.

She is six years old. Girls love trying on clothes. Christie stated.

I smiles back at her daughter in the back seat.

The Big Wedding Ceremony

We had packed our bags, and we were heading to the train station to ride to Kenya, Africa. Christie had become so emotional. Gerald, put his arms around my waist.

He said, "I know you probably thought it would never happen to you. "I nod my head. Gerald said, "I have waited my whole life for someone like you, darling." Adrianna, she wipes her eyes.

She squeezes her husband hand. "Listen to my brother he is such a wonderful man." Adrianna stated.

The train was getting ready to board for the Passengers. We all had a sleeping cart. It took one hold day, and a half to get to Kenya Africa.

They were near to Kenya than Gerald from the Bahamas Island. Christie had told them that she was A Private Investigator. They thought that was unusual, but they were proud of her accomplishment. They went to their sleeping cart because it was night. They both had to work that day of their travel. I bid them goodnight. I told them that Kaylee and I can share a bed together. Gerald, he slept by himself. He just told me to wait until the wedding night. I just laugh. I was tired from the hot roasting sun. I went to take a cold shower, and put on my gown. I ask Kaylee did she need to go to the bathroom. She knew what I meant when I made gestures. She laughs. Shake her head. I lift her up in the bed. She wanted to use the higher level bed. She climbs the ladder. We will be going to the Safari Trail after we check into our hotel. Then, Gerald he was going to meet with the dancers to rehearse their dance routine.

The conductor had announced our Arrival. He spoke some English. He said, "All those who are departing at Kenya will need to get off now." We hurry to get our Bags. As we get off the train. We had to take a cab to our Hotel. We did not need to rent a car, because everything was near the Hotel. Gerald had rented a Limousine for the drive riding around the city of Kenya. The Wedding was being held in the beautiful backyard. Or, the Jungle as they calls it. They had everything set up for the reception. There were Animals roaming around the hotel. This reminds me of an old flick. I had taken some pictures. I felt someone squeeze my hand gently. It was Horace. He said, "I was going to ask you if I could help with the Wedding Ceremony." I would like to do one version from our country. And they do theirs from here."

I put my arm around his neck. I said, "I will be so pleased to have you be apart of my wedding ceremony." A telegram had arrived at the hotel from Great Britain. The telegram says that a relative of Gerald was coming to the wedding. This was an Aunt. She was a Princess. She was the daughter of the great-Grandmother who had married the great-grandfather who was the King of British. She said that she was almost 85 years old. She wanted to see her great-nephew get married. She was bringing everybody she could bring that was still alive. Gerald, he was shouting and rejoicing. He thought that everybody was gone on to another life. He had some relatives still alive. I was crying so hard. He was hugging and kissing everybody. His sister she was happy, too. She did not know if they could find out if they had relatives still alive, she did a search locator any way.

Gerald had not seen the gown that Christie had bought. She had order it from the Bridal shop in Bahamas Island. It had a 10 foot train. She was waiting on it to arrive by the UPS. She had gotten a call from the front desk who told her that her package had arrived. She left to go to the elevator. She went to the Front desk. She says, "I am Ms. Christie Higgins." They gave her the box. She thanks them. She could not speak their language. She went back to her suite where she was sharing with Ann. Who wanted to stay with her until she becomes Mrs. Gerald Labrodereax. She laughs.

She had her name change on her driver license, already. She goes up to her suite.

She goes inside the suite. She had to get dressed for her wedding ceremony tomorrow evening. Tonight was the big African dance show. Gerald he had gone to rehearsal. They had given him a special dance outfit. He had asked if his friend, Manuel could dance with him. So they went to rehearsal together. The show was starting at 8:00 p.m. It was the best dance routine he had ever done in his life.

They had bongo players, all kind of musicians. He was so tired from doing this dance. Everybody they had to eat dinner on their own. We had to be outside for the show. They sit on the lawn but for those who could not sit on the lawn. They had lawn chairs. They were serving refreshments for the show. He went to take him a shower, and hope he could take a little nap. He had not seen Christie all day.

As time passes by they all were meeting outside on the lawn. Someone had announced, "Congratulation is in order for Mr. Gerald Labrodereax and Ms. Christie Higgins on their upcoming wedding." We both smiles and thank the announcer. He said without further ado we want to bring out the African Dancers these are all descendants of Kenya, Africa. Will you show them your love? Everybody claps.

The musicians begin to play the music. Gerald he came out with the others. He was smiling, and he started to do the dance. I had wipes my eyes. As I watch my future husband dance with the dancers. He was so handsome. He was smiling, and the leader had asked if the future wife would join her future husband in the dance?

I did not know how to do the dance. Gerald he takes my hand. He said, "I will show you."

It was fun and I follow his steps. Everyone claps and whistle. They put on a good show that had lasted three hours. Then we all left to go to bed. Tomorrow was the big day.

They had called Gerald down to the lobby early that morning. He woke up his sister.

"Our family has arrived." he stated. He started hugging and kissing them. His great aunt told him to use his royal title. She said, "You should not be afraid that you are a Prince of Great Britain."

He cries. He said, "That he had lived a different lifestyle in the Bahamas Island." She said, "She understood about living in a different culture." Well, when you come there you will be honor as my Nephew, the Prince.

He said, "I will accept that when I get there next week." She hugs him. You look like your Great grandfather. He was one of the most handsome men I had ever seen. I have brought some pictures with me. She stated. Adrianna, you look

like your great grandmother, she was beautiful. She said, "That she was tired."

"I am an old woman, and I must get my rest." Gerald kisses her hand,

and does a bow to honor the majesty. Christie she does a curtsy. She was taught what to do by a member of the family. The Princess she was escorted to her suite.

I was starting to cry again. I was taking out my gown from the box to hang it up. It had a very long train. We had to meet with the two Ministers whom were performing the ceremony. We had to sign for our Marriage license, and Gerald paid him his fee. He was very expensive. He spoke some English. They had an interpreter there just in case some guests did not speak English. I had cried for the second time. I saw all of my friends from NYC and Ann was right there with me in my suite.

There was a huge wedding ceremony. I had become Mrs. Gerald Labradoreax.

Jamal and Manuel had brought in telegrams from the Police department, also the Coast guard. Kenny and Joy had made it there too. They smiled.

All of Brad and Adrianna friends came too.

Conclusion

Mike Arrival

Mike he signs the register book. The consultant said to him. I will get your key card.

He has thick curly black hair. He was sporting a thick mustache. He signs his name.

Here is your key card. You will be on the 21st floor, in suite 2108. Thank you. He had two bags and one garment bag, and a regular duffle bag. He had on a green suit. He picks up his bags, and went to the elevator. She had to face him sooner or later.

He had made dinner reservation tonight. He knew where his daughter was staying. She already was waiting on his arrival. She said, "She would see him at 7:00 p.m. today for dinner. Christie had been down in the lobby. She heard his voice. He stated who he was to the consultant. I went to the front desk. Excuse me, sir.

"Yes he said, smiling at me". "I am Christie Higgins."

He laughs. Yes, I recognize your voice. He gave me a warm hug.

"I was going to call you soon as I get comfortable from the flight." He stated.

"How are you feeling?" I had to ask him.

He said, "I am as well as could be expected. But, I am not complaining. He stated.

"Where were you going?" He had asked me.

"I was on my way to have some breakfast. I heard your name being mention." You are here early. Christie stated.

Yes. I have contacted my daughter. Oh, really? Yes. She was a little bit surprised, but, she is anxious to see me. I am seeing tonight at 7:00 p.m. instead of this afternoon." She said, "She has a surprise for me." I want to rest for a while.

I understand, Mike.

"You are just as I picture you to be, dear. You are quite, beautiful." He stated.

"Thank you for the compliment." "But, I am not beautiful." Christie stated.

He smiles. He said, "You cannot see what we men see, dear." He stated.

Christie smiled.

"And you look way younger in person than on the satellite."

He said, "I have heard that many times."

"That brings me to ask this question?" She asks him. Why do you use that VCR?

He stated. "It gives me character and it is an added feature to communicate instead of over a phone." She pushes the button for his floor. They bid each other goodbye until later on for dinner.

"Okay. I look forward to our dinner tonight." He had stated.

She was married to Gerald now. They had gone a glorious honeymoon. She had a whole new life to learn about his descendants. She had gone to a doctor, and he say that she might be pregnant.

They were waiting for the results. Gerald he was still working with the Police and Coast Guard. He told Christie she could stay at the hotel until he got off work to take her back to his boat. He had to go home to change his clothes for the dinner.

Gerald said, "He wanted to thank the man who made it possible to meet his wife." "You must be tired from the travel. Christie stated,

"Yes, I am a little jet lag. I still have one more place to go. I wish I could have come to your big wedding." Mike stated.

"I have videos I can show you later." Christie stated, "I would like that dear. Right now, I must go rest." She hugs him, gently. He smiles.

"I will not break, Christie." She was crying now.

He hugs her a little better. "I am hopeful that I will be back the way I was before this happen to me. She swallows a lump in her throat. So, do I Mike with all my heart Mike." She replies. I will see you at the Restaurant in a couple of hours.

"I think being able to see my daughter is making me feel better. I still am going to Hong Kong. Actually, I am flying to Mexico for the treatments. I have to see a specialist in Hong Kong."

"Wow. I am praying for you to have a speedy recovery." Christie stated.

He said to me. "Bless your heart, dear."

Mike receives the shock of his life

Mike had taken his nap, and was going to take the cab that was waiting on him in front, of the hotel. He was seeing his daughter, tonight. At least that is what he thought. She knew he was there. She had found her mother, too. They had made up. He was meeting Gerald too.

This was an emotional reunion. He gave Christie a gentle embrace. Stephanie had asked her Mother to join them for dinner. She told her I believe that dad will be happy to see you Mom. He just needed to get over the initial shock of seeing you with me. She stated.

"He was happy to see Christie his niece again after all these years. He told her, you are just as Gerald describe. He is a very lucky man." I am so happy for you both."

He wore a sharp Navy blue suit with gold buttons. He smiles. He looks younger.

Are you feeling alright? Christie asked him.

He said, "Yes I feel pretty good right now."

"I have to tell you something, Mike." She stated.

He said, "Yes what is on your mind."

"Ever since you told me that, you were ill. I have not stop thinking about you."

He smiles. "I was just feeling down that day when I spoke harsh. I would never intentionally hurt you or say cruel words." He stated.

"I believe I will be alright one day and I have the faith."

"I am praying for you, too."

"Thank you." He replies.

I had on a fitted gown and had my hair in a fancy hairstyle. I was waiting on Gerald to arrive to the Restaurant. He had his job with the Coast guard. He had to go to his Yacht to change his clothes for dinner.

A server comes over to the table to take our order.

He introduces himself. I will be your server. "Can I start you out with a cocktail or

beverage? "I would like to order some champagne for the table. Is that alright,

Christie? That is fine with me. But, I rather have non-alcoholic beverage. She had stated. He gives the name of a bottle of Champagne. Bring out one that is non-alcoholic for the lady. He stated.

"Yes, sir I will bring them over to your table." She stated to him.

"I will give you sometime to look at your menu."

She stares at her uncle eyes.

"You are staring at me, Christie." He smiles.

"I did not realize how handsome you were in person." She stated.

"You are making me blush." He was smiling. Where is my nephew Gerald?

"He will be here soon." She stated.

"How have Stephanie been doing since her break up with that man?" Mike asks her.

"She is happier Mike.", she replies. I was staring and smiling at the two women walking into the dining room. I was still waiting on Gerald to arrive there so he could meet my uncle. Mike turns to look around at the two women walking to our table. He was in shocked. He stood up and gave his daughter a kiss and a hug. He was crying when he saw the woman standing beside his daughter.

"Hello, Mike." She said with tears in her eyes too. He gave her a hug. She was crying too. I had started to cry now. I hug Stephanie and Wynona.

"You know this woman-I mean my wife." He asked me.

"Yes, Mike." Christie replies. "She asked me not to tell you anything.

"So, you have kept a secret from me too." He asked me.

"Yes, I felt that it was not my place to butt into your affairs." I had taken the liberty of asking for a table for 3 instead of four. She stated.

He smiles. I think you have miscounted dear. He stated.

I said, "Gerald and I will be dining alone. She stated.

They both were beautiful women. He said, "I am so happy that I cannot stand myself." I saw Gerald walking into the restaurant. He looks so handsome. He had on a white suit tonight. He had broad shoulder and his hair was thicker. He had his hair standing up in the style he wears often. He smiles.

And he walks over to the table. He went straight to Mike. Mike stood up to give him a hug.

He said, "I am Gerald Christie husband."

Mike he laughs. He said, "I am so pleased to have finally met you, young man." I mean my nephew.

"It is the other way around, Mike. You are the one who brought me my wife. And I am so grateful for that—if nothing else." He hugs him again. He walks over to kiss Christie, and hugs the two women.

"You know my wife too?" He smiles.

"Yes, I had the pleasure of meeting this wonderful woman a few days ago."

Are you ready to dine at our table, my love? He asked Christie.

Yes, I said smiling. I had not been feeling the best in a few days.

He held out his hand to mines. I stood up and we walk over to our table. Wait a minute Mike said, "I want to pay for both tables. So do not take out any money." Gerald laughs. "I will accept that offer, Uncle." Mike laughs. He looks happier.

Christie she was crying from seeing them together as a family.

"Are you alright, honey?" He asks her. She said, "Yes I am just so happy."

"Good." He replies. Mike sat down across from his wife and their daughter sat in the center, he touches his wife hand. "I am so glad to see you both here together." Gerald he was wiping his eyes too. He said, "I believe that he is going to get better. Maybe this is what he needed in his life." Christie agrees.

Conclusion

He tells the server, "Please put this bill on my credit card." He laid the card on the table.

"Yes, sir." She replies.

Mike was content with seeing his daughter and wife again. She wanted to be given another chance. She insisted on flying to Hong Kong with her husband. She said, "For whatever the news she wanted to be by his side."

They were leaving for Hong Kong that next day.

Christie, she was waiting on her news from the doctor. Gerald told her that she could continue working as a PI/ Detective. And that he wanted to see her Loft and visit the United States for the first time. Mike was slowly recovering from his illness. He had gone back to his wife, and they were working things out. A Research Doctor had met Stephanie. Christie and Gerald were having a baby next year. Deon and his company had been charged. They were sent to prison.

The End

To Pastor Smith
& First Lady Smith

From: Yvonne Snyder (Author)
October 25, 2010

I am grateful for your warm hearted spirit and encouragement - for being there when I needed. May you both be eternally blessed.